# WEDDING BELLE BLUES

## LIZ MCKNIGHT

T𝐕*Ink*
Thunder Valley

**Wedding Belle Blues**

Copyright © 2023 by Liz McKnight

Published by Thunder Valley Ink

www.thundervalleyink.com

Cover art copyright © cboswell@depositphotos.com and AllaSerebrina@depositphotos.com

Cover and layout copyright © 2023 by Thunder Valley Ink

Cover design by Annie Reed

ISBN: 978-1-954460-01-0



For more information on the author, go to https://lizmcknight.wordpress.com.

WEDDING BELLE BLUES is also available in an ebook edition.

# WEDDING BELLE BLUES

# CHAPTER 1

*E*dwina Morrisey stood at the altar and gazed into the deep blue eyes of the most beautiful man in the world.

He had cheekbones to die for, a strong jaw, and wavy brown hair so deeply hued it looked almost black in the warm glow of the chapel lights. His chiseled chin bore a shallow cleft, and his lips were curved in a nervous yet happy smile. He stood half a head taller than Edwina, which was just about perfect in her book. He was a bit younger than she was, but when a lady reaches Edwina's age, she doesn't quibble about a few years difference here and there.

He stood waiting for Edwina to speak on what was surely the happiest day of his life, and he didn't seem annoyed that she was taking her sweet time. Patience like that was a virtue Edwina definitely appreciated.

No doubt about it, the man with the nervous but happy smile was definitely Mr. Right.

Unfortunately, the soon-to-be Mrs. Right stood at the altar right next to him.

Edwina gave herself a mental shake. She had plenty of time for daydreaming about the perfect man later. Right now, this happy young couple had paid her good money for their ceremony, and she best get on with it.

"Jeremy, Heather," she said, looking from the groom to the bride, who, to be honest, looked just as happy about getting hitched as her almost-husband did. "This is what you've been waiting for." She gave them a wide, happy grin of her own. She loved this part of the ceremony. "By the power vested in me by the State of Nevada, I now pronounce you husband and wife."

No one moved. No one applauded. Instead, everyone—even the bride and groom—seemed to be holding their collective breaths.

In her experience, sometimes the happy newlyweds just needed an extra little nudge.

She looked at the wedding guests seated in the first two rows of pews in her chapel.

"I'd like you to join me in congratulating the new Mr. and Mrs. Jeremy Hillington," she said before she turned her attention to the groom. "Why don't you give your new bride a kiss?"

The guests burst into an enthusiastic round of applause as Jeremy swept the fishing hat off his bride's head and kissed the stuffing out of her.

It wasn't the first time Edwina had officiated at a wedding where the bride and groom wore fishing gear, although it was usually the groom in the fishing hat.

In fact, given that Edwina's Bluebelles Wedding Chapel & Dry Goods, along with the rest of the tiny town of Liberty Springs, Nevada, overlooked the northern shore of Sutter Lake, it was a rarity for Edwina to officiate a wedding where the bride and groom wore anything approaching traditional wedding attire.

Sutter Lake was a twenty-mile long, eight-mile wide natural lake in the middle of the Nevada desert a hundred and ten miles southeast of Reno. Enough trout called the lake home to draw fishing parties from both the northern and southern parts of the state, and the lake was wide enough and long enough to attract sailboarders and water skiers. Every now and then Edwina found herself marrying a bikini-clad bride to a Speedo-clad groom, which really made it difficult to keep her mind on her job.

Jeremy and Heather had been part of a decent-sized fishing party from Yerington, a small Nevada town fifty miles or so to the northwest of Liberty Springs. Even though Edwina was pretty sure Yerington must have a few wedding chapels of its own, Jeremy and Heather had decided to get married on the shores of Sutter Lake, so twenty minutes earlier the whole group had shown up at Edwina's general store, hip-waders and all, looking for a preacher.

Edwina wasn't a preacher, but she was an ordained minister of the Church of God Almighty. Ten years ago the internet ministry had provided Edwina with all the documentation she needed to register with the state to perform marriages.

She had always loved weddings. Back when she was a file clerk in the District Courthouse in Reno, she used to watch all the starry-eyed couples who came to the Clerk's office to buy their wedding licenses. She wanted nothing more than to be there when couples said "I do" and the groom kissed his bride. She'd been holding out for a position with the Marriage Commissioner's office, but the clerk there had shown no signs of ever retiring.

Edwina had been about to give up on her dream when she overheard a couple who were buying their marriage license talk about how they'd wanted to get married by Sutter Lake because that's where they'd met and fell in love, but the wedding chapel in Liberty Springs had been closed and a "For Sale" sign was staked in the little patch of dried-out grass front of the chapel. That got Edwina to thinking.

She'd saved up a bit of money here and there, never really knowing what she was saving it for. Edwina had been single all her life, and she didn't need a whole lot of money. She did some research and found out it was easier than she thought to become a "registered officiate" for civil marriage ceremonies, as the state called it.

She even found out that the asking price for the combined

wedding chapel and dry goods store—who would have ever thought of combining those two businesses? It was like putting a bait shop in a fine wine boutique—wasn't really all that high.

Before she had a chance to change her mind, Edwina made an offer on the property, completed the paperwork for the Church of God Almighty, and started packing up her apartment. She put in her notice with the county the same day she signed the escrow papers for the wedding chapel, and within a month she'd moved to Liberty Springs as the brand-new owner of Bluebelles Wedding Chapel & Dry Goods.

Not bad for a former file clerk who'd left thirty behind in the rearview mirror more than a few years ago.

A little of the shine had worn off the woodwork, as her father used to say, now that Edwina had kissed forty goodbye and was squinting at fifty.

Edwina's problem was that she was an incurable romantic. In the ten years she'd lived in Liberty Springs, she'd performed enough marriages to figure out that she might never meet a Mr. Right of her own.

How could she? The only Mr. Rights she ever met had their own soon-to-be Mrs. Rights standing next to them.

It wasn't like she hadn't tried to find her own Mr. Right, but the pickings in Liberty Springs were a bit on the sparse side. The town only had a population of five hundred twenty-seven, soon to be five hundred twenty-nine when Bessie Tigg delivered her twins, which should be any day now.

Edwina _had_ already crossed off the few single (and age appropriate) men who called Liberty Springs home. She'd dated most of them, and Mr. Right they weren't.

Horace Wedgeworth's idea of a romantic evening was grilling hotdogs on his Hibachi while they watched _American Idol_ on satellite TV. Chuck Long had at least taken her to a movie down in Hawthorne, which was the big city—at least compared to Liberty Springs—at the southern end of Sutter Lake. Too bad the movie had been the latest remake of _The Texas Chainsaw_

*Massacre.* The rest of the single men in Liberty Springs were either gay, like Jerry Parker, had taken a vow of celibacy like Father Mills, or were just a few years out of high school like Joey Hamilton.

The only other men who passed through Liberty Springs on a regular basis were delivery men and truckers. The UPS guy was married, although he did have cute legs. Edwina had to give a man credit who'd wear shorts even in the middle of winter when he had to chain up that brown UPS delivery truck. As far as the truckers went, Edwina figured out what they wanted just by taking a good look at their mud flaps. Raquel Welch she was not.

The fishermen and sportsmen who came out to the lake didn't interest Edwina either. They all had their own lives elsewhere, and she had no desire to be someone's vacation fling.

She'd been surprised at first at how well she'd adjusted to life in a tiny town like Liberty Springs after growing up in Reno. Not that Reno was a big city like Las Vegas, but it might as well have been compared to Liberty Springs, a place that didn't even have much in the way of sidewalks to roll up when the sun went down.

If it wasn't for the fact that the major highway—no one in their right mind could call it a freeway—between Reno and Las Vegas ran right past Liberty Springs, and that Sutter Lake was always a big draw, Liberty Springs' businesses wouldn't have much business at all. Her dry good store and wedding chapel would never make Edwina rich, but she didn't mind. When she'd moved to Liberty Springs, she'd found her place in the world.

As much as Edwina liked Liberty Springs, she absolutely loved Bluebelles.

The wedding chapel hadn't exactly been rundown when she'd bought it, but it didn't have much in the way of personality either. If anything, it looked like an old married woman who'd slapped on too much makeup in an attempt to reignite the spark of new love.

The chapel comprised one half of a long, rectangular building that stretched alongside Liberty Springs' main road. The entrance to the chapel was on the side of the chapel half of the building. The entrance itself had been constructed to look like the front of an old-fashioned church, complete with steeple over the double doors.

The whole building must have been painted white during the Reagan administration, from how bad the faded and chipped paint had looked when Edwina took over. Some budding artist had added a mural featuring cartoon caricatures of a happy (demented?) bride and groom on the long side of the chapel that fronted the road, and a neon sign over the cartoon couple pointed to the chapel entrance. As if it wasn't obvious.

The other half of the building—the dry goods half—had been decorated with caricatures of a horse tied to a hitching post and a cowboy—hitching up his jeans—headed toward the store's entrance, which was highlighted with another neon sign that pointed to a set of double glass doors at the far end of the dry goods half of the building.

Back when Edwina bought the place, the inside of the wedding chapel had looked as garish as the mural and the neon sign on the outside. The wooden pews had been painted hot pink, the walls a faded white, and the floor was a stained and warped hardwood that looked like it belonged in a saloon in Virginia City. The altar had been decorated with faded plastic plants and flowers, and the whole interior had been accentuated with neon-colored spotlights shining down from can lights suspended from the ceiling. The patch of lawn outside the entrance had dried out in the summer heat, and the potted plants on either side of the chapel's double wooden doors were more faded plastic.

Edwina had rolled up her sleeves—literally—and gone to work to make the chapel a warm and welcoming place that would be part of a happy couple's cherished wedding memories, not a knock-off of a quickie wedding chapel someone got married in after a night on the town that featured way too much alcohol.

She'd stripped the pink paint off the pews and sealed the natural wood with a shiny varnish that made the woodgrain glow.

She'd repainted the walls a warm off-white, and accentuated the paint with wallpaper borders featuring a delicate bluebell pattern. She'd replaced the neon bulbs in the can lights with soft, low-wattage lights, and covered the floors with a hardy, warm-toned gray carpet, promising herself that someday she'd refinish the hardwood floors underneath the carpet.

Then she'd gone about upgrading the altar itself.

She'd never been overly religious, but she believed an altar where people pledged to love each other for the rest of their lives should honor that solemn commitment. She'd bought quality linens to cover the altar, and then she'd embroidered a linen table runner to go on top, choosing a delicate bluebell pattern that matched the wallpaper. She'd decorated the altar with simple taper candles topped with electronic flames—no reason to tempt fate with real flames in a dry desert climate—and upgraded the old boom box sound system with a discrete built-in system that had an iPod dock so that her customers could choose their own music.

Over the years, she'd been surprised at some of the music her customers had requested she play while they tied the knot, but whatever made them happy, that's what counted.

Jeremy and Heather hadn't requested any special music, so Edwina had opted for her one of her personal favorites—an acoustic version of "My Way," an old Sinatra song her father had been fond of. It might have seemed an odd choice for a wedding song, but considering that the fishing hat was back on the bride's head as the wedding party filed out of the chapel, Edwina thought it fit.

The bride and groom were the last out the door. Edwina followed them, intending to lock up. It was five o'clock, time she locked up the chapel for the night. She'd keep the dry goods store open until seven. Memorial Day was coming up fast, a big three-day weekend around these parts since it was the official start of the summer tourist season for Sutter Lake, and Edwina had a lot of new stock to inventory and shelve.

The bride started down the few steps to the dirt parking lot in front of Bluebelles when she turned around and gave Edwina a big hug.

"Thank you!" Heather whispered into Edwina's ear. "I'm going to remember this day for the rest of my life, and you're a big part of it. Where else could I get married in this silly hat?"

Edwina was still beaming when Heather and her Mr. Right got into his pickup truck and drove away.

# CHAPTER 2

That night Edwina sat in a big easy chair in her tiny house, her tired feet propped up on an ottoman she'd inherited from her parents, and stared at her laptop. She'd pulled the chapel's website up, intending to spruce up the site a bit for the coming summer season, but she couldn't get past the home page.

Not that there was anything wrong with the home page. It featured a flattering picture of the chapel entrance complete with a freshly whitewashed steeple and real plants bracketing the double-door entrance. She paid a couple of locals to repaint the building every couple of years—the caricatures of the demented bride and groom and the cowboy with the perpetually low-riding jeans were things of the past—and the outside of Bluebelles always looked fresh and clean and welcoming.

The picture on her website had been taken a year ago in the spring when the little bit of lawn on the chapel side of her building was still a vibrant green before the summer desert heat dried the grass out. Edwina had planted petunias in the flower boxes on each side of the double doors, and their cheery pink and purple blooms had certainly livened up the picture. Bluebelles looked inviting, which was what Edwina wanted, but when she looked at the picture with a critical eye, she could tell something was missing.

She wasn't in the picture.

Sure, her name was in the text beneath the picture of the chapel, and the website even had another page devoted entirely to her since she was the licensed officiate, but her picture wasn't on that page either.

Not that Edwina didn't like the way she looked. She'd had over forty years to become comfortable with the fact that she just wasn't a conventionally beautiful woman but someone who was on the handsome side. Kind of like Sigourney Weaver when she'd been in all those science fiction movies when she'd been younger. Except Edwina was a little older, a little sturdier, and couldn't imagine handling one of those big guns like Sigourney had in the movies. Edwina wore jeans and plain T-shirts underneath her minister's robes, and if any of the couples she married noticed that tennis shoes, not high heels, peeked out from beneath the hem of her robes, they never mentioned it.

If Sigourney Weaver owned Bluebelles, she'd probably put her picture on the website.

The real question was, would Sigourney Weaver ever discover her own Mr. Right standing at the altar one day?

Probably not.

Sigourney Weaver would hitch up her own jeans and go looking for him.

Edwina? Not so much.

And that was her problem.

Just like her father used to tell her, she didn't put herself out there in the world.

"You need to mingle," he used to say. "Meet new people. You'll find someone when the time is right."

He'd meant well, but Edwina had never done well on dates even when she'd been younger. People never seemed real on dates. It was like they were trying to impress the other person with how perfect, how special they were, just to cover up the fact that they really didn't think they were all that special after all.

"You're one to talk," Edwina muttered to herself. "If you thought you're good enough, why don't you put your picture up there for the world to see?"

Was it because she wasn't *Mrs.* Edwina Morrisey?

Because she was worried what people would think of a wedding chapel owner who'd never been married herself? After all, someone who'd never even attempted to find true love for herself really couldn't really believe in marriage. Could she?

"I most certainly do," Edwina said in an attempt to quiet the annoying little voice in her head. "I always have."

So why she wasn't she willing to put herself out there now and take a chance? What did it matter what total strangers thought? She was happy with herself, right?

With the life she'd made for herself in Liberty Springs?

"I most certainly am."

Well, all except for the one thing she was missing in her life—a true love of her own.

The chances that Mr. Right would find her in Liberty Springs without a little help were slim to none. It was time to stop hiding, and not just on the chapel's website, but in life. She wasn't getting any younger, and daydreaming about finding her own Mr. Right wasn't getting her any closer to finding a happily-ever-after of her own. If she wasn't careful, if she didn't make an effort to meet people like her father had wanted, Mr. Right would turn into Mr. Never, and that wasn't something Edwina wanted to think about.

Okay. She'd do it.

But how?

What would Sigourney Weaver do?

Certainly not internet dating. Besides, what internet dating service would actually serve a tiny, out-of-the-way place like Liberty Springs?

How about craigslist?

Shirley Evans had sold her old pickup on craigslist last year. A classic car collector had driven all the way from Stockton, California, to buy it. He'd said he intended to spruce that old truck up for a classic car competition he entered every year up in Reno.

Edwina didn't feel like a beat-up classic that needed to be spruced up before decided she could go out in public.

Sigourney Weaver would never advertise on craigslist.

Edwina leaned back in her chair and sighed. She wanted to change the chapel's home page. She also needed to meet an eligible man who wouldn't mind relocating to Liberty Springs. And not just an eligible man, but someone who had as much romance in his heart as Edwina did.

Wait a minute. She didn't need a site like craigslist. She already had a website, and she really should put her picture up anyway.

She needed to think about her sudden brainstorm. Not too long—after all, she hadn't thought about buying the chapel and moving to Liberty Springs for too long before she did it, and she still considered that decision the best thing she'd ever done for herself—but this new idea of hers was even crazier than that, so she needed a minute or two to consider how it all might turn out.

In the meantime, she needed a picture of herself. She didn't have any recent ones that she could think of, so she brought up the laptop's built-in camera.

Her face appeared on the screen.

Edwina blinked.

Was that what she really looked like at the end of the day? Were those *bags* under her eyes? Good lord, no wonder she couldn't...

Edwina made herself stop. She took a deep breath, and then scooted around in the chair until the light from the lamp next to her chair illuminated her face in a more flattering way.

The bags beneath her eyes didn't quite disappear, but at least now they looked like they might fit in an airplane's overhead compartment instead costing her an additional charge for over-sized luggage.

She ran her fingers through her hair—shoulder-length dark

brown and going gray around her temples but still thick and mostly manageable—and practiced her smile until she was satisfied the image on the computer screen made her look more like a confident, happy woman than a crazed serial killer.

She clicked the laptop's touchpad and took the picture. She deleted the picture when she realized she'd been looking at her fingers rather than at the camera.

She reposed, smiled her "I'm a confident, happy woman" smile, and tried to remember to look at the little camera lens at the top of the laptop's screen while she clicked on the touchpad to take the picture.

Easier said than done.

Finally, after the fifth try, she took a picture she was happy with. She resized it so that it wouldn't overwhelm the picture of the chapel and then loaded it on the website, first on her own page above the text that described her background and experience, and then on the home page below the picture of the chapel.

Okay. Decision time.

Take a chance, or play it safe?

She knew what her father would say.

She opened a text editing program just as a small chat window opened on the laptop's screen and a soft chime sounded.

Reverend Thomas was online and asking if she wanted to chat.

He owned a wedding chapel in Lovelock, Nevada, the most perfect name ever for a town, as far as Edwina was concerned. She'd met Reverend Thomas in an online forum for wedding chapel owners and operators right after she'd closed the deal on Bluebelles. He'd been a veritable font of knowledge when she needed it, which had been right around the time she realized she had no idea about the nuts and bolts of running a wedding chapel.

He'd talked her down from an incipient panic attack more than once back then. He was such a calming influence, and he could always be counted on to make her laugh when she most needed it.

He wasn't really a reverend, not the way most people would think, he'd confided to her once, although his real name was Thomas. He said people around town had started calling him "Reverend" because the title had come with his officiate papers, and the handle had just stuck.

Even though they'd never met in person—she'd never even done a Google images search on his name—Edwina considered Thomas a good friend. They chatted most nights if they were both online. Edwina supposed they could have picked up the phone and actually talked to each other, but there was something comforting in talking to someone in a chat window. And comfortable. Whenever she saw his name pop up in a chat window, she couldn't help but smile.

*Give me a minute*, she typed in the chat window. *In the middle of something.*

*Take your time* came back a few seconds later.

What a perfect response. Why couldn't she meet an eligible bachelor who was as nice and understanding as Thomas?

She turned her attention back to the text editing program and considered what she wanted to say. This might end up being the most important thing she'd ever written, and she wanted to get it right

*Don't beat around the bush, say what you mean* had been another of her father's favorite sayings. He'd been chock full of them, but as she'd gotten older, Edwina realized that as clichéd as those sayings were, her father had been right. Well, most of the time. She had a feeling he'd be right now, too.

Okay, so don't beat around the bush. Say what you mean.

If she wanted romance, she'd have to ask for it.

She could do that.

She put her fingers on the keyboard and began to type.

# CHAPTER 3

The Reverend Thomas Trask used to love his work. No, he didn't preach sermons on Sunday mornings, and he didn't wear a priest's collar. What he did was perform weddings for couples who wanted to get married and married couples who wanted to renew their vows.

At first he'd felt odd calling himself "Reverend." The title was purely honorary. The certificate he'd received from the internet chapter of the Grace Church of Louisiana that authorized him to officiate at wedding ceremonies had bestowed the title on him, the very same certificate that (in the fine print) also required him to use the title "Reverend" in association with his name if his name appeared in any advertising for his wedding chapel.

So he'd become Reverend Thomas, the guy with the wedding chapel and the little gift shop in Lovelock, Nevada.

A far cry from his roots as the son of a miner—and very briefly a high school football star—in the tiny town of McGill in eastern Nevada.

His McGill football star days were pretty far back in the rearview mirror these days. He still had most of his unruly brown hair, and he'd managed to keep middle-aged spread at bay by running a few miles every morning.

He'd never been one of those muscle-bound linemen types, just a scrawny running back—in McGill, all the kids who tried out for football, no matter their size, usually made the team—so he didn't have to worry about trying to maintain an insane body-building regime. In high school, he'd been disappointed to discover that he just wasn't one of those guys who could bulk up. Now he was pretty happy with the fact that all he needed to do to stay in shape was go for a daily run.

In fact, these days the only thing that didn't make Thomas happy was the one thing that used to make him the happiest of all.

It all started with that certificate that bestowed the title "Reverend" on him all those years ago.

The Grace Church of Louisiana used to be located in New Orleans. After Katrina, the church had relocated to Atlanta. He'd expected—hoped, really—that the church would rename itself to match the new location and would reissue Thomas's certificate. His original certificate had yellowed around the edges and was stained in one corner where water from melting snow had leaked through the chapel's roof during one early spring thaw. It would have been nice to have a shiny new certificate.

But that hadn't happened. Even with its new home in Atlanta in the beautiful state of Georgia, the church had remained the Grace Church of Louisiana, and Thomas was stuck with his old certificate. Unless he wanted to spend fifty dollars (plus shipping and handling) to have the church provide him with a duplicate copy of his original certificate.

While Thomas's dual businesses provided a reasonable living, the frugal part of him—the part that had grown up in McGill with parents who'd had to scrimp and save to afford his football uniforms—didn't want to spend the money to replace something he already had that worked just fine.

Except that it didn't. Not anymore.

The time-worn certificate made him look long and hard at the rest of his time-worn life. He'd been performing civil wedding ceremonies for nearly twenty years, and pretty much the same civil wedding ceremony for all that time. Sure, he had a few standard variations—the starry-eyed newlywed version, the renewed-vows version, the quasi-religious version, and the quick-and-simple version (which Thomas privately thought of as the "down and dirty so we can get on with the honeymoon" version)—but that was pretty much it.

His chapel only had two rooms to conduct ceremonies in, so there wasn't a lot of wiggle room there, either. He'd decorated one room to resemble an Old West church, complete with rough-hewn wooden pews, an unfinished pine altar, and wallpaper with a log-cabin print. The other room was decorated to look like an outdoor garden in a much greener place than most of Nevada and with a much more temperate climate than the Nevada desert. Fake greenery and flowers climbed a whitewashed arbor that covered the spot where the bride and groom stood, and the wallpaper provided a panoramic view of a tree-shaded, springtime meadow, complete with a fish pond featuring floating lily pads. Pots with fake plants placed strategically along the walls gave the garden mural an illusion of depth. Instead of pews, guests in the garden room sat on wrought-iron chairs that had been painted white.

Thomas offered his customers a choice of room for their wedding, and the choices were split pretty much evenly between the two, even though he could see how someone could look at those rooms and see how tacky they really were.

Or maybe that was just him. His customers always seemed to go away happy.

As much as he used to love his work, Thomas was starting to think he'd spent his life pretending to be something he wasn't. He certainly wasn't a reverend. His chapel wasn't either an Old West log cabin or a peaceful garden. And after a lifetime of bachelorhood, what did he know about being married?

After all, a person could only marry so many people before he began to notice the gaping hole in his own life.

This year's Lovers Lock Plaza Anniversary Celebration hadn't helped.

The town of Lovelock, Nevada, where Reverend Thomas had his wedding chapel and gift shop, had had a serious identity crisis of its own back in the '80s when Highway 40 that ran through the middle of the two-square-mile town was bypassed by the brand-spanking-new Interstate 80. A few years after that, the railroad depot closed, and that was nearly that for Lovelock.

Until the town decided to reinvent itself as a tourist destination, complete with historic buildings like the Pershing County Courthouse that dated back to 1919, and special events like the annual Lovers Lock Plaza Anniversary Celebration.

Someone had come up with the idea to capitalize on the town's name, and the little park behind courthouse had been promptly changed to Lovers Lock Plaza. Wrought-iron pillars were installed, painted green, and green-painted chains looped between the pillars formed a never-ending chain. Once a year on Valentine's Day, the city threw a love-locking ceremony officiated by Reverend Thomas where couples could get married and couples already married could renew their vows, after which they'd place a specially designed lock on the green chains to symbolize their love.

The chains in Lovers Lock Plaza were practically bristling with locks these days, which should have cheered Reverend Thomas immensely.

His wedding chapel did brisk business in February, which made up for the rather dismal business it did the rest of the year. Lovelock wasn't exactly the kind of tourist destination that Las Vegas and Reno were, and while Lovers Lock Plaza was a pretty place to get married, not a whole lot of people stopped in Lovelock to get married unless they wanted the town's name on their wedding license.

Reverend Thomas had come to the conclusion that the only reason most people knew Lovelock was even on the map was because O.J. Simpson had been incarcerated at the correctional center outside of town.

Maybe he needed a change of scenery. He couldn't remember the last time he'd taken a vacation.

Or maybe he was just experiencing his own brand of mid-life crisis.

Thomas settled down in front of his computer with a bowl of tomato soup and a grilled cheese sandwich. Comfort food, his mother would have called it, and tonight she would have been right.

After his computer booted up, Thomas checked the discussion boards on the "Join Your Hands Together" forum.

Thomas was a long-time member on the website. He'd been a big believer in networking even before the term had become popular. The forum was a way for wedding chapel owners all across the country to connect. Owning a wedding chapel in a small town like Lovelock left little in the way of opportunities to meet other people who knew the ins and outs of the wedding chapel business, especially when that business, like Thomas's chapel, was combined with another business that had very little—or nothing at all—to do with weddings.

Like Edwina Morrisey's combination wedding chapel and dry goods store.

If Thomas didn't know better, Bluebelles Chapel & Dry Goods sounded like something the writers of the old television show *Northern Exposure* might have dreamed up. But Thomas had been chatting online with Edwina for years. He'd seen the pictures of her chapel on her website. He'd even met a couple who'd come to town one year on Valentine's Day to renew their vows who said that they'd been married a year earlier at Edwina's chapel, and it had been such a nice ceremony that they'd decided to do it all over again at the Lovers Lock festivities.

Bluebelles Chapel & Dry Goods might not be a conventional wedding chapel, but it was certainly real.

But if Thomas was honest with himself—and who should be

more honest with himself than a reverend? Even if the title was just honorary—he chatted with Edwina for more than just an opportunity to network.

He enjoyed Edwina's company. She had a down-home, dry wit that he appreciated, and she lived in a town that was even smaller than Lovelock. She had what Thomas liked to call a "gentle soul." She still believed in romance and, he was fairly sure, true love.

Not in the fairy tale, happily-ever-after way where no one ever thought about what happened to the loving couple after they rode off into the sunset. True love, the kind that lasted in the real world—at least from what Thomas had seen—was grounded in honest affection, comfortable companionship, and an abiding knowledge that you'd found the one right person in all the world that you were supposed to be with.

Conversing with Edwina never failed to brighten his day. Over the years, he'd found himself looking forward more and more to the time he spent on the computer talking to her through that little chat window.

Thomas hoped that most of the couples he married had found true love, but he was enough of a realist to know that probably wasn't the case. Marriage was easy in Nevada, but so was divorce, and some days it seemed like as many people passed through the doors of the courthouse on their way to get unhitched as stood in the plaza behind the courthouse on Valentine's Day to tie the knot.

Now, that was a truly cynical thought for a man in his business.

He closed the page for the forum. Tonight was not the night for him to attempt to give any wedding chapel owner advice on how to run his or her business. He put down his sandwich, opened a chat window, and checked to see if Edwina was online.

The smile that lit up his face when he saw that LibertyBelle was available to chat was the brightest one he'd had all day.

*Good evening*, he typed. *What's up in your neck of the woods?*

It took Edwina a moment longer to respond that it usually did.

*Give me a minute*, came back in the little dialogue window. *In the middle of something.*

*Take your time*, he typed back.

He'd nearly finished his soup before a new line of text appeared on his screen.

*Spruced up the website tonight. Thought I should get ready for a big influx of customers on Memorial Day. ;)*

Thomas smiled. Edwina had told him that she married quite a few couples who went to Sutter Lake to fish or water ski and decided to tie the knot on the spur of the moment after seeing her chapel when they went to restock supplies at her dry goods store. Memorial Day weekend was coming up fast. Lovelock had its own festivities planned, although Thomas doubted they would increase the call for spur-of-the-moment weddings. Like most every month except February and December, he'd probably sell more postcards and T-shirts than wedding licenses.

*Sounds good*, he typed. *Let me go take a look.*

*No!* Edwina typed almost immediately.

Thomas's eyebrows rose. That didn't sound like Edwina at all.

Before he could type a reply, she replied to her own chat.

*Oh, that was silly. I'm just a little nervous is all. I did something I'm still not sure about.*

His eyebrows rose further.

*You really don't want me to look?* he typed.

Another long pause before she typed, *No, it's okay. Really. I'd like to know what you think.*

Thomas had Bluebelles' site saved as one of his favorite places. In fact, it was probably his most favorite place on the internet, if he was being honest with himself.

He opened a browser window and called up the chapel website.

At first he didn't see anything different. The website had a soft blue background bordered by a thin vine of slightly darker blue flowers. Bluebells, he supposed, although even after all his years in the wedding business, he couldn't identify any flower by name except for roses and daisies.

The focal point of the Bluebelles webpage was a photograph of the chapel itself, which occupied one half of the building that also housed Edwina's dry goods store. Not that he could tell from the photograph that the other side of the building even housed another business. From the front, the chapel looked very much like a tiny version of a church—inviting and friendly, much like Edwina herself. All that was missing in the photo of the chapel was Edwina.

Thomas was about to ask her what she'd done to the website because he couldn't see anything different when he caught the top edge of a second picture at the bottom of his screen. He scrolled down until the new picture was centered in his browser window.

Edwina. It had to be.

She had finally put her own picture up on the website.

And good lord, was she beautiful.

Edwina's face was a perfect oval, her chin just a bit on the stubborn side, her lips full and curved into what Thomas could only think of as a saucy smile. Her hair was dark brown with just a little gray at the temples, and worn down loose around her shoulders with a wisp of bangs across her forehead. She looked to be in her late thirties or maybe early forties with just a hint of laugh lines around her mouth and at the corners of her eyes.

It was her eyes that took his breath away. Dark like her hair and wide set, her eyes held not only the same saucy sense of humor that played around her lips, but a combination of confidence and tenderness that Thomas hadn't seen in many people in his life.

The photo wasn't a studio portrait or a staged outdoorsy snapshot. Instead, it looked like Edwina had been sitting relaxed in her favorite chair and simply looked up at the camera and smiled. For a moment Thomas wondered who took the photo, and if Edwina always looked at him like that.

The thought produced an unexpected pang in the region of Thomas's heart.

Before he could think too much about his reaction, a new message appeared in the chat window.

*Well?*

Thomas cleared his throat even though he wasn't talking to her on the phone. *You put your picture up,* he typed.

*Well?* she typed again.

What to say? Pick something professional, he decided. Friendly, but professional.

*Wonderful decision. I've always thought you should have your photograph up. It's a very lovely picture of you.*

He winced as he finished typing. That sounded like something he'd say to his mother.

*That's all?* she typed back after a slight hesitation. *What about the rest?*

The rest?

He scrolled down a little further. He'd been so mesmerized at seeing what a beautiful woman he'd been chatting with all these years that he hadn't even noticed the new text below Edwina's picture.

*Wanted!* he read. *One man, age not a factor.*

What?

The text went on.

*Romance required.*

*Must have own teeth.*

The ad finished with a request to contact LibertyBelle at an email address Thomas didn't recognize.

Apparently Edwina had set up a free email account for responses to her ad for...

Edwina was advertising for a man?

On the internet?

Was she serious?

Thomas sat back in his chair, totally at a loss of what to think.

In the space of a few moments he'd gone from being knocked

on his heels by the realization that he'd been chatting for years with the most beautiful woman he'd ever seen, to wondering who in the world she had in her life who could get her to smile like that, to having the rug pulled out from under him by finding out that she was advertising for a man.

On the internet!

He knew that Edwina was single, and in fact, just like him, had never been married even though she believed in love enough to make it her career. She'd never complained about being single, although on one occasion she'd confessed that she was a little too old for a date to think he could get a free feel of second base just because he took her to a horror movie so she'd get scared and lean on him.

Then she'd apologized profusely for sharing that kind of information with a reverend, which was when he'd told her that his title was honorary, and that he'd probably heard (and said) far worse than that himself on more than one occasion.

Of course, he didn't tell her that most of those occasions had been when he was still playing high school football.

So why all of a sudden was she advertising for a man?

Why would such a beautiful woman even need to advertise for a man?

On the internet, no less!

What in the world was she thinking?

# CHAPTER 4

"What in the world were you thinking?" Nellie Watkins asked Edwina the next morning when Edwina stopped by Nellie's diner for hot chocolate and the daily special, which happened to be a cinnamon-raisin waffle. "Don't you know there are a lot of kooks out there on the internet?"

Edwina sat down on one of the six stools at the counter. The Lickety-Split Cafe, like most businesses in Liberty Springs, was on the small side. The counter sat six. The three booths lining the front windows and the two two-person tables that sat along the left-hand wall provided additional seating, but not all that much. Nellie took the orders and did the cooking unless a big party came in, and then she rustled her husband away from his fly tying so he could wait on tables while Nellie took care of the kitchen.

Most days, the Lickety-Split did just enough business to let Nellie try out a new special menu item while leaving Gus to tie his Woolly Buggers and Bead Head Pheasant Tail nymphs in peace.

Edwina only knew the names of the flies because she stocked a few in her store. While fishing flies weren't precisely dry goods, Edwina knew her customer base, and it paid to keep the customers happy.

Nellie certainly kept Edwina happy. Nellie always had

Edwina's order ready by the time Edwina walked in the diner's glass front door at seven-thirty so that Edwina would be done and at the dry goods store a block away by eight. Today the cinnamon-raisin waffle was especially tasty. Edwina didn't even need to use the syrup Nellie kept on the counter.

She wasn't quite as happy about the unwanted advice that was sure to come, but that was Nellie for you. Except for her inexplicable need to mother Edwina even though Edwina was the older of the two by a good ten years, Edwina couldn't ask for a better friend.

Nellie refilled Edwina's hot chocolate without asking.

Technically it was already too late in the season to be drinking hot chocolate, especially in the middle of the Nevada desert, lake or no lake right next door. But Edwina figured if people could drink hot coffee all year long, she could drink hot chocolate whenever she wanted to. Especially Nellie's hot chocolate. Nellie had a secret recipe for her hot chocolate that she wouldn't even share with Edwina.

Not that Edwina would ever ask. That would just be rude.

She spoiled herself by eating breakfast every morning at the Lickety-Split. The locals tended to support local businesses like the diner whenever they could afford it. Plus, with the summer season starting up soon, Edwina could use some spoiling. She kept the dry goods store open every day of the week from Memorial Day through Labor Day, working by herself, and popped over to the chapel as the need arose.

"I guess this means you saw the website," Edwina said between bites of waffle.

"Seen it? Shirley called me this morning because she got a call from Bessie who'd been up all night cause the twins were kicking up a storm again—have I ever told you how glad I am that Gus never wanted kids?—because Bessie had cruised by your website and saw the picture, and then saw the *ad*." Nellie leaned in close over the counter and lowered the volume on her otherwise boisterous voice. "What got into you, advertising for a man like that?

Don't you watch the news? There are crazy people out there just cruising the internet, looking for some gullible woman to take advantage of."

Only one other person was in the diner—Cal Jenkins—and he was sitting at one of the two-person tables with his nose buried in a paperback, and it looked like he'd forgotten his hearing aids at home again. Cal was pretty much deaf as a doornail without his hearing aids. It must have been a lot of fun for Nellie to take his order, but there was no reason now for her to whisper.

"I do watch the news," Edwina said. "And I'm not a gullible woman." She picked up the hot chocolate and licked at the whipped cream before she blew on the cocoa a bit to cool it off. "I also took a good long look at myself and realized I'm not getting any younger." She lowered her voice to match Nellie's. "I'd like a little nooky before I die. I don't think that's too much to ask." She shot a sideways glance at Cal. "I'm certainly not going to get any from the men around here."

Nellie tried to look shocked, but a small giggle escaped anyway. "You're not going to give Chuck another try?"

"I didn't know there was another horror-movie marathon playing down in Hawthorne," Edwina deadpanned.

"That bad, huh?"

Edwina hadn't told Nellie all the gruesome details of her movie date, and she wasn't about to start now. "It wasn't pretty," she said, and figured that would suffice.

The only good thing about the whole date with Chuck had been that he'd realized how mismatched the two of them were too, and he hadn't asked her out on a second date. As a matter of fact, he hadn't even looked her in the eye the next time he came into the dry goods store until Edwina broke the ice. He'd seemed grateful that she had.

"Gus has a cousin down in Pasadena," Nellie said. "I could ask him—"

"Don't you dare." Edwina put down the mug. "No man in his right mind is going to want to leave Southern California for the likes of Liberty Springs, and I don't want to leave. I just want—"

"Nooky," Nellie said and sighed. "Trust me. It's overrated."

Edwina didn't believe that for a minute.

Gus was fifteen years older than Nellie, had a face like a boxer who'd spent more of his time in the ring on his back than on his feet, and probably hadn't seen his hairline in the mirror in a couple of decades. Nellie was still cheerleader pretty, right down to the rosy cheeks, pert little nose, and natural blonde ponytail. She had a figure that hadn't been damaged all that much by time, gravity, and her own good cooking. Gus and Nellie looked like the last two people on earth who should have ended up together, but their differences didn't matter one iota. Nellie loved the stuffing out of Gus and he loved her. Edwina had no doubt the nooky between those two was something special.

"Well, I'd like to find out for myself," Edwina said. "A woman should be able to do that if she wants."

She'd said something along the same lines to Reverend Thomas last night, only without the nooky reference.

She'd been so nervous about him seeing her picture. Why, she didn't know. It wasn't like she'd ever seen *his* picture.

The only pictures on the Lovers Lock Wedding Chapel website were of the chapel itself, a rustic-looking thing meant to resemble a log cabin in snow country complete with a sharply-sloped roof and a wooden front porch, pictures of the chapel's two available rooms, and pictures of the locks on the chains in Lovers Lock Plaza. And the chance they'd ever meet in person were somewhere between slim and none.

He was a good friend, no doubt about that, but he was her online friend. He lived too far away for either of them to drop in on the other on a casual basis.

The one time she'd asked him if he fished or water skied, thinking that he might make a sporting trip to Liberty Springs someday so they could finally meet, he'd said he was all thumbs when it came to fishing lines and two left feet when it came to any type of sporting activity that involved coordination beyond simply running. She'd been more disappointed than she should have been.

Just like she'd been more relieved than she should have been when he'd said her picture was lovely.

Things had gone so well with the picture, she never expected to get such strong opposition from him to her want ad.

*You can't be serious,* he'd typed after a long and rather pregnant pause.

She'd paused with her fingers poised over the keys. She hadn't known what to say.

Reverend Thomas had never been so blunt about any of her ideas before. If he thought there was a better way to do something she wanted to do, he always gave his advice in a gracious, understanding way. He never criticized her, and he was never sarcastic. It was one of the things she valued most about their friendship. He made her feel like all her ideas had value, even if the things they discussed might improve her ideas a little—or a whole lot.

*I most certainly am,* she'd typed back, deciding if he could be blunt, she could too. *You have no idea how hard it is to meet anyone here.*

*It's difficult to meet the right person anywhere,* he'd typed. *Advertising on the internet is not the way to go about it.*

*Dating services use the internet all the time,* she'd replied.

She could almost see his frown in the little chat window. It probably matched the one that had creased her own brows.

*Dating services at least do a little pre-screening,* he'd typed.

In other words, the only people who could possibly be attracted to her were weirdo stalker types. He hadn't exactly said it that way, but Edwina was sure that's what he'd meant.

Lovely picture, indeed.

Edwina didn't seriously believe that any internet-savvy, crazed stalker types would travel all the way to Liberty Springs just to harass her. She wasn't a gullible teenager. She was an adult woman, fully able to take care of herself.

And she'd post her ad if she wanted to.

Not that anyone would notice.

Maybe the ad was a bad idea, but at that point, she hadn't been about to admit it. Not to anyone. Especially not to the man who was supposed to be one of her best friends.

Even if she had no idea what *he* looked like.

*I doubt anyone is going to answer my ad anyway,* she'd typed into the chat window.

Then she'd said a brief goodnight and logged off the chat program without letting him get another word in.

She'd sat in her favorite chair for a long time afterward and debated pulling down the ad.

She did have her doubts whether anything would come of the ad. The people who clicked on the chapel's website were looking for a place to get married, not a person to get married to. Besides, if a man did click on the chapel's webpage, that meant he already had a fiancé. A man who'd already met the love of his life would think her ad was just part of a quirky marketing campaign for the chapel. He wouldn't think Edwina was serious.

She'd decided to sleep on it and figure out what to do in the morning.

On the short walk to the cafe, with the cool desert morning air brushing against her face and the first faint put-put of a motorboat engine echoing across the lake, the whole idea of advertising for romance seemed more than a little silly.

She'd almost decided that when she got to the dry goods store after breakfast, she'd take the ad down. She'd leave up her picture though. Reverend Thomas had been right about that. She should have always had her picture up, if not on the website's main page with the photograph of the chapel, then on one of the sub-pages. Edwina and her chapel were a package deal—both a little quirky, both a little down home, and both definitely friendly and welcoming.

But the ad?

She could chalk the whole thing up to too much time by herself with nothing but the television for company.

At least that's what she'd decided *before* breakfast.

Then Nellie had basically reiterated the same objections as Reverend Thomas had the night before. That brought out Edwina's stubborn side.

She was a grown woman, for goodness sake. She had a right to go about looking for romance in any way she decided, and this was the way she'd decided.

Her two best friends in the world might not like it, but right about now Edwina wouldn't take that ad down for the world.

# CHAPTER 5

Thomas couldn't get Edwina off his mind.

He daydreamed about her when he should have been dusting the stock in his gift shop.

He imagined what the feel of her hand might be like while he placed fresh flowers in the vases at either side of the garden room altar in his chapel.

He vacuumed the carpets in the whole place, his normal mid-morning, mid-week, you've-got-no-customers-so-why-not chore, and wondered if her hand would fit best nestled in the crook of his elbow or held firmly but gently in his own hand as they walked side by side, talking about life in general the way they did online.

Thomas was still considering that question when the vacuum stopped abruptly. Startled from his daydream, he frowned down at the machine. He'd had the vacuum for a long time, and they'd logged a lot of miles together keeping his chapel clean. Had it finally given up the ghost?

He nearly smacked himself in the forehead when he realized what had happened. He'd been so intent on imagining Edwina's hand in his that he hadn't even noticed he'd come to the end of the cord.

The vacuum had quit working simply because he'd pulled the

cord out of the socket. He knew he had to change sockets halfway down the aisle in the Old West room. He'd just forgotten.

This was silly. He was used to thinking about Edwina from time to time during the day, particularly when he was doing routine things like counting the gift shop's inventory of shot glasses, souvenir spoons, and T-shirts. But now that he had a face to go with Edwina's name, he couldn't stop thinking about her.

And her quest for romance.

How could an otherwise smart woman do such a ridiculous thing as placing a "romance wanted" ad on the internet?

Especially a woman who'd told him more than once that she'd decided to perform weddings for a living because she believed in true love?

A person couldn't advertise for love. Finding your one true love just didn't work that way.

Now, a person might find someone they could become infatuated with like that. Infatuation happened all the time.

Every so often when a couple came to his chapel to get married, Thomas could tell they weren't in love, they were just infatuated with each other. Often such couples got together at the end of a long night spent gambling and drinking at one of the local casinos. By the time morning rolled around, they'd convinced themselves that each was the other's long-lost soulmate. They'd tell Thomas they'd fallen in love at first sight, but Thomas knew what they'd really found was alcohol-fueled mutual lust.

He'd still marry them. They were adults, after all, capable of making their own decisions, and as long as they were sober, far be it from him to judge whether the infatuation they felt for each other wouldn't turn into love someday.

The only couples Thomas ever turned away were the ones who were obviously still intoxicated. He gave those couples a coupon for fifty percent off the wedding ceremony of their choice, provided they came back the next day. Many of them didn't.

True love, now that was something special.

Something to be nurtured.

Something to be treasured.

Something that took time and patience and understanding, not something to put in a want ad.

Edwina deserved better than she would get by advertising for romance on the internet. She was a kind and loving person. She was beautiful. She shouldn't have to settle. She deserved someone who truly loved her, and how could anyone she met through a want ad on the internet understand what a wonderful woman she was?

Thomas plugged the vacuum cord in the correct socket with more force than he intended. The vacuum sprang to life, and he resumed pushing it across the carpet, only with a little more oomph this time.

He was working so hard that he didn't hear the door to the chapel open.

"What did that carpet ever do to you?" a woman shouted over the vacuum noise.

Thomas turned around to see the Honorable Julie Wilkins smiling at him.

Julie Wilkins was the lone District Court judge for the Nevada counties of Pershing, Humboldt, and Lander. She was sixty years old if she was a day, and her tanned, lined face made her look like a grand old dame in her seventies.

Not that Thomas would ever tell her that.

Besides, Julie was as robust and hearty as a woman half her age. Little more than a hair over five feet tall and as wiry as they came, Julie wore custom-made cowboy boots beneath her black judicial robe, and she always had an oblong turquoise and silver ring as big as Thomas's thumb on the ring finger of her left hand. Today, like most days, she was dressed in a multi-colored broomstick skirt, the kind that had gone out of style a couple of decades ago, and her red blouse was something Thomas thought of as gypsy chic: light and airy, and as full as the skirt.

Julie always pulled her gray hair back into a tight bun while she was on the bench. It gave her a stern look she said was all the better to sentence criminals by, but when she wasn't in court, she let her hair out of its austere prison. Today it hung to the middle of her back in waves as unruly as Julie herself.

If someone who didn't know Julie encountered her on the street, they might think she was a poet or an artist, not a judge. Thomas had an idea that was one of the reasons she dressed the way she did.

He stepped on the vacuum's power switch with his foot to turn the machine off.

"I didn't know you were scheduled to be in town today," he said, smiling and holding his arms wide.

Julie stepped into the hug. "I wasn't, but criminals are entitled to a speedy trial, so what can I do?"

The Honorable Judge Julie H. Wilkins presided over criminal and civil trials and hearings in three of the largest but most sparsely-populated counties in Nevada. Julie, just like the other judges who covered more than one rural district, traveled on a set schedule from one county seat to the next to conduct court business. If someone's divorce went to trial in Lovelock, the trial date was scheduled—often months and months in advance—for a day when Julie would be in town. Criminal cases were scheduled on the same timetable except in rare instances when the accused refused to waive the right to a speedy trial as a tactic to force a plea bargain. When that happened, Julie made an unscheduled trip to Lovelock, much to the dismay of defense counsel.

As Julie often said, some people never learn.

Thomas didn't ask what case had brought her back to Lovelock. She wouldn't tell him, and he really didn't want to know. He preferred to think about people who found true love, or at least who had become infatuated with each other and decided to give it a go. Julie had told him once it was one of the things she liked most about him.

She stepped back out of the hug. "Can I buy you lunch? Court doesn't start until tomorrow, and I'm famished."

"Absolutely," Thomas said.

He put the vacuum away and stuck a *Be Back at 1:00* sign on the gift shop door. He didn't have to worry about locking up the chapel.

Unlike Edwina's side-by-side chapel and dry goods store, Thomas's chapel was at the rear of the gift shop and didn't have a separate outside entrance. The set-up allowed him not only to operate both businesses at once, but also funnel the newly-married couple and their wedding guests out through the gift shop just in case someone wanted to buy a memento of the happy occasion. Edwina, on the other hand, had to close her dry goods store whenever she got a wedding party.

And there he was thinking about Edwina again!

Thomas really didn't understand why. He hadn't chatted with her in two days.

Not that he didn't want to. She just hadn't been online.

Or maybe she just hadn't logged into the chat program.

Thomas hoped she wasn't still angry with him. She'd signed off so abruptly the last time they'd talked, not that he could really blame her.

In retrospect, he'd been far too blunt about her decision to advertise for romance. That was so unlike him. He'd never dismissed any of her ideas like that before. He'd told himself at the time that it had just been his honest reaction, and he'd always been honest with Edwina. Wasn't honesty the bedrock of their friendship?

Looking back on that conversation, though, he realized he'd been rude. And dismissive. And totally callous about what must have been a very difficult decision for her, even just to put her picture on the website, much less the want ad.

Why in the world had she done that anyway? She didn't seem like a woman who did things on a whim.

Although she *had* purchased her wedding chapel on something very much like a whim.

That brought him up short.

How much did he really know about Edwina? She had a pretty face—a very pretty face—and he'd always enjoyed her sense of humor. She was just the sort of woman he thought he could be interested in. If she lived in town. Or anywhere near town, but Liberty Springs was over a hundred miles away. And besides, he'd always been so comfortable chatting with Edwina online, he really didn't want anything other than friendship.

Right?

Even if seeing her want ad had given him a rather odd feeling in his—

"You are a million miles away," Julie said, interrupting his thoughts.

Thomas blinked. She was right.

They had walked all the way down the street, turned the corner, and were nearly at The Player's Club, their usual lunchtime destination, and Thomas hadn't even noticed.

He felt his cheeks heat up, and it had nothing to do with the noonday sunshine beating down on his head.

"You're right," he said with a sigh. What in the world was wrong with him? Julie was too dear a friend for him to ignore her like that.

Julie made a humming noise while she peered up at him. Thomas got the distinct impression she was studying him much like she studied the people whose cases she tried. For the first time in their long friendship, her gaze made him a bit uncomfortable.

"I thought so," she said at last. The corners of her mouth tipped up in a little grin. "You've met a woman."

Now his cheeks really heated up. No, it wasn't like that.

Was it?

"Well, not so much 'met,'" he said. "More like 'can't stop thinking about.'"

One of Julie's eyebrows lifted. "Now, this sounds like a story I want to hear."

They reached the front door of the sandwich shop, which gave Thomas a reprieve. He held the door open for Julie, and she nodded her thanks.

The Player's Club was Julie's favorite place to eat when she was in town. Stan Otto had named all the sandwiches on his menu after card games. Thomas usually ordered the Texas Hold 'Em, which was a barbecued beef sandwich on a poor boy roll, hold the onions. Julie preferred the Solitaire, which resembled a regular club sandwich but with a wider variety of vegetables and a choice of only one type of meat. Julie usually picked smoked turkey.

A few people were in line at the counter waiting their turn to order lunch, but The Player's Club wasn't crowded. It rarely was, but Stan never seemed to mind. He'd won a tidy sum of money a few years ago at a poker tournament in Reno. No one in town knew exactly how much—opinions varied widely—but it had been enough to let Stan retire from his job at the correctional center and open his sandwich shop. Gossip had it that his winnings funded all his expenses, and the sandwich shop just kept him busy and out of his wife's hair.

The change in careers seemed to agree with him, at least judging by the extra twenty pounds he'd packed on around his middle.

"Judge!" Stan said with a smile when Thomas and Julie got to the front of the short line. "Nice to see you back in town. Your usual?"

Julie nodded at him. "You know me well."

Stan turned to Thomas. "Woah! You been out in the sun, Reverend?"

Like most of the locals, Stan called Thomas "Reverend" even though he'd tried to tell Stan to just call him by name. Thomas stifled a sigh and gave the man a smile.

"A little," Thomas said. Apparently his cheeks were still on the ruddy side. He'd hoped the short time in line, which had effectively prevented him from having to talk about Edwina, would have let the flush he'd felt fade away.

In fact, the flush *should* have faded away. He really hadn't been all that embarrassed at Julie's prodding.

Had he?

Good Lord, did he actually have that "glow" people always talked about? The one he noticed on the couples who seemed to be truly in love?

Hoping to forestall any further discussion about his complexion, he said, "I'll have my usual."

While Stan went about making sandwiches for his lunch crowd, Julie and Thomas got their drinks at the little self-serve soda machine and found an unoccupied two-person table off to one side of the shop.

Instead of looking at Julie's expectant face, Thomas poked his straw through the lid of his iced tea, rolling the wrapper into a tight little ball. Then he pressed down around the top of the lid to make sure the lid was snapped on tight. The last thing he wanted was a lap full of ice even on a hot—

"You're stalling," Julie said.

He sighed and glanced up at her.

"I've never seen you this nervous before," she said. "It's not like I have you on the stand and I've just shredded your attorney into a quivering mass of overpriced goo."

Thomas had to chuckle. Julie had told him once that one of her favorite things was to put egotistical, misogynistic attorneys—and the criminal defense bar in rural Nevada seemed to have more than their fair share—in their place.

She wasn't doing that to him. She was just interested in his life, like any good friend would be.

So why was he so nervous?

Why did he have a glow that even Stan could see?

And why couldn't he stop thinking about Edwina and that

want ad of hers, the one that had made him feel so unsettled inside?

He knew the answer, of course. He recognized the symptoms in other people, he just never thought it would happen to him.

He quit playing with his iced tea and put his hands flat on the table. If there was anyone in the world he could talk this over with, it would be Julie.

Thomas looked her in the eye, shrugged his shoulders, and gave her a sheepish, goofy grin.

"I'm pretty sure I've gone and fallen in love," he said. "And I have no idea what to do about it."

# CHAPTER 6

$\mathcal{E}$dwina snuck into her dry goods store through the door at the back of her chapel that connected the two. Before this week, she had rarely used the connecting door. It was more like an emergency exit at the movie theater—nice to know it's there, but not something she ever thought of using.

Over the last two days it had become a necessity.

If it wasn't coming up on Memorial Day weekend, Edwina might have closed the dry goods store. But the last weekend in May, with its influx of fishermen and late spring water sports enthusiasts drawn by the clear blue of Sutter Lake, made up for the poor sales Edwina and every other business in Liberty Springs suffered through all winter. She couldn't afford to keep the store closed.

No matter how many geezers waited for her in the parking lot outside the store.

Edwina peered through the windows at the front of the store. Luckily the windows weren't floor to ceiling plate glass, just over-sized wood frame windows like someone might have in a fancy living room. The day had dawned hot and bright, not a cloud in the desert sky. She hadn't turned on the lights in the store yet, so she hoped none of the men gathered by the front door could see her in the gloomy interior of the store.

She counted twelve men out there, which was more than the seven who had waited for her yesterday.

And that didn't count the number of single men who'd shown up at the store throughout the day.

Her little advertisement for romance had been successful beyond her wildest dreams.

Or perhaps that should be beyond her worst nightmare.

She wasn't sure how it had happened—did anyone really know why something went viral on the internet?—but Liberty Springs was being inundated with geriatric Lotharios, and each and every one of them showed Edwina his teeth in lieu of a normal "hello."

It was like living in a town overrun by zombies who were all trying to smile.

The only motel in Liberty Springs, the aptly-named Liberty Springs Motor Lodge, had filled its eight rooms the day after Edwina's ad hit the worldwide web.

There was a recreational area, complete with campgrounds, on the north shore of Sutter Lake about a mile away from town, but the campgrounds wouldn't open until tomorrow. So once the motel filled up, Edwina's would-be suitors had set up camp in the desert outside of town. She sold out of tents and chemical toilets within a day.

After that, Father Mills had opened up the rec hall next to the church for the overflow, and Edwina had sold out of sleeping bags, blankets, and travel pillows.

Not to mention every sort of over-the-counter remedy for sore muscles and stiff backs.

Who knew there were this many single men willing to travel to an out-of-the-way place like Liberty Springs?

And most of them were in their seventies. If not their eighties!

Had she really looked that old in her picture?

And hadn't she specified that they contact her by email? She'd even created a new freebie email account for herself just for the occasion. Leave it to a man—or several dozen men—to ignore the instructions.

"The next time you get a bright idea, have a glass of wine instead," she muttered to herself.

The very worst thing was she just couldn't bear to send them all home. For all she knew, Mr. Right was somewhere out there waiting for her to rub his sore muscles with a little liniment.

Not that they were *all* quite that old. Edwina had met a few of her wannabe suitors who'd actually been in their late fifties or early sixties. One man who'd told her he was fifty-nine said he'd been a widower for five years, and he didn't want to be alone for the rest of his life. He'd actually brought her a box of candy.

Edwina thought that was sweet, even though he hadn't peeled the price tag off the wrapper, so she knew the candy had come from a grocery store in Hawthorne.

She'd actually considered asking him if he wanted to get a piece of pie with her at Nellie's, but his attention had wavered to the display of fishing flies on the wall next to the counter while he was talking to her.

So much for romance.

At least he'd made a personal effort. Almost every other man who'd answered her ad thought romance meant flowers.

The chapel was overflowing with flower arrangements prepared by the same florist in Fallon that Edwina used. UPS had to put another driver on the route to handle all the deliveries.

Edwina had put the unopened box of candy on a shelf beneath the register. One down, an ever-increasing number to go. And the worst thing was, now they were all starting to ask for her hand in marriage before they even said hello!

She couldn't even walk to the Lickety-Split for breakfast without some man dropping to one knee, grinning a teeth-baring smile, and declaring his true love for her.

True love? Not in her book.

True love didn't happen like that. You had to get to know a

person. Become friends. Have fun together. Spend long hours talking to each other about nothing and everything.

In other words, she wanted a relationship like she had with Reverend Thomas, only with love and nooky, and preferably not the online kind. Was that too much to ask?

How in the world was she going to get to know any of these men long enough to figure out if he was Mr. Right?

Someone rapped on the door.

Edwina peeked out from behind a display of canned beans and chili.

"Open up!" Nellie shouted.

She was holding a large covered Tupperware.

What was Nellie doing here?

As Edwina watched, one of the men waiting for her outside the store bared his teeth at Nellie. He had to be seventy if he was a day. He wore black-rimmed glasses with coke-bottle lenses, and he had a large hearing aid behind one ear.

"Still has his own teeth, my patootie," Edwina muttered.

Nellie held up her left hand—complete with the ostentatious wedding ring set Gus had splurged on because he thought all women liked gaudy jewelry—to the man, then to all the men in general.

"I'm not her," Nellie said loud enough even Edwina heard. "Do you think I look like the picture on the internet?"

The old guy shrugged.

Edwina winced. This so wasn't going according to plan.

Not that she'd ever really *had* a plan.

She sighed. She couldn't leave her friend all alone out there with a bunch of rabid retirees.

"Fifteen minutes!" Edwina shouted as she unlocked the door for Nellie. "We open in fifteen minutes." She made herself smile. All these men were all here because of her, after all. At least she could be polite. "Thank you for your patience."

Another car pulled into the parking lot as Edwina was shutting the door behind Nellie. The car was a modest sedan, silvery-blue in color, and had dusty Nevada plates. Edwina couldn't remember seeing it before. It certainly didn't belong to anyone in Liberty Springs.

Oh, great. Another one.

Edwina locked the front door. "I don't even know what to say."

Nellie had a broad smile on her face. "I do." She thrust the Tupperware at Edwina. "Have some breakfast. On the house. You deserve it."

Edwina cocked an eyebrow. "How come?" she asked as she took the dish from Nellie's hands.

"This is the busiest my place has been in years. I can't keep up. Gus has been waiting on so many tables, I'm going to have to buy him new shoes. Tonight we're going to start serving food for the people staying at the rec hall. I talked to Lois last night, and even she's been busier than normal. And it's all thanks to you."

Lois ran a diner in Hawthorne at the other end of the lake. Lois's diner hadn't been doing all that well since the McDonalds everyone drove by on their way to or from Las Vegas upgraded their ordering system and doubled their staff. Lois made delicious travel food, but most people seemed to like familiar, cookie-cutter takeout rather than taking a chance on a local restaurant's version of a BLT.

"They're invading Hawthorne, too?" Edwina asked.

Nellie nodded. "You must have a magic touch. Maybe I should have you do a website for the Lickety-Split."

"Very funny."

Edwina took the top off the Tupperware. Strawberry waffles, complete with only partially-melted whipped cream, along with a to-go cup of hot chocolate were nestled inside. Breakfast looked wonderful, but Edwina didn't have much of an appetite. She put the Tupperware down on the counter next to the cash register.

"What am I going to do with all these men?" she asked.

"See if one of them is the one you're looking for, of course."

"How? I can't possibly go out on a date with every single one of them. It would take weeks!"

Nellie sighed. "I see your point. We could do a spreadsheet. Gus is pretty good at that. He does all the books for the diner."

A spreadsheet? "What for? I'm not taking bids." Edwina's idea of romance was taking a beating as it was. She certainly wasn't going to put herself up for auction.

"No, no, that's not what I meant." Nellie leaned against the counter. If she noticed that Edwina had simply put the Tupperware down without taking a bite, she didn't seem upset. "Every woman has ideal things they look for in a man. Hair, eyes, body type." She gave Edwina a wicked smile. "Teeth."

Edwina snorted. "Please don't ever mention teeth to me again."

It had seemed like such a whimsical line when she'd put it in her want ad. Never in a million years would she have guessed that she'd see more teeth in a few days than a dentist did in an entire month.

"Okay, not teeth," Nellie said. "But you get the idea. Well, we could make up a spreadsheet that would tell us how many brown-haired men are here, if that's your thing, or how many are over six feet tall."

"Have you seen the men out there? If there are more than three in the brown-haired column, I'd be surprised."

Besides, physical attributes weren't all that important. Edwina doubted that any of Gus's physical attributes would have made it onto Nellie's own personal spreadsheet, but they sure did love each other.

Speaking of Gus...

"Did you leave your husband all alone at the diner?" Edwina asked. She couldn't imagine Gus trying to run the kitchen. In fact, she didn't even know if Gus could cook.

Nellie smiled. "Today's special is scrambled eggs and bacon. It was the one thing Gus knew how to cook for himself before we got married. He'll be fine until I get back." She nodded at

Edwina's untouched breakfast. "That's the only waffle I've made all day, and by the looks of it, I've lost my touch."

Edwina winced. "Not your cooking, believe me." She gestured at the parking lot. "I've got to get a handle on this. I caused this mess. I can't exactly sneak out of town in the middle of the night."

"Gus would suggest a lottery. He's always watching the California lottery, just waiting for it to get big enough to make it worthwhile to drive across the border to buy a ticket." Nellie shook her head. "That man has a perpetual sense of optimism. He's absolutely convinced that if he buys a ticket, he's going to win."

A lottery was too much like putting herself up for auction, or like bingo night at the church rec hall, just waiting for the right numbers to be called.

At least the last time Edwina had gone to play bingo, she'd won a nice handmade afghan the church had raffled off to raise money to send the choir—all five of them—to Sacramento for an interfaith choir competition. They'd come in second place in the small ensemble division. The entire town of Liberty Springs had shown up at the church to welcome them home.

Wait a minute. That gave Edwina an idea.

"Not a lottery," she said. "A raffle."

"What?"

Edwina took her breakfast out of the Tupperware. "You mind if I borrow this?"

Nellie looked uncertain. "Depends on what you're going to do with it."

Edwina snorted. "Nothing you won't approve of." She rooted around on the shelf beneath the cash register and came up with a box of pens and two pads of plain white paper she kept for making notes to herself. "Everyone who comes in here and shows me his teeth is going to write his name on a piece of paper and put it in the Tupperware."

"And you're going to draw a winner," Nellie said, then she

frowned. "I don't see how that's going to help you find the right man. You do want to find the right one, don't you?"

Edwina most certainly did. The influx of suitors might have put a strain on her nerves, but she still believed in true love. Somewhere out in the world, Mr. Right was waiting for her to discover him. The only way to do that was to get to know all the men who'd come to meet her.

She couldn't date each one in the conventional sense, that would take too much time. But she did need to meet each of them, and without the distraction of a bunch of other guys hanging around.

"I'm not going to draw a winner," Edwina said. "I'm going to give everyone an audition. Ten minutes, repeat performance at my discretion." She held up the Tupperware. "Let's get some names in this tub and see who I talk to first."

# CHAPTER 7

Thomas still couldn't believe he'd driven all the way to Liberty Springs.

It was all Julie's fault.

"You have to go meet her, of course," she'd said after Thomas had told her about his longtime friendship with Edwina and his recently discovered feelings.

Julie had eaten nearly all of her Solitaire by the time Thomas had finished talking about Edwina. He'd barely touched his Texas Hold 'Em even though it looked as delicious as Stan's sandwiches always did.

"I can't just show up and declare my undying love for her," he'd said. "What if she doesn't feel anything but friendship for me?"

Or worse.

What if she never wanted to talk to him again because he'd been so rude to her the last time they'd chatted?

"But what if she does?" Julie had smiled gently at him. "You of all people must know how rare it is in this world to find the one person you can truly be yourself with. The one person you can love unconditionally who will love you unconditionally in return.

Why would you chance missing an opportunity to find out if she's that one person for you?"

"I value our friendship too much to risk it," he said.

"Oh, poppycock."

Thomas blinked at her.

"Your friendship is already undergoing a sea change," she said. "You've recognized feelings in yourself that you weren't aware of before. Even if you never tell her, which I think would be criminal, you will always know that things have changed. Your friendship can never be what it was before. There's nothing to risk except the possibility of discovering that she feels the same way about you."

There was the possibility of getting his heart broken, but Thomas didn't say that. He didn't have to. Julie was as aware of that as he was. She obviously thought it was an acceptable risk to take.

He must have, too, or he wouldn't be here.

Although it had been a close call. He'd almost turned around more than once, especially when he hit Fallon.

The sun had just come up, turning the desert that soft, warm, golden shade it only got at the first light of day. He usually saw the sunrise through his kitchen window while he was enjoying his first cup of coffee, and a new thought struck him.

What if Edwina didn't like coffee?

What if she didn't even like the smell of it?

There were so many things they didn't know about each other. Was she an early morning person, or was she a night owl? Occasionally they chatted on the computer until midnight, but that didn't mean Edwina always stayed up until the wee hours of the morning. Could a morning person and a night owl find happiness together?

And what if she was more religious than he was?

She'd told him that she'd gotten her minister's license online just as he had, but what if she took her ministry more literally? He'd never talked to her about religion other than confessing to her that the title "reverend" was just that—a title, not a vocation. Had that been a mistake?

These questions and more had plagued him the entire drive from Lovelock to Liberty Springs. One hundred miles had never seemed so long.

In the end, Thomas had forced himself to keep on driving only by imagining the disappointed look on Julie's face if went back home without at least saying hello to Edwina.

He finally turned off the two-lane highway onto the road that led to Edwina's dry goods store a little after seven-thirty. Edwina opened her dry goods store at eight. Thomas had left Lovelock early enough to make sure he arrived at the dry goods store before Edwina. It might have been cowardly, but he wanted to see her before she had a chance to see him, and he figured his best bet was to wait in his car in the parking lot and watch her while she opened the store.

And hope that she didn't think he was a stalker.

He couldn't have been more surprised to discover that he wasn't the only man waiting for Edwina in the parking lot, only most of them weren't still in their cars.

A good dozen men were crowded around the front door of Liberty Springs Dry Goods & Sporting Supplies, all of them older than Thomas by a good ten years, most of them by considerably more.

A short blonde woman stood in the middle of the huddle of men, holding a large Tupperware container over her head.

She wasn't Edwina. Even if the woman's hair wasn't Edwina's dark brown, Thomas would have known it wasn't her. The blonde woman was cute, but she wasn't Edwina's brand of beautiful.

The door to the store opened, and the blonde woman slipped inside. The door shut again quickly, but not before Thomas caught a glimpse of the woman inside.

Edwina.

He was surprised at how much his pulse quickened at just that brief glance.

He'd never felt like this about a woman before, and he hadn't even officially met her yet, at least not in person.

He wasn't sure what to do. He didn't want to join the group at the door. He had no doubt they'd come to Liberty Springs for the same reason he had—he'd seen more than one of them bare their teeth at the blonde, which had been the one whimsical part of Edwina's want ad that had almost, *almost*, made Thomas laugh —but he was amazed that anyone had even seen Edwina's ad, much less driven to Liberty Springs to answer it.

This many men wanted to marry Edwina? He'd hoped to get a chance to talk to her alone, but that was impossible now.

Thomas sat in his car and considered what he should do next. He'd driven all this way. He had to figure out a way to meet her.

He was still thinking about that when the blonde woman stepped back outside. She had the Tupperware in her hands along with a small sign. She was saying something to the men gathered around the front door. Thomas rolled the car window down so he could hear her.

"...name on a piece of paper and drop it in the Tupperware that I'm going to leave on a stand right inside the door. No monkey business. We're all gentlemen here, right?"

"Damn skippy!" said one of the men, an old guy wearing black-framed glasses with thick lenses.

That drew a few laughs from the crowd.

The blonde smiled in return. "Good to hear it. Now starting at noon today, we're going to be drawing names out of the Tupperware, and you're going to be meeting with Edwina, one at a time, in order of the way we draw. She wants to meet with all of you, so you'll all get your turn. We're going to put this up in the window"—she shook the small sign—"so that anyone who's not here knows what we're doing. We'd appreciate if you'd let them know. We'll have another sign like this at my diner and over at the rec hall. In the meantime, Edwina would appreciate if you gave her a little breathing room. Feel free to shop in the store, but no marriage proposals, understand?"

That raised more laughter from the group.

"She'll be talking to everyone," the blonde said. "So put your name in the hat, so to speak, and come back at noon. It's that simple. In the meantime, enjoy the town. Do a little sight seeing, or come over to the diner. Scrambled eggs and bacon are the special today."

She ended by handing everyone a slip of paper and a pen. While the men were busy writing their names on the paper, she taped the sign to the window beside the door.

Thomas sighed.

Edwina wanted to be left alone, which probably meant these men weren't the only ones who'd answered her want ad. These were just the men who'd shown up first thing this morning, just like Thomas had.

He wasn't going to be able to spend any quiet time alone with her, not now. He'd seen a group of tents near the road on his drive into town. He'd figured the tents belonged to fishermen here early for the long holiday weekend, but now he wasn't so sure.

He had no place to stay. He hadn't even thought about making reservations, and he doubted there was room available anywhere.

What should he do?

He knew what Julie would say. He'd wanted time alone with Edwina to talk to her in person. Julie wanted him to tell her how he felt, but he certainly couldn't do that now. From the sound of things, it seemed like Edwina was getting marriage proposals left and right. Thomas didn't want her to discount his feelings just because he'd arrived in the middle of a deluge of suitors.

When you got right down to it, there was only one thing he could do.

He got out of the car. His muscles were stiff from the long drive, but his legs felt much more wooden and clumsy than a long drive should have made them. Nerves, he told himself.

By the time he got to the front of the store, half the men had already placed their names in the Tupperware and left. Thomas got in line behind the old guy in the black-framed glasses and waited his turn.

When he got to the front of the line, the blonde handed him a piece of paper and a pen. Instead of writing his full name on the paper—much less the "reverend" part—he simply wrote "Tom T" and dropped it in the Tupperware.

His heart was pounding as he walked back to his car.

There. That was the most he could do for now. He'd come back at noon with all the other men and wait his turn so he could talk to Edwina.

He just hoped that by the time he actually got to meet her in person, she hadn't already decided someone else was her one true love.

# CHAPTER 8

 $\mathcal{E}$ dwina had a small office in the chapel off to one side of the altar. She used the room to complete the paperwork she had to file with the county about the weddings she performed.

Originally the room had come furnished with a gray metal desk, a garage sale office chair, and a rickety metal filing cabinet whose drawers never shut properly. Over the years she'd replaced the desk with small wooden one with drawers on both sides of the cubbyhole for her feet and a big enough top to write on. She'd splurged on a comfortable desk chair, one that supported her lower back and felt positively sinful when she sank into it. The metal filing cabinet had long since gone to wherever rickety filing cabinets went when you donated them to Goodwill. Now a sturdy wooden filing cabinet was nestled in the corner of the office behind her desk, complete with sprawling spider plant on top.

The spider plant was the companion to a pint-sized ponytail palm that sat on her desk. The plants got just enough light through a small window high on the office wall and added a bit of green to her otherwise comfortable but sparsely furnished office.

And at this point, non-aromatic green plants were a welcome

change from the flowers that were rapidly overwhelming the chapel.

At the back of the office, next to the connecting door to the dry goods store, stood a good-sized, free-standing closet. The collection of robes Edwina wore while she performed weddings shared space in that closet with janitorial and restroom supplies, and one well-used Elvis costume.

Edwina refused to perform a wedding ceremony dressed as Elvis. Instead, she offered her happy couples a choice of color of the robes she wore. Some people wanted white, some wanted black, and she even had a royal blue robe she wore when the couple had no other preference.

The Elvis costume wasn't really Edwina's. It had come with the chapel. The officiate who'd operated the chapel before her must have performed themed weddings because there'd been a variety of costumes in the closet when she bought the place. She'd given away the cowboy outfit and the outer space outfit, the Old World monk's outfit and the stage magician outfit, but she hadn't been able to part with Elvis. Something about it struck her funny bone. She kept threatening to dress up one year for Gus's birthday since he was a big Elvis fan, but so far she hadn't followed through.

If she lost her mind during this whole audition process, she might bring Elvis out of the closet just long enough to see if any of the men who professed to love her still meant it when they saw her in Elvis drag.

Since noon, Nellie had brought a steady stream of suitors through the connecting door. Edwina didn't have a visitor's chair in her office—no visitors ever came back here—so Nellie had loaned her a folding chair from the card table set she and Gus used for Tuesday night board game nights. (The diner closed early on Tuesdays to give Nellie a night off.) The chair was metal with barely enough padding to call it padding, and probably uncomfortable as all get out, but none of her suitors had complained.

Edwina had met with each of the men who'd come all the way

to Liberty Springs to woo her with a gradually sinking heart. They were all pleasant and attentive—sometimes a little too attentive—and Edwina had been polite in return, but it quickly became apparent that none of the men she met were anywhere close to Mr. Right.

The clock on the wall next to the free-standing closet told her it was now nearly three o'clock in the afternoon, and Edwina was tired. So tired, in fact, that she let a little of her exasperation show.

"I don't understand," she said to the man currently auditioning for a chance to date her. "Why would so many men make the trip out here just to meet me?"

He had the good graces to look a little sheepish at her question, and she felt momentarily bad about asking it. After all, he had made the trip out here as well, and he seemed nice enough.

Well, more than nice enough, if she was being honest with herself. In fact, the only strike against him so far was that he seemed a little on the shy side. At least he was far younger than any of the other men Edwina had met with. Which meant he looked to be about her age, or maybe just a year or two older.

He was also pretty easy on the eyes.

Not smoothly handsome in a movie star way, or ruggedly handsome like he'd ridden in off the range and had left his horse in the parking lot. He had a full head of light brown hair that looked like it might bleach easy in the sun, and soft brown eyes with laugh lines at the corners. He was clean shaven, his cheekbones and jaw strong but not aggressively so. He was taller than Nellie, which would make him taller than Edwina, and he was trim without being lean. He wore a simple blue short-sleeved shirt, dark blue jeans, and dark brown work boots, not cowboy boots, and he hadn't doused himself in aftershave or body spray.

Edwina really appreciated that last part. A few of her suitors had overdone the body spray to the point she wished the little window in her office opened, even if the afternoon had turned out hot and dry.

This man had held out his hand to her when Nellie had

brought him into Edwina's office. For a moment, she thought he was going to kiss her fingers—it wouldn't have been the first time someone had kissed her fingers that day—but he shook her hand instead. She'd liked that.

In fact, she rather liked him. A lot. She just hadn't felt any sort of spark.

Not that there needed to be an immediate spark—plenty of couples who stood at her altar told her they'd been friends for a long time before they fell in love—but a spark would have been nice.

A spark certainly would have made this feel less like she was interviewing potential employees instead of potential dates.

Instead, talking with this man had felt more like talking with an old friend. Except for his shyness, he was pretty easy to talk to. Maybe that's why she'd vented a little without even meaning to.

"I'd really like to know," she said, deliberately making her tone a little more gentle. "Why travel all this way for a woman you've never met?"

After all, it wasn't like she had a lot of cash or a body to die for.

"That's a good question," the shy man said.

Edwina wished she could remember his name. She hadn't wanted to write the names down on a piece of paper when Nellie introduced each man to her—that really would have made the whole process seem like a job interview—but now she wished she had. All the names had begun to blur about an hour ago, and she didn't want to appear rude and ask him what his name was again when he'd told her only a few minutes ago.

"All I can do is tell you why I came," he said. "I don't know for sure about the rest of them, but if they're at all like me, it's because we all hope we can find that one special person who will make the rest of our lives worthwhile. The one person in the whole world we're supposed to be with. That love—true love—is possible at any age. For a man who believes in true love, a trip to

Liberty Springs to find out if you're that one special person doesn't seem like all that much of a hardship."

A flush had colored those strong cheekbones by the time the shy man quit talking, and he dropped his gaze from hers, like he was afraid he'd said too much.

Edwina was stunned. He got it. He understood. That was exactly why she'd written her silly ad in the first place, because she believed in the possibility that true love existed somewhere in the world for her (no matter how old she was), and if she couldn't leave Liberty Springs to go find it, true love would have to come to her.

She could see herself spending time with him. Getting to know him better (even though part of her felt like she already knew him, which was completely irrational since she was pretty sure she'd never seen him before in her life), and maybe snuggling up next to him in a darkened movie theater like teenagers who couldn't wait for the lights to go down.

That thought gave her a pleasant tingle, and she smiled at him.

Okay, so she hadn't felt a spark when their fingers touched, but that tingle had definite possibilities. He was very, very easy on the eyes, after all, close to her own age, and not the least bit over-bearing. And he believed in true love! What he'd just said didn't sound like a canned speech. No one could talk about love like that without believing in what he was saying.

Out of all the men she'd met so far today, this guy was the first one she wanted to give a second chance—an actual date complete with movie tickets and a bucket of popcorn.

She was about to suggest just that when Nellie came through the connecting door.

"We've only got one more out there," she said, "and I need to get back to the diner. Gus is threatening to divorce me if I don't get back to give him a break." She seemed to notice for the first time that the shy man was still there. "Oh, I'm sorry." She glanced at the clock on the wall behind Edwina's head. "I thought the ten minutes were up."

The shy man stood up. He held out his hand again, and Edwina took it without thinking. He had nice hands, too. Soft but strong, like he worked inside most of the time but not at a typical desk job. She realized she hadn't asked him what he did for a living.

"It's been a pleasure to finally meet you," he said.

His brown eyes held some emotion Edwina couldn't quite identify, like he was working hard to keep himself in check.

"I'm sorry you had to wait so long," she said. He'd been waiting around the store for nearly three hours, after all.

"Not a problem," he said, giving her a warm smile. "It was worth it."

He let go of her hand and walked toward the door the led into the chapel, like all the men she'd met before him.

Only he wasn't like all the other men she'd met on this long and frustrating day. He was special.

"Don't leave town just yet," she called after him. "I mean, if you don't have any other plans."

He turned around, and she felt an honest smile play around her lips.

His grin widened. "I don't intend to."

She wanted to ask his name, but she didn't want to break the spell by admitting that she couldn't remember it. Besides, even if she didn't know his name, he'd be easy to find in a town the size of Liberty Springs. Even though the town was overrun with all the men who'd come to meet her, this guy would stand out.

After he shut the door behind himself, Edwina sighed a happy little sigh. She really didn't want to meet anyone else. She liked how she felt after talking to him, and she didn't want to spoil it by meeting with someone who'd turn out to be a totally unsuitable suitor.

"Wow," Nellie said, studying her. "I guess he was a good one, huh?"

Edwina could deny it, but what was the point? "Yeah, I think he could be."

"He did seem kind of nice, for an older guy."

Older guy? Sometimes it was easy to forget that Nellie was younger than Edwina was. "He couldn't be any older than Gus," Edwina said.

Nellie grinned. "Like I said, for an older guy. I happen to like my older guy."

Edwina knew it was more than "like," but she wasn't about to quibble. "You said there was one more?" She'd really like to send him away, but that would just be rude. She could, however, cut the interview short.

Nellie waggled her eyebrows and her grin turned just a touch wicked. "There most certainly is. Wait until you get a look at him."

"Why?"

"You'll see. And I'll see you later. You want me to lock up the store on the way out?"

"Might as well," Edwina said.

The suitors had pretty much cleared her out except for the kind of things that sold only once in a blue moon. She'd placed an emergency order for all the regular staples, like canned goods and flour and freeze-dried, ready-to-eat meals. The delivery was supposed to arrive tomorrow, which would give her just enough time to restock the shelves before the weekend—and all the normal tourists—arrived.

"You got it." Nellie paused at the connecting door to the dry goods store. "Although I'm tempted to stay to watch your reaction, I really have to go. Don't do anything I wouldn't do," she said, and she winked.

She actually winked.

What in the world was Nellie up to? She had never, ever acted like that, not even when Edwina had mentioned, in passing, that she'd finally broken down and accepted a date from Chuck Long to a horror movie. If anything, that should have opened Edwina up to all sorts of teasing from Nellie, but Nellie hadn't even raised a suggestive eyebrow. She'd simply told Edwina to have a good time.

Now she was winking. What in the world was waiting on the other side of the connecting door?

Of course, Nellie could just be tired. Lord knows, Edwina was tired, and she hadn't done much beyond sit behind her desk all day and talk to men. Who knew auditions for the part of Mr. Right could be so exhausting?

What she really wanted was a long, hot bath, complete with bubbles, a nice glass of ice tea, and a few candles burning softly for atmosphere. Edwina had no idea whether a candlelight bubble bath was romantic and relaxing, or more trouble than it was worth. The movies always made it look romantic.

Maybe she should do a test run tonight after she got home, just in case things went really well with the shy man—why couldn't she remember his name? Was it John, or maybe Dan? Tim? Tom? She was fairly sure it was something short like that— she'd already know if taking a bubble bath together would be romantic or just plain silly.

Edwina shook her head. Talk about silly. Here she was, imagining romantic interludes with a man she'd just met. She hadn't done that in years, not since she'd been a love-struck teenager fantasizing about marrying her favorite movie star. She was far too old for ridiculous ideas like—

That thought fizzled as the connecting door opened, and the closest thing to a movie star Edwina had ever seen stepped into her office.

Tall. Blond. Muscular.

Startling blue eyes that held more than just a simple twinkle.

And at least a good ten years younger than she was.

He smiled at her—a smile that was sure to stop traffic, as her mother used to say—and held out his hand.

"Edwina?" he said, his voice pleasantly deep. "I'm Rufus Monroe, and I am *very* pleased to meet you."

## CHAPTER 9

Thomas found a quiet spot on a bench by the lake where he could sit for a while by himself and wait for his heart to resume beating at something approaching a normal pace.

He'd actually talked to Edwina.

Not only talked to her, but shared far more than he'd meant to about the way he felt.

And the earth hadn't opened up and swallowed him whole. Nor had Edwina scoffed at what he'd said. To the contrary, she looked like she understood exactly what he'd meant.

"And," he muttered, "she has no idea who I am, which was an absolutely *brilliant* idea." Note to self: never do that again.

Thomas didn't usually resort to sarcasm, but he was still pretty rattled by how absolutely wonderful and utterly horrible his conversation with Edwina had been.

She was going to be furious with him when she found out he'd deceived her. If their situations were reversed, he knew he would be. What kind of a friend blindsided another friend like that?

Years ago he'd watched a movie called *You've Got Mail*, which had been billed as a romantic comedy. Thomas liked romantic comedies, and he thought Meg Ryan was in her element when she was playing the female lead in that type of film. *When Harry Met Sally* was one of his favorite films of all time.

Of course, now with the perfect clarity of hindsight, he realized the reason that movie was his all-time favorite was because longtime best friends had finally fallen in love. Talk about his subconscious trying to send him a message.

So Thomas couldn't wait to rent *You've Got Mail* from the video store, back when Lovelock still had a video store. That night he'd popped a bag of microwave popcorn, made himself a fresh pitcher of iced tea, and sat back in his recliner, ready for an enjoyable movie about two people falling in love.

Two hours later, he was ready to snap the DVD in two, and would have if he'd bought the thing instead of merely rented it.

How could Tom Hanks' character deceive Meg's poor character that way? She was just a businesswoman trying to keep her bookstore afloat. She'd asked for advice from her online friend, who—unbeknownst to her (and him, at the time)—was the owner of the new mega-bookstore that was putting Meg's business out of business. Okay, as a set-up, that was a credible meet-cute, the industry term for boy meets girl, which another great romantic comedy, *The Holiday*, had taught him.

The problem with *You've Got Mail* arose after Tom Hanks' character learned who his online friend really was. Not only had he not revealed his identity to her, he'd purposefully used their online friendship to manipulate her. What kind of a friend would do a thing like that?

And what kind of a woman would forgive him? Because of course by the end of the movie, Meg Ryan's character had not only forgiven his deception so that the characters could have their happily ever after, she'd done it immediately without even a hint of the annoyance any real woman would have felt.

What a farce!

One of the reasons Thomas liked romantic comedies was the happily ever after. In romantic comedies, no one ended up before a character like his friend, the Honorable Julie Wilkins, arguing about who got the china and who got the silverware in the divorce. In romantic comedies, when the guy got the girl at the end of the movie, you knew they were going to stay together for the rest of their lives.

Thomas couldn't imagine how the movie of his life could have a happily ever after, not after what he'd done today.

He'd manipulated Edwina. Maybe not as badly as Tom Hanks' character had in *You've Got Mail*—after all, their chapels didn't directly compete with each other, and the advice he'd given Edwina over the years really had been with the best of intentions —but he should have told Edwina who he was the moment he walked in her office.

He should have introduced himself—well, not really introduced himself, since they already knew each other, but at least given her his full name instead of a shortened nickname that he never, ever used—and told her that he wanted to meet her in person before another man swept her out of his life. He didn't have to tell her right away that he'd only recently realized he'd had feelings for her all along.

No, that would have been as bad as what all those men Thomas had waited with in the dry goods store planned to do.

They'd bragged to each other about whose marriage proposal would be more romantic, who had more to offer Edwina, or, conversely, who needed a woman like Edwina more to take care of them in their declining years.

If Thomas had walked into Edwina's office and declared his undying love for her, even if he'd told her who he really was, she would have thought he was out of his mind.

Either that, or she would have thought it was a cruel *I told you so*, and that he'd only come to show her how really wrong her decision about her ad had been.

What he should have done was simply tell her who he really was. Then he could have used his ten minutes to just sit and talk with her, like they'd done all these years.

But if he'd done that, he wouldn't have been able to tell

whether her reaction to him had been for her friend, Reverend Thomas, or just to one random stranger who'd responded to her ad.

And she had responded well to him. In fact, he thought she'd been about to suggest a second meeting before the blonde woman who was handling the appointment schedule came in to tell Edwina that her time with Thomas was up.

Wonderful. Just wonderful. He'd blown his chance to make a good first impression as the real-life Reverend Thomas.

That was the problem with hiding your identity. One day, you had to give up the deception and shoulder the responsibility for hurting everyone you'd deceived, or else you'd be stuck in the fake persona's life for the rest of yours.

The sun was still pretty high in the clear western sky even though it was past three in the afternoon. The day was hot, but not as hot as Thomas guessed it would get once summer really got here. Sutter Lake was big—twenty miles long, Thomas had read back when he first learned where Edwina lived—and a startling deep blue. Little waves lapped at the shore, and as Thomas watched, a flock of pelicans skimmed across the water looking for dinner.

Thomas had never been to this part of the state before, but it didn't look all that different from home, even with the big desert lake. The town had taken some pains to make this part of the lake inviting. The bench where Thomas sat was one of a number of iron benches scattered along a walking path that hugged the north shore of the lake. A few sparse trees had been planted here and there along the path, none of which were big enough to provide shade. Instead, simple open-air lean-tos covering each bench gave a bit of relief from the sun.

No fishermen were out on the lake. Off in the distance, a powerboat cut through the water hauling a lone water skier behind. The whine of the boat's engine sounded like an angry insect buzzing around his ear.

He imagined the lake would get a lot busier tomorrow. The

campground at this end of the lake was still closed. The sign hung on the locked gate listed the camp's season as the Friday before Memorial Day to the Monday after Nevada Day, which was the end of October. Bad timing for all of Edwina's suitors—including himself—who'd arrived in Liberty Springs one day early.

Liberty Springs was far smaller than Lovelock. He supposed it would be, what with only five hundred or so people living in town on a year-round basis according to the population count on the *Welcome to Liberty Springs!* sign on the main road into town. Still, he thought he might like it here. He'd never lived by a lake before. Liberty Springs didn't have a casino, and there was only the one diner.

He'd driven down to Hawthorne at the other end of the lake after he'd put his name in the Tupperware that morning. He'd needed to work off some nervous energy, and driving had always worked for him. Hawthorne was a bigger town—it even had a bowling alley and a modern-looking McDonalds. He imagined that's where the residents of Liberty Springs went when they wanted to blow off a little steam. Not that he'd ever bowled a game in his life, but he could always give it a shot if Edwina liked to bowl.

If she liked to bowl.

Thomas laughed at himself. What in the world was he thinking about?

Here he was, getting to know the place like he might be moving here. As if Edwina might invite him to stay. She didn't even know he was her friend, Reverend Thomas.

Well, there was only one way to fix that.

He'd just have to tell her and deal with the fallout.

Because now that he'd met her in person, he was absolutely sure she was the one true love of his life.

# CHAPTER 10

$\mathcal{E}$ven as Edwina took Rufus Monroe's out-stretched hand, she thought it must be a joke. No one this good looking would ever respond to her ad for romance. He was probably someone's cousin, or nephew, or distant relative who enjoyed playing practical jokes.

He had the deepest blue eyes Edwina had ever seen. His blond hair was the color of a summer sunrise and brushed straight back from a shallow widow's peak to where it was held in place with a strip of leather at the nape of his neck. His shoulders were broad, his smile full of the kind of honest good humor that lent a sparkle to his eyes, and when he spoke, his voice resonated with a deep, pleasant accent that Edwina couldn't immediately place. He was tall—well over six feet, if she had to guess—and tan, but not in an artificial, tanning-bed kind of way. Her hand looked tiny in his, and she'd never considered herself a small-boned woman.

He was also quite a bit younger than she was.

How could this not be a joke?

"Are you sure you have the right place?" Edwina asked.

He chuckled, then bent over to place a soft kiss on the top of her hand. "I definitely have the right place," he said.

Oh, my. The back of her hand was actually tingling.

"Have a seat," she managed to say when he released her hand. She was not at all surprised that her voice came out breathy.

The metal folding chair on the far side of her desk creaked with the solid weight of him. She doubted there was a lick of fat beneath the plain black T-shirt stretched tight across his chest. He looked like he was solid muscle, from his jean-clad legs to the tantalizing bit of chest she could see in the V-neck of his shirt. He was the perfect embodiment of a romance novel cover model.

Or a superhero.

In fact, that's exactly who he reminded her of—one of the Avengers. When Nellie had bought the DVD, she'd invited Edwina over one night to watch the movie. Gus had been thrilled that his wife actually wanted to watch a superhero movie, at least until it became clear that she was more interested in ogling the actors than in following the plot.

Edwina understood the attraction. The whole cast was ridiculously attractive.

"Has anyone ever told you that you look like—" she began.

His smile grew wider. "All the time. But I don't carry a hammer with an unpronounceable name."

Oh my, indeed.

"Rufus," she began, then she stopped. She had no idea what to say. He might be far younger than she was, but she felt like an inexperienced schoolgirl who'd attracted the attention of the star quarterback.

He sat watching her, the same smile on his face, the same twinkle in his eye.

Patience. A good quality in a man.

She considered whether it would be rude to just sit and stare at him for ten minutes. He certainly was easy on the eyes, to put it mildly.

"Edwina," he finally said. "May I call you Edwina?"

She nodded.

"I can see that I'm the last thing you expected, but I want you to know that I am serious. I'm here with the best of intentions."

"Why?"

Okay, that was probably beyond rude, but her brain wasn't functioning well, and she couldn't seem to be able to look away from his eyes. Had she noticed before that they were the deepest blue?

"I mean, I can't be your ideal woman. Can I? I mean, look at you." She made a vague gesture in his direction. "You can't tell me you have any trouble at all meeting women."

Especially women his own age, but she didn't say that.

His smile dimmed. "You're right. I meet lots of women. Just not the right woman."

He leaned back in the chair, and the chair made an alarming creak. He didn't seem to notice. He crossed his legs so that one ankle rested on his knee, and he hooked his thumbs in the pockets of his jeans. If he was nervous at all about meeting her, it didn't show.

"I've been living in Las Vegas for a few years now," he said. "I got a job at Caesar's Palace. Sometimes I'm on stage, other times on the casino floor. Definitely not a career, but it is a lot of fun." His expression turned mischievous, with one eyebrow raised, and the twinkle was back in his eyes. "You should see me in Roman armor."

"I can imagine," she said, her voice breathy again.

And she could, right down to the helmet, the little red cape, and the skimpy golden codpiece, or whatever the Romans used to call it.

Was it getting hot in her office? Maybe she should open the window.

"I meet a lot of women at work," he said. "But the women in Vegas, at least the ones I meet..." He shrugged. "Any one of them could be a fashion model. I know, tough life, right? You'd think a guy like me would be eating that stuff up, but I'm not in college anymore. I gave up frat parties and all-night keggers. That's not what I'm interested in. I moved to Vegas because I wanted a change, but as it turns out, I suppose I'm a product of my upbringing."

He laughed, a short, self-deprecating sound that didn't make him seem at all self-indulgent, but rather self-aware. Edwina wondered what he'd majored in in college. Psychology?

"Of course, I can't tell my father that. I'd never live it down. You'll keep my secret, right?"

Edwina smiled. "Already, you're asking favors. Should I be alarmed?"

Good lord—she was practically batting her eyelashes at him!

She made an effort to get herself under control. These meetings were supposed to be simple auditions with an eye toward an actual date. She needed to keep with the agenda.

Then again, Nellie had said Rufus was the last name in the hat today. Why shouldn't Edwina enjoy herself?

"You should never be alarmed with me," Rufus said. "At heart, I'm pretty old-fashioned. I want what my dad found. I'm tired of women who are too thin and too shallow, women who wouldn't be caught dead without their makeup or who can't wait for some plastic surgeon to fix an imagined imperfection. Not that you're not beautiful," he added quickly, one hand raised as if to hold back any imagined slight. She wasn't offended, but then again, she didn't think she was beautiful either. "By anyone's standards, you are amazingly gorgeous, but what attracted me is what you do here."

"What I do?"

"Run this chapel. Marry people. I mean, you spend your life surrounded by people in love."

Not all of them were in love. Some of the couples who came in to get married were simply in lust, an emotion Edwina was rapidly becoming intimately acquainted with, thanks to Rufus and his amazing and apparently inherent sex appeal.

"The chapels down in Vegas—I have a friend who works in one of the themed chapels," Rufus said. "With those kind of places, it's all about the splash. About the upsell. Part of my friend's job is to try to convince people they need services they don't really want. A gold-embossed marriage certificate. Imported champagne. Live music to walk down the aisle to, or a celebrity impersonator to conduct the ceremony. Expensive flower arrangements. Anything to make the chapel a little extra money. That's not the feeling I got when I looked at your website. When I saw your photo and read your ad. With you, I think it's all real. All you care about, really, are the people. What's important to you is love."

He stared deeply into her eyes, and Edwina couldn't seem to look away.

This was getting a little too real too fast, and a part of her was still nonplussed that he might be even younger than she'd initially thought. She needed to lighten the mood.

"Would you be disappointed to learn that there's an Elvis costume in my closet?" She nodded at the free-standing closet behind him.

He blinked and glanced away. "Not at all, but I'm guessing you wear it for Halloween." When he looked back at her, the intensity was gone but the smile that lit up his eyes remained. "I overdid it, didn't I?"

Oh, thank goodness. He wasn't really this intense all the time. Otherwise she might really melt.

She held up her hand, her thumb and forefinger almost touching. "Just a little," she said with an answering smile. "You do give good audition, though."

"That's what the human resources director at Caesar's Palace said back when I was interviewing for a job I thought I really wanted. But I think I'm done with that kind of life. It's not what I'm looking for."

"And what are you looking for?" Edwina asked.

He paused, like he was trying to think of the right words. For the first time since he walked through the door, he looked unsure of himself.

"Something quieter than Las Vegas," he finally said. "A life I can feel good about."

Edwina understood the need to move on from a life that wasn't emotionally fulfilling. After all, she'd done the same thing when she'd bought Bluebelles, although her old life hadn't been filled with men who looked like extras from the movie *300*.

"So no more skimpy outfits?" she asked.

He flashed her a quick grin. "No, but honestly, after a while, the costume was more like a company uniform than anything else."

She supposed she could understand that. When she performed her first wedding ceremony, she'd felt odd about putting on the robe. Now it was just part of who she was. Not exactly a company uniform, but no longer uncomfortable to wear.

"So what happens next?" Rufus asked.

Edwina gazed at him, trying to determine whether she should pursue this any further. She'd told Nellie she wanted some nooky before she got too old to enjoy it, and while she had a feeling nooky with Rufus would be amazing, there was still that nagging issue of age.

Well, if that was all that was bothering her, might as well get that issue out of the way.

"How old are you anyway?" Edwina asked.

He laughed, an honest-to-God belly laugh.

"I mean, I'm no spring chicken," she said. "You had to know that when you saw my picture, right?"

"I didn't run away screaming, if that's what you meant," he said when he got himself under control. "I turned thirty last month."

Thirty!

She didn't have to work at doing the math. He was nearly twenty years younger than she was!

"Yes, I know I'm younger than you are," he said. "But my mother's twelve years older than my father. They've been together for thirty-five years."

Edwina blinked. That explained a lot, but his mother and father had obviously married when his mother was still young enough to have children. All Edwina wanted was romance and a husband.

And there she was, getting ahead of herself again.

Some of what she'd been thinking must have shown on her face. Rufus sat forward in the chair, his foot dropping to the floor.

"Look, I know I'm not what you were expecting," he said. "Last week I wasn't expecting that I would ever meet anyone like you. Then my friend who works at the wedding chapel, he sent me a link to your website. Not to set me up, but just to show me the kind of chapel that would never make it in Vegas. He's always sending me links, and most of them I ignore. Something made me click on yours. I'm still not sure why, but I'm glad I did. I'm glad I drove out here to meet you. I have a feeling we would be good together, but I understand that you're not sure. Neither am I. That's what getting to know another person is all about. I hope you'll give me—give us—the time to find out."

Would she? She'd only met one other man—the shy man whose name she couldn't remember—that she thought she might like to see again. With Rufus, there was no doubt she wanted to see where this might lead. The difference of a few years (a few years? Talk about deluding herself!) wouldn't be that bad, would it? After all, his parents had made it work.

She smiled at him as she stood up, and took a deep breath to steady her nerves.

"Tonight's movie night at the church rec center," she said. "I don't know what they're showing, but I'm fairly sure it'll be a full house. Would you like to accompany me?"

He stood up as well. "Edwina," he said. "It would be my honor."

# CHAPTER 11

The walk from the lake to Bluebelles Chapel & Dry Goods was a short one—probably not much more than a mile. Easy stuff for a guy who went for a run every morning to stay in shape.

Well, every morning except this one. Thomas had been too nervous to go for a run before getting in his car and driving to Liberty Springs. He'd worked off some of his nervous energy by driving down to Hawthorne and just generally exploring the area before meeting with Edwina.

After meeting with her? He'd had enough nervous energy to fuel the entire town.

The walk to the lake had worked off some of his nerves. Now that he'd made up his mind to come clean to Edwina and tell her who he really was, the walk back to the wedding chapel was fueled by a whole different type of nervous energy.

The afternoon had been hot, but Thomas was used to the Nevada heat. Now that the sun was closer to the mountains in the west, an afternoon breeze had sprung up, cooling the air down as it blew toward town from the lake.

He liked the quiet of his morning runs, but late afternoons

were his favorite time of day. The hour or two after lunch always felt lazy, like the world was napping. He rarely performed weddings between one and three in the afternoon—people just didn't seem to want to get married then—and sometimes he was tempted to take a nap himself. He always threw off that lethargy around three, and by four he felt energized again.

It was close to four now, he could tell without looking at his watch. He felt the same familiar energy coursing through him, only now it was coupled with his new-found resolve and an anticipation he hadn't felt in...well, he couldn't ever remember feeling anticipation like this, and it was all because he was going to see Edwina.

Only one other car besides Thomas's was still in the parking lot next to the chapel and dry goods store. The car was a classic El Camino with Nevada plates. Thomas couldn't see Edwina driving a car like that, but it was possible. It was also possible that the car belonged to the woman who'd brought the Tupperware that morning. Thomas hadn't seen her arrive.

If she was still here, he should check in with her first. Edwina might not like it if he just barged into the chapel, especially not if she was still conducting auditions.

Still meeting men, you mean, Thomas told himself.

The thought made him uncomfortable. He didn't want to think about the fact that Edwina might meet another man she could be attracted to.

Of course, since that had been the whole point of her ad, it was entirely possible that she might meet someone she liked. Someone who wasn't Thomas.

The nervous excitement in his stomach started to turn into an uncomfortable ball of dread. He should never have left without telling Edwina who he really was. Even if he hadn't told her how he felt, she deserved to know his name. He hoped it wasn't too late.

Thomas walked up to the door of the dry goods store. He was

about to reach for the handle when he noticed the *Closed* sign in the window.

Right next to the *Closed* sign was a hand-printed sign that read *If you're here in response to Edwina's ad, tomorrow she will be talking to everyone she didn't get to today. Leave your name in the Tupperware bowl. We'll post a schedule of interviews tomorrow morning at eight. Good luck!*

The Tupperware bowl had been duct-taped to a gumball machine next to the dry goods store's front door. The lid of the Tupperware had been taped to the bowl to make sure no one took the lid off, and a rough slit had been cut in the top. Thomas could see a couple of slips of paper through the semi-transparent plastic of the bowl.

Had he missed Edwina then? No one was in the dry goods store as far as he could tell. He didn't want to rap on the glass. For all he knew, the store had an alarm system he might set off.

Edwina might still be in the chapel, though. Just because the dry goods store was locked up tight didn't mean that the chapel was closed as well.

Thomas walked down the parking lot to the other side of the building and the entrance to the chapel. He had to admit that the design of the two businesses was clever. It reminded him of duplex apartments, only instead of the front door for each half of the duplex being side by side, the front doors to the two businesses were on the narrow ends of the rectangular building. The long side of the building that faced the street had a sign with an arrow for each business that pointed to the appropriate front door.

The dry goods store had a covered wooden walkway on its narrow storefront. The storefront for the chapel, on the other hand, looked like a miniature church, complete with a few steps leading up to the door. He had to admit he hadn't noticed a whole lot of these details on his way out after meeting with Edwina.

Thomas walked up the steps and tried the chapel doors. When he discovered the doors were unlocked, he let himself inside.

The scent of flowers hit him almost like a physical force. He'd smelled the flowers earlier when he'd talked to Edwina in her office, but when he exited through the chapel, he'd been too head over heels at how well that meeting went to even notice the flowers. Now that he was all alone in the chapel and more than a little nervous, he couldn't help but notice that the chapel was practically stuffed to the gills with flower arrangements.

Had everyone who'd come courting Edwina sent her flowers?

Should he have sent her flowers?

The answer came easily enough.

She hadn't kept any of the arrangements in her office, like a woman would if the flowers came from someone who was special in her life. No, Edwina had arranged her flowers along the sides of the chapel, behind the altar, and along the back wall on either side of the doors.

The flowers weren't all that special to her, but she wasn't about to waste them, either. So she'd used them to decorate her chapel.

If he had brought her flowers, they would have just become another decoration in the chapel, along with dozens of others.

As Thomas considered the flowers, he realized she'd also arranged the bouquets in the chapel according to color. The arrangements that were mostly red roses and pink carnations were placed around the altar. Multi-colored arrangements lined the outer walls, and the arrangements with bluebells and white carnations were placed near the rear of the chapel so that anyone who came in through the chapel doors would see those flowers first.

Bluebells for the Bluebelle. It all made sense.

It also told Thomas just how much care Edwina put into maintaining her chapel.

He'd known that she'd given up a life in Reno which, while it wasn't nearly as big as Las Vegas or Sacramento, was a pretty big town by Nevada standards, to move to Liberty Springs. He'd wondered more than once if she didn't have a reason behind the move that she never told anyone about. Most people had a secret or two they didn't tell anyone, and Thomas didn't like to pry.

But now that he had the time to pay closer attention to Edwina's chapel, he could see why she stayed.

She loved this place. She hadn't spruced it up just to attract customers, which Thomas had to admit he'd done with his own chapel. When he'd bought the place, there had been no gift shop out front. He'd added the shop as a way to attract the tourists who passed through town and—if he was being truthful with himself—to make a little extra money from the Love Locks festival participants. Edwina had added details to her chapel that wouldn't matter to anyone except herself.

She'd painted tiny bluebells in a rambling vine on the sides of each wooden pew. Since the long sides of the building had no windows, she'd added window-sized landscapes on the walls where windows would have been, and then framed each of the landscapes with real draperies.

Thomas knew the previous owner hadn't done any of this. Some of the first conversations he'd had with Edwina were about how rough the chapel had been when she bought it, which was why she could afford it in the first place. It had been her own fixer-upper project, and she'd obviously poured a lot of herself into it.

She might work in the dry goods store, but she lived in the chapel.

No wonder she wouldn't leave Liberty Springs, even if she was lonely.

The door to Edwina's office opened, and Thomas heard voices. Edwina's was one; he didn't recognize the other, although it sounded like a man with the remnants of a west Texas accent.

Thomas was torn. He didn't want to seem like he was out here stalking her, but he didn't want to leave without talking to her either. He felt very exposed just waiting in the chapel all by himself. It felt like he was invading her space without her consent, and he wasn't comfortable with that.

He hurried to the door and slipped outside, hoping that neither of them had seen him. He could wait for her in the parking lot. After all, he had a reason to be there since he'd left his car in the lot when he went down to the lake.

He was nearly to his car when he heard voices again. They must have reached the chapel's outer doors.

Thomas turned around, trying to make the move seem casual in case Edwina spotted him.

He needn't have bothered.

Edwina's full attention was on the man at the bottom of the chapel steps. He was taller than she was, but standing at the foot of the steps while Edwina was still in the chapel doorway made their height almost even. She was looking at him with a broad, almost bemused smile on her face, and the man was smiling back at her.

"So I'll pick you up here at seven," the man said. "Will there be popcorn, or should I bring some?"

She laughed before she said something in reply. Her voice wasn't as powerful as the man's. Thomas couldn't understand what she was saying, but he'd heard enough.

Edwina had made a date with this man.

Thomas's heart sank.

He'd missed his opportunity.

She looked happy, and that made her even more beautiful than she'd been when Thomas had met her. She wouldn't want to hear about how Thomas had deceived her. Not now.

And he didn't want to tell her. As disappointed as he was for himself—he wasn't ready to admit the hollow ache he felt watching the two of them together was anything more than disappointment—he didn't want to do anything to interrupt her happiness.

Thomas got in his car and shut the door. Here he'd been so worried that Edwina would meet someone before he got to

Liberty Springs, when it turned out she'd met someone she liked better after she'd met him.

He'd had his one shot, and it hadn't worked out.

He started the car, and after one last look at Edwina, he drove away from Bluebelles.

# CHAPTER 12

Rufus brought a single yellow rose for Edwina when he came to the chapel to pick her up for the movie.

She had no idea where he could have bought it. She was convinced that all the flowers in this half of the state were currently gracing the inside of her wedding chapel. She'd spent the last half hour making sure all the arrangements had enough water. Most of them did, but it was a way to work off the case of the nerves that had set in while she'd been waiting to see if Rufus really would show up.

Why hadn't she made a date with the shy man instead? They'd had a definite connection, something that felt like an old, comfortable friendship that could definitely turn romantic given half a chance.

And she'd been more than willing to give it that chance. Until Rufus walked through her office door.

"In lieu of popcorn," he said as he handed the rose to her. "Butter yellow. For friendship."

"Friendship?"

She felt an odd little pang of disappointment. Hadn't she made it clear that this was a date?

"It's a place to start."

That was better.

"You had me worried there for a minute," she said.

He held out his arm. "I don't want you to think I'm easy," he said with that mischievous smile.

Could he really be what he seemed? Could anyone really be such a charming mix of old-fashioned values wrapped in a drop-dead gorgeous, sexy, thirty-year-old body?

She'd spent more time talking with him that afternoon than with any of the other men who'd shown up. It helped that since he was the last one of the day, she didn't have Nellie keeping her on the strict ten-minute interview schedule. Edwina had actually lost track of time while she was talking to Rufus, and she'd been surprised to see that she'd spent more than an hour with him.

In all that time, she hadn't detected any hint that he might not be exactly what he seemed—a truly nice guy. An old soul.

Who honestly seemed interested in her.

Maybe she'd been living in Liberty Springs too long, but with Rufus this all seemed too easy to be real.

As excited as she was to actually be going out on a date, she couldn't shake the feeling that this was all a dream and she'd wake up any minute to discover all of this—including her harebrained idea to put a want ad on her website—wasn't real.

The problem was it was all happening too fast. Nothing happened that fast in Liberty Springs. Even the couples who came in to get married spur of the moment in the middle of a fishing trip had at least planned their trip to Sutter Lake.

Edwina hadn't really planned any of this. It had been less than a week since she'd come up with the idea for her want ad in the first place, and here she was, going out on a date with the most gorgeous man she had ever seen in her life, including all the men she'd seen coming into the clerk's office back in Reno for their marriage licenses, much less any of the men who came to her chapel to get married.

She wanted to slow down, catch her breath, and get used to the fact that men—*men*, not just one lone man—were courting her.

But she couldn't ask any of them to wait for her to get her head around the idea of a man in her life after all the years she'd spent alone. Half of the men who'd come to town to meet her were living in tents next to the lake, and more were sleeping on cots and in sleeping bags in the rec center. It wouldn't be fair to them.

Sure, they'd come out here all on their own with no guarantees, but at the very least, she owed them a speedy answer.

Today had been all about meeting these men for the first time. She'd told herself they were just auditions, but they were more like job interviews, and now she was giving one of the top candidates his second interview. Maybe if she thought about it like that, she could keep herself on an even keel.

Besides, as auditions/job interviews/dates went, Rufus was doing pretty darn well. She ought to at least give him a sign.

She tucked her hand in the crook of his elbow and smiled at him. "Where have you been all my life?"

He laughed. "I'll take that as a compliment."

"It was most certainly a compliment," Edwina said.

His arm felt wonderfully strong, and he smelled fantastic. Not overwhelming, like he'd showered with cologne, but a more subtle scent that was part clean soap, part strong coffee, and part fresh outdoors—without a single whiff of Ben Gay.

In fact, now that she was a lot closer to him than she'd been this afternoon, she realized she might not be able to maintain such an even keel after all.

She'd never been this close to anyone as handsome as Rufus Monroe.

Tonight he'd let his hair loose from the little ponytail he'd had it in earlier. It brushed the shoulders of the navy blue sport coat he wore over a light blue polo shirt. She wondered if he kept his hair this long for his role as a Roman soldier at Caesar's Palace, or if he was just comfortable wearing it like this. Not that Edwina minded, not one bit. The long hair didn't make him look any less masculine. If anything, it made him look more like a certain movie star than ever.

He led her to a car parked in the lot. Before he could unlock the door, Edwina stopped him.

"The rec center isn't far from here," she said. "Would you like to walk?"

Besides, she liked the feel of her hand on his arm. Walking with her hand on a man's arm might seem old-fashioned, but she liked it. It made her feel like she was going on a real date to a real theater.

He smiled down at her. He really was tall. Edwina hadn't paid attention when she'd walked him out of the chapel that afternoon, but walking beside him now in her comfortable flat shoes, she couldn't help but notice. Not that his size was such a bad thing. If anything, it felt natural.

"I'd love to walk," he said.

Liberty Springs didn't have much in the way of sidewalks. Most of the streets were bordered by a dirt or gravel shoulder, which would have made walking difficult if Liberty Springs had any traffic to speak of. Edwina and Rufus simply walked on one side of the road. The rec center was only three blocks from the chapel on the desert side of the main street through town. The heat of the day was bleeding off into what promised to be a very comfortable night, at least from a temperature standpoint.

Once they left the chapel behind, Edwina's stomach began tying itself into increasingly pleasant knots of anticipation.

She was actually on a date. A real date with someone she was becoming increasingly more attracted to.

"I bet you can actually see the stars here," Rufus said, interrupting her thoughts. "It's far too bright in Vegas to see anything but the brightest stars. Here I feel like I might be able to see all of them."

Edwina looked up at the sky. The sun hadn't set quite yet. It wouldn't be long until the first stars of the night would be clearly visible in the east. A sliver of a moon was already out, still riding low on the horizon. Insects were gearing up for their nighttime symphony out in the sagebrush and desert scrub, and the sound of laughter drifted in from the direction of the lake.

"It's pretty out here," she said. "A lot of people wouldn't like it. Not enough things to do at night." She chuckled at the thought. "Heck, there's not a lot of things to do during the day, either. We're busy during tourist season, but most of the time, life passes us right on by."

She glanced at him, a little embarrassed by the unintended emotion in her voice. She hoped he wouldn't think she was complaining that life had passed her by.

He was looking down at her with a thoughtful expression on his face. "But you like it," he said.

"I do. Guess I'm a small-town girl at heart."

"At heart. So you weren't born here."

She shook her head. "I was born in Sacramento, then my family moved to Reno when I was thirteen." She smiled. "I used to think *that* was a small town, and I suppose it was, compared to Sacramento, but I liked it. It was friendly. All the neighbors knew each other. My parents locked their doors at night, but I think that was as much because they always had before we moved. Half of my friends' parents left the doors unlocked for their kids after school."

"Amazing," he said. "Where I live in Vegas, half the businesses have bars on the windows."

"What about where you grew up?"

He smiled. "A little town in west Texas not much bigger than this. Well, actually on a ranch outside of town. My brother still lives there with my parents. I think they're grooming him to take over running the place."

"You didn't want to do that?"

"I wanted to go to college. I got a football scholarship to

UNLV—Running Rebels—that paid for nearly the whole thing. I worked odd jobs while I was in school to pay for everything else."

Football. "What position did you play?" she asked.

If he said quarterback...

When she'd been in school, only the prettiest girls had dated the quarterback.

"Wide receiver," he said. "I'm actually pretty fast on my feet."

Hadn't Thomas told her that he played football in high school? What position had he played, again? She couldn't remember. She'd have to ask him the next time she talked to him.

She gave herself a mental shake. Why in the world was she thinking about Thomas when she was actually on a date with another man?

A man Thomas no doubt would not approve of. Especially considering she'd just met him only a few hours ago.

"Did you ever play pro?" she asked Rufus.

He chuckled. "No. I was good enough to keep my scholarship, but I never wanted to go pro. Football was a means to an education. A way to get off the ranch and out into the world."

"And now you're here," she said. "Back in a little town the size of the one you left behind."

He stopped walking and turned toward Edwina. She let go of his arm, and he surprised her by reaching down to take her hand.

"I had the exact same thought when I pulled in off the highway. Except for the mountains, you have no idea how much this reminds me of home. I'd forgotten how quiet a place like this gets at night. How you can smell things besides car exhaust and cigarette smoke, and the night air cools you off without having to turn on the air conditioning or walk though those little misters they have on the sidewalks on The Strip." He looked at the empty road. "Here I don't have to dodge drunk drivers."

Or any drivers. The main road to Liberty Springs continued on into the desert and eventually circled the lake down to

Hawthorne, but no one ever drove that way. The only cars on the road to Liberty Springs were actually headed to Liberty Springs.

He shrugged, smiling. "I think I needed the time away from a small town to appreciate the good things about living in one." He squeezed her hand. "One of the best things about this small town is standing here next to me, holding the rose I gave her and wondering if I'm an idiot."

Edwina chuckled, she couldn't help it. "Not an idiot, but I am wondering why you'd even consider moving back to some-place you wanted so badly to get away from."

"Maybe I've grown up. I certainly did my share of acting like an idiot in college."

He had mentioned keggers this afternoon. She imagined he'd done a lot of things in college—and after college—that he wouldn't want to tell a woman about on the first date.

Fair enough. While Edwina hadn't lived what she considered a wild life, she had lived an independent life. She'd gone to college, too. She had vague memories of certain parties at certain frat houses that she wouldn't be telling anyone about anytime soon. If ever.

She supposed some men did hit thirty and decide it was time to grow up and settle down. She hadn't had any great epiphanies at thirty, or even forty. It was that looming fifty that got to her.

Why did she have to think about that now?

As if she wasn't having a hard enough time not feeling like a dirty old woman for going out on a date with a much younger man. She'd even put on more makeup—and spent more time doing it—than she had in years! And now that she thought of it, she'd been walking with her hand on his arm the way her father held her grandmother's hand when he used to help her walk down the sidewalk. The last thing she wanted—well, one of the last things—was to feel like he was helping her down the street. Or for anyone—especially Rufus—to think that he was.

She shifted her hand in his grip until their fingers twined

together. "How about we go watch the movie now?" she asked him.

He smiled at her, and she could swear his eyes twinkled in the fading daylight.

"My pleasure," he said.

# CHAPTER 13

*T*homas made it twenty miles out of Liberty Springs before he pulled his car over to the side of the two-lane highway and read himself the riot act.

He'd been a lot of things in his life, but he'd never been a coward. Sure, he'd convinced himself that Edwina had found someone else and it would be better off for everyone involved if he just went back home to Lovelock and stuck with chatting with her online. Things could go back to normal, and no one would be the wiser.

Except he would know.

And his friend, the Honorable Judge Julie Wilkins, would know. That fact alone would keep things from ever going back to normal.

Every time he talked to Edwina online, he'd remember that he hadn't been able to bring himself to tell her who he really was. That he'd had a chance to meet her as himself, not simply online as Reverend Thomas, and he'd been too afraid to do it.

That he'd used a flimsy excuse to cut and run when things got tough.

Eventually their friendship would sour. He wouldn't want to chat with her as often, and she'd never know why. Maybe she'd think she'd done something wrong to upset him, which would only make him feel worse. And things would just go downhill from there.

Julie had told him once that with most of the couples who filed for divorce, it wasn't big things that came between them. It was something small. Some little disagreement that got blown all out of proportion. Some small slight they'd let fester until it became the most important thing in the world, and they let that little thing drive a huge, permanent, irreconcilable wedge between them.

He didn't want to drive a wedge between himself and Edwina.

And besides, just because it looked like she was having fun with someone who wasn't him, that didn't mean this guy was the right guy for her. Thomas wasn't even sure if *he* was the right guy for her. He knew she was the right woman for him—his feelings for her hadn't changed—but he was too much of a realist. He knew that a lot of the time, love went unrequited. Even when people got married, it didn't mean both people were really in love or that even if they were, the love would last.

What if he drove all the way home only to find out that Edwina hadn't decided yet if she really liked any of the men who'd answered her ad?

Just because she was going out on a date with this guy didn't mean that he was *the one*. People dated people all the time without falling head over heels. She might decide after spending the evening with him that they weren't compatible at all.

Thomas had to face the fact that he could be leaving for no reason except his own aching heart (and somewhat bruised ego). If he really loved her—and he knew he did—that wasn't good enough.

He needed to give her a chance.

He sat in his car staring at the long road in front of him. There wasn't a whole lot of traffic on the highway, and the cars he did see were a long ways off. He'd left Sutter Lake behind, and out here it was all desert and sagebrush. The landscape looked barren, but he knew it wasn't. All sorts of insects lived in the desert. Lizards and snakes lived out there too, along with coyotes and jackrabbits and even wild horses and big horn sheep.

Things weren't always what they seemed at first glance.

What had Edwina said to him? Don't leave town. And here he was, doing exactly that.

What if she went looking for him later?

What if she wanted to go out on a date with him, and he never gave her the chance?

He sighed and checked the highway in both directions. He wasn't a coward. He wasn't sure where he would stay tonight or what he would do, but one thing he wasn't going to do was run away.

He put his car in gear, flipped a U-turn, and headed back to Liberty Springs.

~

By the time Thomas made it back to Liberty Springs, his stomach was rumbling. He hadn't eaten since the lone sunny side up egg and piece of whole wheat toast he'd had before he left home at the crack of dawn that morning.

He'd been too nervous to eat before his meeting with Edwina, although he'd had plenty of time, and he'd been too excited afterwards. Then once he'd made up his mind to leave town, he didn't even stop long enough to get a soda. He had bottled water in the car and figured that would be good enough. It wasn't like he had any appetite left.

Now that he'd decided to stay, at least for the night, his appetite had come back with a vengeance. He hadn't seen any fast food franchises in Liberty Springs, not even a Starbucks. He'd seen a McDonalds in Hawthorne, but he didn't want to drive another twenty miles past Liberty Springs just for a fast food burger and fries.

When he'd been driving around the area that morning, trying

to acclimate himself to Edwina's hometown, he'd seen a couple of restaurants. Well, not restaurants like in Fallon or even Lovelock, but something like The Player's Club—a little diner or a sub sandwich shop where he could sit down and grab a bite to eat.

While he'd settle for a sub sandwich, he'd prefer something a little more substantial, so he decided to try the Lickety-Split. He liked the down-home name, and the diner had looked inviting enough. Plus, it was only a short walk from Edwina's chapel and dry goods store. He could see both of them from the diner's parking lot.

Yes, he definitely had it bad. Wanting to eat in sight of Edwina's businesses like a kid who went out of his way to walk to school past the house where the girl he had a crush on lived.

Not that Thomas had ever done something like that himself.

Until now.

When he'd driven by the Lickety-Split earlier in the day, the place had looked moderately busy. Now the parking lot was packed to the gills. He had to park on a side street a half-block away. He took that as a good sign.

The inside of the diner was stuffed wall to wall with men, most of them well past the age to qualify for a senior discount. Those who didn't have seats at the counter or in booths or at the few tables were standing around holding plates of food. Which all appeared to be either hamburgers or scrambled eggs.

The blonde woman who'd been at Edwina's earlier, the one who'd brought out the Tupperware container and managed Edwina's appointments, was in the kitchen working next to a harried-looking older man (although he looked like a teenager in comparison to most of the diner's customers). The only other woman in the place was an extremely pregnant young brunette sitting on a tall stool by the front door.

She gave Thomas a tired grin.

"Standing room only," she said. "And I'm afraid they're down to hamburgers or eggs. Or pancakes. I think there's still pancake batter left."

Thomas's stomach rumbled louder. "A hamburger sounds wonderful."

The brunette let out a surprisingly loud whistle. The woman in the kitchen looked up, and the brunette pointed at Thomas, then held up a finger. The woman in the kitchen nodded and went back to work at the grill.

"That will be six dollars," the brunette said. "I hope you have change."

This was the oddest diner Thomas had ever been in, but then again, he'd never be to a diner in a town that had been unexpectedly overrun with geriatric suitors.

He handed the brunette a ten dollar bill. "Keep the change," he said with a smile of his own.

He found a place to stand in between two small tables at the far side of the counter and settled back to wait for his burger.

The overall noise in the diner was louder than even the overcrowded conditions should have made it, but then again, it looked like most of the diners were wearing some type of hearing aid and those who weren't, should have been. Most of the men ignored him, either busy with their own food or attempting to carry on a conversation. That made it easy for Thomas to engage in one of his favorite pastimes: people watching.

He'd perfected his people-watching skills over the years he'd operated his gift shop. When he was performing weddings, he kept his attention on the bride and groom, but when he was in the gift shop, he had an opportunity to stand behind the counter and just watch the customers who came into his store.

He could tell the browsers from the shoppers, the bargain hunters from the people who'd just won some money and didn't care, for the moment anyway, what something cost. He could usually tell how long his customers, especially the ones with kids, had been on the road that day, and whether they had a good relationship with their kids. He learned about all sorts of things by overhearing their conversations, from the best way to get rid of a ketchup stain to the reason premium gas was better for some cars and with others was just a waste of money.

What Thomas learned people watching the other diners in the Lickety-Split was that most of them wanted to talk about anything else, like their various aches, pains, and medical problems, rather than talk about the woman they'd come to town to meet.

They discussed how things were "back in my day" or how the old neighborhood just wasn't the same anymore.

Not that Liberty Springs was anyone's neighborhood.

To hear them talk—and Thomas couldn't help but hear them, given the decibel level of the conversations going on around him—most of them had come from Reno or Carson City or Gardnerville, with a few from Fallon and Bakersfield, and all of them couldn't wait to get back home.

After "that woman" made up her mind, of course, and decided who she wanted to go home with.

Thomas was truly surprised.

Didn't any of these men understand how important the chapel was to Edwina? That she wasn't advertising for a new place to live, but someone to share her life in Liberty Springs?

The man closest to him, another one of the standees, was just finishing up the last of his hamburger. He looked like he was in his early sixties. He'd been talking to the two elderly gentlemen sitting at one of the tables about fly fishing. He'd also mentioned that he couldn't wait to get back home to Reno.

"Your hamburger looked good," Thomas said, by way of breaking the ice. It was also an honest remark. Thomas's stomach had taken up a steady rumble since he'd walked in the diner and smelled the wonderful aroma of grilled meat.

The man smiled at him. "That woman in the kitchen makes a real good burger. My wife, God rest her soul, wouldn't let me eat burgers. Said they were bad for my cholesterol." He patted his round belly. "Skinny as a rail, that woman was, but I'm still here."

Thomas nodded. "What did you think of Edwina?"

The man's smile got wider and was tinged with something just a bit unpleasant. "Beautiful woman. A man could do worse than spend the rest of his life looking at something like that, you know what I mean?"

Thomas was afraid he did. "So she's someone you could stay here for?"

The man snorted. "Stay here? Are you kidding me? And do what…run that chapel of hers? The dry goods store, maybe, but running a wedding chapel out in the middle of nowhere's not good business." He put his empty plate down on the table on top of the empty plate that belonged to one of the men sitting there. "Look, business is business, whether it's marrying people or selling sporting goods, am I right?"

The man looked like he expected Thomas to agree, so Thomas nodded.

"And the number one rule of business is—"

"Keep the customers happy," Thomas said.

"Profits," the man said.

In Thomas's experience, happy customers equaled profits, but the man was on a roll, and Thomas didn't want to argue.

"Overhead's probably low out here, but so's volume. When a place sits empty like that—I've been here two days and I haven't seen her do one wedding in that time—it's a drain. No income, no profits. You get enough of those days strung together, and you're out of business."

While what the man said was fundamentally sound, business wise, Thomas wasn't sure the simple basics were all that was involved in running a wedding chapel. There was an emotional side as well. He decided not to mention that. As far as this man was concerned, emotion no doubt had as little place in business as crying did in baseball.

"Look, if she wants to run a wedding chapel, more power to her, but there are plenty of places to open up shop in Reno. I'm not about to move out to the middle of nowhere and rely on some rinky-dink business to augment my retirement years."

Thomas's spine stiffened.

Bluebelles Wedding Chapel wasn't a rinky-dink business to Edwina. It was her baby. It represented the thing that was most important to her—true love—and Thomas felt outraged on her behalf.

This man would never understand how important her wedding chapel was to her, no matter how many times someone explained it to him. Thomas didn't even try.

Were all the men here this selfish?

Did they all want Edwina to move back to their homes, without a single thought for the fact that she might not want to leave Liberty Springs and Bluebelles behind?

Were they all that unworthy of her?

And on the heels of that thought...

Did the man she was going out with tonight expect her to move away with him?

The pregnant brunette brought Thomas his hamburger along with a side of fries. He took the plate, even though he didn't feel all that hungry anymore.

When she started clearing empty plates from a nearby table, Thomas offered to help, but she declined.

"Eat your food," she said. "The exercise feels good. Maybe it'll convince these two that it's time to come out and say hello to the world."

Twins. No wonder she looked so very, very pregnant. He couldn't help but notice that she wasn't wearing a wedding ring. Some women had to take their rings off when they were expecting, but her finger didn't have the telltale tan line a longtime wedding ring would leave behind.

He wondered what her story was, and if she truly was going to be raising two babies alone.

Not that it was any of his business.

"Congratulations on two," he said. "I wish you the best."

She beamed at him. Clearly she was happy about her babies.

"Thank you," she said. "I can't wait to hold them with my

arms instead of in here." She pointed at her belly. "Can I get you anything else?"

Thomas thanked her and said no.

He decided he should eat, whether or not he still had an appetite.

The one thing he didn't want to do was talk to any of the other men in the diner. He'd had enough of their selfish, self-centered ways.

The burger turned out to be one of the better burgers he'd eaten in his life. Amazing, considering the circumstances. He wondered what the cooks in this diner could do on a normal day, and then he wondered if he'd ever have a chance to find out.

If Edwina didn't forgive him for deceiving her, he doubted he'd ever come back to Liberty Springs. He really needed to come clean about who he really was.

From what he'd overheard of their conversations, Edwina had arranged to meet the guy he'd seen her with outside the chapel at seven. It was only a little after six. He had time to go see her now, but even if he'd known where she lived, which he did not, he wouldn't go bother her before her date. That would just be rude, and would make him as thoughtless as the men he'd met in the diner.

So when was he going to tell her? Tomorrow morning? When a whole new army of suitors would be lining up to meet her?

And that brought up another issue.

If he was going to have to wait to see her until tomorrow, where was he going to spend the night tonight?

He'd assumed that he'd be able to check into a motel if he decided to stay overnight in Liberty Springs, but the only motel he'd seen in town had the "No Vacancy" sign lit up. Once he'd seen the crowd at Edwina's dry goods, he'd understood why. He hadn't brought a tent or even a sleeping bag, and the shelves in Edwina's dry goods store that normally held such things had been empty, along with shelves for most other useful camping supplies.

Although if push came to shove, he could sleep in his car.

Definitely not his preference. He had too many aches and pains on a normal day—all part and parcel of being on the downhill side of fifty—to even want to think what he'd feel like in the morning after spending the night trying to sleep in the back seat of his car.

The men who'd been sitting at the table next to Thomas got up and left.

Thomas sighed. His feet were sore. There was a reason he kept a stool behind the counter in his gift shop. Thomas had flat feet, just like his father had. At least he hadn't inherited his father's male pattern baldness.

He gave up and sat down, thankful that the businessman from Reno had left as well.

In fact, all around Thomas, the other men who'd crowded the diner were leaving. It looked like they all had places to go and things to do tonight.

What did elderly men do in a strange city after dark? Play poker? Liberty Springs didn't have a casino. Did they sit around a campfire and tell ghost stories that most of the other men were too deaf to hear? Thomas doubted that whatever passed for local law enforcement would allow them to start a campfire in the desert, and the official campgrounds weren't open yet.

Probably they just went to bed, wherever that bed was.

His mother complained that his father went to bed earlier and earlier these days, and that pretty soon he'd be going to be before he got up in the morning. Thomas had told her his dad had earned an early bedtime. They both had. His parents had both worked hard for decades and lived frugally. They were both still relatively healthy, given their ages, and as far as Thomas was concerned, it was way past time for his parents to enjoy life. If that meant his dad climbed into bed at six in the evening, well, that should be fine with everyone.

That didn't mean Thomas wanted to climb into bed that early. Although tonight he'd be grateful to just have a bed.

The pregnant brunette began bussing tables. The blonde

Thomas had seen at Edwina's came out from the kitchen, poured herself a huge glass of iced tea, and sat down at the end of the counter near Thomas. The nametag on her uniform read "Nellie."

"Excuse me," Thomas said. "Can I ask you something?"

Nellie turned her head to look at him. He'd expected the weariness he saw in her eyes, but he hadn't expected her tired grin. "This was pretty amazing here tonight, wasn't it?"

"Uh...yes," Thomas said.

"I mean, standing room only. That's for rock concerts or really good movies, not a diner. Especially not *my* diner. Good thing the health inspector wasn't out here tonight. He would have had a cow." Her eyes narrowed, then her grin got bigger. "Hey, I remember you. You were in with Edwina right before..."

Right before the man Edwina was going out with tonight.

Something in Thomas's expression must have given away his thoughts.

"Oh, hey," Nellie said. "I'm sure you're still in the running. I probably shouldn't tell you this, but she didn't talk that long to anyone else today, not like she did with you. She must like you."

Well, at least that much was good to hear, although Edwina had talked a whole lot longer to the man who'd come in after him. Thomas forced himself to smile, even though his heart wasn't really in it. "I just didn't expect so much competition."

"No one did. Edwina expected to be roundly ignored."

"She did look a little overwhelmed," Thomas said.

"That's putting it mildly. The whole town's been over-whelmed, but everybody's pitching in. We haven't had this much excitement in years."

"I miss my wooly buggers!" shouted the man still in the kitchen.

Wooly buggers?

Nellie laughed. "What are you complaining about?" she shouted back. "Everybody loved your cooking."

She shot Thomas a sideways glance. "That's Gus, my

husband. Most days I handle the diner by myself, and he gets to stay home and tie flies. Edwina sells some, and he loses some in the lake, but he's still got tons of little Tupperware containers full of the things."

Ah. Wooly buggers must be fishing flies.

Thomas had never been into fishing himself. He was grateful Nellie had explained that, at least in passing. A whole different image had popped into Thomas's head before her explanation, something that involved a furry creepy crawly thing that lived in the desert and liked to burrow inside sleeping bags.

Maybe it was a good idea he hadn't planned to spend the night outside. That still left the problem of where he would be sleeping.

Which had been the original question he was going to ask Nellie.

"You said the entire town was pitching in," he said. "I don't suppose any of those helpful people are giving Edwina's suitors a place to sleep, are they?"

"Gus!" she shouted at her husband. "Does the rec center have any cots left? Do you know?"

Even from where he was sitting, Thomas could see the exasperated look Gus gave his wife. "How in the world would I know? You've had me stuck in this kitchen all day."

She just looked at him.

"Okay, okay," Gus said. "They might have one or two left. Cecil called a couple of hours ago looking for extra blankets and pillows. I gave him that afghan your aunt gave us last year for Christmas." The expression on the man's face made him look like a guy who'd managed the coup of the year. "Told him to keep it."

Nellie laughed. "Good for you! That was the ugliest thing she's ever made. I'm glad it's going to a good cause."

She turned back to Thomas. "The rec center set up cots and sleeping bags for the overflow. If you head over there now, you might miss the rush."

Thomas got directions to the rec center and left a generous tip on the table.

He might actually have a place to stay that didn't involve the back seat of his car.

"Have some popcorn for me," the pregnant waitress said as he reached the door. At his quizzical expression, she added, "It's movie night at the rec. They've got an old-fashioned popcorn machine, and their popcorn's the best I've ever tasted. Can't have any for another couple weeks." She rubbed a possessive hand on her stomach. "Thanks to these guys, it gives me indigestion."

Movie night.

Was that where Edwina was going to the movies with her date? She'd mentioned popcorn.

The rec had set up cots for the overflow of suitors. If she was going to the rec, she'd be on a date with a bunch of her suitors acting as chaperones.

Including Thomas.

The thought made his heart skip a beat.

He might not be on a date with her tonight, but at least he'd get to see her. And he'd get to make sure her date treated her right.

Then tomorrow—somehow—he'd tell her who he really was.

He had a plan. Finally.

He left the diner with a big grin on his face. For the first time since he'd left the chapel that afternoon, he felt like everything might work out just fine.

# CHAPTER 14

*I*f Edwina hadn't been holding Rufus's hand when she walked through the doors of the rec center, she would have turned right around and walked out.

The place was filled with row after row of men—all the men she'd interviewed that day plus a bunch more, from the look of things.

All she wanted was a quiet date with Rufus so she could get to know him a little better. See if there might be something more to her attraction to the man besides the tantalizing prospect of nooky with a guy who looked like a certain movie star. While that might be fun—might be extremely, fantastically fun—in the end it wasn't what Edwina was really looking for, and she knew it.

And so far, what she'd learned about him and his intentions (what an old-fashioned word!) made her believe there might be something more than amazing nooky with this guy. Might actually—dare she admit it?—be a future with him.

*If* she could get over the feeling that she was a dirty old lady for dating such a young, handsome man.

She wanted to carry on the conversation they'd been having on the way to the rec center, but that looked like it wasn't going to happen. How could it when the rec center was packed to the gills with a bunch of old codgers all carrying on conversations at decibel levels that made intimate conversation impossible?

The rec center used to be the Liberty Springs Regatta Celebration Hall thirty years or so ago, Nellie and Gus had told her. Which explained the sailboat murals on the walls.

Back in those days, the town council (all three of them) had decided the best way to put Liberty Springs on the map was to hold sailboat races on Sutter Lake, complete with a post-race dinner/dance celebration. They'd arranged for discounted rooms at the motels in Hawthorne and even as far away as Fallon and Minden and Gardnerville to the north. They'd even renovated the building that was now the rec center but what used to be an old boating and off-road vehicle retail store that had gone belly up. The county owned the property, since the previous owners had defaulted on their taxes, and hadn't been able to sell it. The town council worked a deal with the county to lease the property for a nominal amount per year. The city renovated the place, turning it into a dance hall with a rustic mountain lake theme—something that looked like it belonged more at Lake Tahoe than Sutter Lake, since Lake Tahoe was actually surrounded by trees instead of sagebrush and rabbit brush.

The town figured that after the Regatta, they could charge local groups a small fee to rent the place for their own shindigs. That plan worked well for a couple of years. Then the economy fizzled, the sailboat races became a thing of the past, and the dance hall, renamed the Liberty Springs Rec Center, stood vacant most of the year.

Except for the once-a-week movie nights, and even then not a lot of people turned out. Most of the ones who did just wanted a chance to gossip and eat popcorn.

The center had one large room with a well-worn wooden floor and an elevated stage up front, a kitchen area off to one side complete with appliances that had been state of the art thirty years ago, and a small storage area behind the stage. A few years ago, the pastor at the local church took advantage of the large room and the elevated stage, and started bringing in a portable DVD player one night a week for free movie night. The town council didn't charge the pastor for using the rec center, given the tax-free status of his church, and in return, the pastor refrained from preaching to the moviegoers, most of whom went to church on Sundays anyway.

Movie night was a low-tech affair. The pastor hooked up the DVD player to a projector someone had donated to the church and speakers that looked like they might have been salvaged from an old car. The movie was projected on a large piece of whitewashed drywall set up on stage. Whoever showed up helped the pastor haul out folding metal chairs from the storage area behind the stage, and shortly after eight, the pastor would start whatever movie struck his fancy that week.

The best thing about movie night was the fresh popcorn made in an old-fashioned popcorn machine leftover from the rec center's heydays as the Regatta Celebration Hall.

Of course, everyone who came to movie night could have watched the same movie in the comfort of their own home, thanks to mail-in DVD rental companies and streaming video, but movie night was more about getting out of the house and being social than watching the movie. If Edwina had thought it through, she would have realized that being social tonight would involve the men who'd come to town to be social with *her*, not just the few people she was used to seeing whenever she went to movie night by herself.

Besides, there weren't a lot of other things to do at night in Liberty Springs, and it looked like a lot of these guys were set up to sleep at the rec center. Rows of cots were lined up in the main room behind the chairs, on the walls on either side of the makeshift movie theater, and even up on stage behind the screen.

"Oh, crap," Edwina muttered, stopping dead in her tracks just inside the main room.

Rufus turned his head to look at her.

So did every other man in the place.

Edwina felt heat rising in her cheeks. She wasn't used to this kind of attention, and she was pretty sure she didn't like it.

Someone in the mass of masculinity wolf-whistled, someone else called out her name, and finally, the whole group started applauding.

"This is ridiculous," Edwina said. "I don't deserve applause."

"The whistle was for you," Rufus said, "but I'd like to think the applause is their way of congratulating me for being lucky enough to get a date with you." He leaned closer and whispered in her ear. "Relax and enjoy it. I have a feeling you've hidden yourself away for far too long. You deserve to be the center of attention."

Edwina was about to protest that she had not hidden herself away, that she was the center of attention when she conducted weddings, but that wasn't particularly true, now was it? Sure, she stood at the front of the altar with the bride and groom, but how many people paid attention to the minister at a wedding? Unless he (or she) was in an Elvis costume, the minister was just part of the stage dressing. All eyes were on the bride and groom, as they should be.

No wonder Edwina was having such a hard time adjusting to the fact that all eyes were now focused on her. She'd never wanted even fifteen minutes of fame. She just wanted someone to grow old with who was as big a romantic as she was.

She took a deep breath. She'd gotten herself into this, after all, whether or not she anticipated just how big "this" would get. She just had to concentrate on the good parts—like walking into a room holding the hand of someone who was as drop-dead gorgeous as Rufus—and not let the rest of it get to her.

She pasted a smile on her face, which only made the crowd applaud louder.

Two of the men sitting in the front row got up and gestured at their seats. The meaning was obvious.

"Perfect," Rufus said.

Edwina glanced up at him. He had a broad smile on his face. He was clearly eating up all the attention. Then again, he was used to walking around at work wearing little more than a speedo and a cape. A shy man wouldn't last long at a job like that.

Speaking of shy men, Edwina wondered if the shy man she'd had such a good meeting with that afternoon was in the audience. She hadn't given much thought to him since she'd met Rufus. She felt a little guilty about that. She had, after all, asked the shy man not to leave town.

If he was here, she should be able to spot him. Most of the men in the audience were either balding, totally bald, or had enough snow on the roof for Santa's reindeer to make a soft landing. The shy man's light brown hair should make him stand out in this crowd.

Edwina tried to locate him in the audience as Rufus led her to her seat, but she didn't see any brown-haired men except the pastor, who was waiting patiently at the DVD player.

Her disappointment must have shown on her face because Rufus gave her an odd look as they sat down. She gave him a quick grin and squeezed his hand. It wasn't fair to him to let her attention wander like that.

"This is still pretty overwhelming," she said. "I thought most of these men would be on their way home by now." Especially the ones with the obviously false teeth. She'd put that line in her ad as an attempt at humor, and instead it had become an easy way to weed out the men who apparently didn't think a requirement like that applied to them.

"Hope springs eternal," Rufus said, then he chuckled. "I just used a cliché, didn't I?"

"You did."

The mischievous twinkle reappeared in his eyes. "You really want to discourage them?"

Edwina blinked. "You're not going to kiss me in front of all these men, are you?"

He leaned in toward her. "When I kiss you for the first time, I want it to be special. I don't want you to be distracted. So no, I'm not going to kiss you." His breath ghosted over her shoulder. "Yet."

A little shiver ran down her spine. Oh my...

"I have something a little more PG in mind," he said.

He let go of her hand, and the next thing she knew, he'd wrapped his arm around her shoulders, drawing her in close.

Edwina hadn't been held like that in...well, she couldn't remember the last time. She fit well beneath the hollow of his arm. He was just tall enough to make it comfortable. His body was as muscular as she'd imagined, and the steady rise and fall of his chest was soothing.

She could get used to this.

The lights in the room dimmed, and the pastor turned on the projector. The menu screen for the DVD appeared on the white-washed drywall.

*When Harry Met Sally.*

Edwina almost laughed. That movie was one of her friend Reverend Thomas's favorites. She'd teased him often about his love of Meg Ryan romantic comedies, and he'd shot back that she shouldn't expect anything different from a man who conducted weddings for a living.

She hadn't chatted with him online since the night she'd posted her ad. She'd been a little disappointed—no, it was more than that; she'd been hurt—by his reaction to her ad. She'd already had misgivings about the whole thing. She'd wanted encouragement, and if not that, at least an acknowledgment that it took guts to put herself out there like that. That's what friends were for, right? Someone who was in your corner, no matter what?

So she'd purposefully avoided logging into the chat program the next night. It wasn't quite the same as giving him the cold shoulder—she just hadn't wanted to talk, that was all.

And then once the men started actually showing up in town in response to her ad, she'd been too busy and too embarrassed to admit that maybe the ad hadn't been such a good idea.

Come to think of it, this was the longest she'd gone without talking to Thomas in years. He must think she was really angry, and she wasn't. At least not anymore. Maybe when she was done with her date, she'd log in and let him know everything was okay between them.

She certainly hoped it was.

What if she wasn't the only one who'd been upset? What if he was angry at her about the whole silent treatment?

And if he did talk to her, what would he say about what she was doing now? Sitting here with a man she'd only met a few hours ago. A man she'd only talked to twice, who currently had his arm around her shoulders and who'd flat out told her he planned on kissing her later. When they were alone.

A man she was probably more than a little in lust over.

Okay, there...she'd said it. Or thought it, and that was practically the same thing.

As interesting as Rufus was, the real reason she was on a date with him was because she'd promised herself some nooky before she hit fifty. Only...

That wasn't all she really wanted. While there was nothing wrong with lust—or the nooky that went along with it—she wanted to fall in love. She wanted to find a man she could see herself growing old with. She was pretty sure Rufus Monroe didn't fit the bill.

Sure, he'd said that his mother was a good deal older than his father, and they'd had a long, wonderful life together. So maybe he was in it for the long haul. But with her? She just couldn't see it.

Edwina didn't have the kind of role models in her life that Rufus had in his. Her father was only a few years older than her mother. All the friends she'd had when she was growing up, their fathers had all been older than their mothers. While that didn't guarantee a long-term relationship, since half her friends' parents got divorced before their kids got out of high school, older father and younger mother had been the norm for Edwina. The last thing she felt like, or *wanted* to feel like, was...what was that offensive word for an older woman who preyed on younger men? A cougar?

Her emotions had been a confused jumble the last few days, but she was definitely certain she didn't feel like a cougar, all appearances to the contrary.

On screen, Harry and Sally had just been ditched by their best friends. The two friends, who were supposed to be on dates with Harry and Sally, had just taken off together in a cab, obviously too much in lust at first sight to worry about how Harry and Sally might feel at being ditched in the middle of their dates.

Of course, Harry and Sally couldn't help but wonder what was wrong with them. Why they weren't dating material. Edwina could relate. She'd spent a lot of time alone wondering why she hadn't found Mr. Right, although once she'd moved to Liberty Springs, the answer was painfully obvious: lack of eligible, not to mention desirable, single men.

Well, Edwina had solved one problem—the lack of single men. She might have solved the lack of desirable men problem, too, but that was a harder call.

Rufus was certainly desirable, but would the I-want-to-jump-his-bones kind of desire last? Did it have a shot at mellowing into the comfortable kind of desire where both of you were happy just curling up on the couch next to each other, reading a good book?

How could you even tell if something like that was possible with the kind of audition/speed dating/round-robin thing she and Nellie had set up?

Even going out on this date, it didn't seem to Edwina like she had enough time to discover whether the attraction she felt for Rufus would burn out just as quickly as it had ignited. After all, she hadn't been out on a date in a long, long time. She could just be experiencing a delayed hormonal reaction to one too many viewings of all the *Avengers* movies.

Harry and Sally wouldn't know they were perfect for each other until the very end of the movie. They were too used to just being friends. According to the philosophy of the movie, love could hit a person any old way, either immediately, like the two friends who had ditched Harry and Sally after the disastrous double date, or by sneaking up on you so gradually that by the time you realized you were in love, it seemed like you'd always been in love.

Of course, that was how it happened in the movies. When in real life did people fall in love the way they did in romantic comedies?

She wished she could talk to Thomas about all this. Nellie might be her best friend in Liberty Springs, but Thomas was really Edwina's best friend. They'd talked almost every night for years, and it didn't matter that they'd never spoken on the phone or seen each other in person. She felt totally at ease talking to Thomas in a chat window. She supposed part of it was the anonymity of the internet, but they weren't just anonymous screen names. They knew where each other lived, what each other did for a living, and it would be pretty easy for either of them to call the other one or just show up to say hi if they felt like it.

That was actually a pretty good idea. She should call Thomas. Nothing was stopping her from picking up her phone and just calling him. He had an after-hours contact number on his chapel's website, after all. If she was so worried that he was angry with her, why not?

The thought of finally talking to him on the phone gave her a happy little thrill that had nothing to do with the fact that Rufus was still holding her.

As soon as this date was over, that's exactly what she would do.

# CHAPTER 15

The pastor who seemed to be in charge of sleeping arrangements at the rec center found an empty cot for Thomas in the kitchen between an industrial-sized refrigerator and a free-standing counter. The kitchen was a decent-sized room, clearly a place meant for a half dozen people to be working comfortably together. Still, there was barely enough room to fit the cot between the refrigerator and the counter. He was going to have to crawl off the end of the cot to get out of bed.

"You'll be all right here?" the pastor asked. "I'm afraid it's movie night, and I have to go get the popcorn machine started or I'll have a mutiny on my hands." He handed Thomas an obviously handmade quilt, a folded rainbow-print sheet, and a small pillow that looked like it had come from the back of someone's couch. The pillow had a matching rainbow-print cover that was twice as big as the pillow. "We're running a little low on emergency bedding."

Thomas took the bundle from the pastor's hands. "This is so much better than sleeping in my car. I thank you. My back thanks you."

The pastor smiled. "You and your back are welcome. Good luck to you, my son."

Before Thomas could respond, the pastor darted through the swinging doors between the kitchen and the main room.

Thomas sighed. The pastor was younger than Thomas. He wondered if the pastor called all men "my son," even if they were old enough to be the pastor's father.

There certainly were a lot of other men in the rec center. The crowded diner had been one thing. The crowd in the rec center was at least twice as large and still growing.

Apparently all the men who were camping out by the lake had heard about movie night, too. Some of the men who'd followed Thomas through the rec center's front door had a couple of days' worth of stubble and smelled a little on the gamy side.

This was how they expected to win a woman as special as Edwina? Thomas felt insulted again on her behalf.

Or maybe he was just being overprotective.

Or jealous.

Or...

He didn't really have a clue. His emotions had been all over the place for days, it seemed like. Ever since she'd put that ad on her website.

He really was too old to be feeling like a rattled teenager trying to deal with his first serious crush.

Wasn't he?

Now that he was at the rec center, he'd changed his mind about watching a movie, and he'd definitely changed his mind about watching Edwina on her "date." He didn't want to go find a seat in a room crowded with the same kind of men he'd eaten dinner with at the diner.

The locals had apparently decided to stay home tonight. Thomas had scanned the group in the rec center's main room while the pastor ducked into the storeroom behind the stage in search of bedding for Thomas's cot. Not a single woman in sight. Without a woman in the crowd, the men were free to make whatever comments they liked about Edwina, including the kind they might have stifled in the diner considering the very pregnant waitress and the very self-assured Nellie, who ran the place.

He didn't want to hear anyone talk about Edwina like that.

He put the bedclothes down on the cot and considered whether he should just try to get some sleep. He'd never been an "early to bed, early to rise" kind of guy. When he and Edwina chatted online, they always started late at night. It was only a little after seven now. Even though he'd left Lovelock at the crack of dawn to drive to Liberty Springs that morning, he still wasn't tired enough for sleep at seven in the evening.

He might have solved the problem of where he was going to sleep tonight, but he still didn't know what to do with himself until then. He didn't want to leave the rec center and risk losing the cot to another one of Edwina's suitors, but he was at a loss of what to do with himself for the next couple of hours. The kitchen was spotless, so he couldn't offer to clean the place in exchange for his bed. He hadn't even thought to bring a book with him, and he didn't have a smart phone. His cell phone was just that—a cell phone. For the first time in his life, he envied people who carried around an entire library of digital books in their back pocket.

Maybe the pastor had a book—besides the Bible—he could lend Thomas. Just because some of the people in Lovelock called Thomas "Reverend" didn't mean he studied the Bible every night. He read from it often enough so that he could accommodate couples who wanted Bible verses quoted as part of their ceremony, but when he did a little light reading, novels suited him just fine.

He was about to go ask the pastor about a book when the crowd in the main room broke into a round of applause. He even thought he heard a wolf whistle.

He raised an eyebrow. That certainly was one appreciative crowd for a popcorn machine. The waitress must not have been kidding about the quality of the rec center's popcorn.

The door between the kitchen and the main room of the rec center hung on hinges that let it swing both ways. It had a small porthole window in the top half, no doubt in order to make sure someone entering or exiting the kitchen wouldn't run headlong into someone headed in the opposite direction. Thomas peeked through the porthole, looking for the pastor, and instead saw something he wished he hadn't.

Edwina, hand in hand with the man Thomas had seen outside the chapel, walking toward the front of the crowd.

Thomas sighed. What had he thought about keeping an eye on her to make sure her date treated her right?

He just couldn't do it, not with the sudden tight hurt in his chest at seeing the two of them together.

And they were definitely together. As soon as they sat down, the tall, blond-haired man leaned toward her, and the next thing Thomas knew, the man had put his arm around her shoulders.

Thomas couldn't seem to catch his breath.

He wanted to be happy for her, he really did. She was his best friend. She'd apparently been lonely for a long time. She'd never mentioned that, not once in all the years they'd chatted online, but he should have figured it out on his own. She had talked about going on a date once or twice, but the dates had never seemed to work out. He'd had a few dates of his own that had gone badly, and they'd joked now and then about how difficult it was, as a person who performed weddings, to actually meet someone who wasn't already taken or didn't think the title "minister" or "reverend" meant no sex ever, nuh-uh, no way.

Even through the small porthole window in the kitchen door, he could see that she looked radiantly happy now. She must really like this man. Thomas was pretty sure that the Edwina he knew wouldn't let that man keep his arm around her shoulders if she didn't like him all that much.

He wanted to be happy for her, but his own feelings kept getting in the way.

What kind of a friend was he if he couldn't put her first?

The lights in the main room dimmed, and he could just see

the edge of the menu screen for *When Harry Met Sally* appear on what looked like a piece of drywall propped up on the stage.

The irony wasn't lost on Thomas.

Edwina's first date was to a movie about two friends who fell in love and lived happily ever after. What better way for the universe to let Thomas know that he'd waited too long to tell Edwina how he felt about her than with a movie that showed him how things should have worked out between them but now never would.

*When Harry Met Sally* was one of his favorite movies. Or at least, it had been. He doubted he would ever watch it again. He certainly wasn't in the right frame of mind to watch it tonight.

No other cots were set up in the kitchen. There really wasn't room. The pastor had only made room for Thomas because he knew Thomas had nowhere else to spend the night. That meant none of the men in the main room should be coming in here after the movie was over. Good. Thomas wasn't in the mood to be around anyone right now, much less another one of Edwina's erstwhile suitors.

He padded over to the wall and flipped the switch that turned off the overhead lights. He thought about turning off the light over the stove, too, but he didn't think he'd be able to find his way around the kitchen without that light once night really settled in.

He went back to the cot, spread out the sheet, and then laid down on the tiny pillow and pulled the quilt up to his chin.

He needed to be a better friend to Edwina. He wanted to be the kind of friend she'd thought he was when she told him about her ad. He promised himself that he would be that kind of friend again, but just not tonight. Tomorrow. He'd make sure that she was really happy with this new man in her life tomorrow, and then he'd go back home for good.

Tomorrow he'd put her feelings first, but tonight, he just couldn't do that.

Tonight he was too tired to do feel anything other than sorry for himself that he'd never get to hold Edwina like he wanted to and tell her how he felt.

He'd be a better man tomorrow.

He turned off his cell phone, curled up on his side, and closed his eyes.

Even though it wasn't even eight at night, by the time Sally met Harry yet again in the bookstore, Thomas was fast asleep.

The movie was over by nine-thirty, and by quarter to ten Edwina was standing on the front porch of her house, saying goodnight to Rufus.

Once she'd relaxed, she'd actually had a good time at the movie. Except for the times when it occurred to her that the throng of men in the rec center were all in town because of her, and they were probably watching her more than the movie. Whenever that happened, she tried to concentrate on Harry and Sally's dysfunctional love affair and not the odd state of her own romantic life, and eventually the feeling of being constantly watched went away.

By the time the movie was over, Edwina had a whole new appreciation of how celebrities must feel being constantly in the public eye. She'd never wanted to be famous, and now that she'd gained a bit of local notoriety, she definitely knew she never wanted a life like that. Ever.

Rufus had been a very good sport about the whole thing. He seemed to have an inner strength that she found admirable. He just took things in stride.

Even her somewhat abrupt "goodnight" when they reached her front door.

She couldn't help it.

During most of the final act of the movie—when Sally and Harry "broke up" after having gone to bed together for all the wrong reasons—Edwina had thought about nothing other than how she might have botched up her friendship with Thomas for good. Rather than looking forward with nervous anticipation to kissing Rufus goodnight, she just wanted to get home, get their goodnights over and done with, and power up her computer so she could try to contact her best friend.

Yes, she'd decided earlier that a phone call might be better, but after tonight, she wanted the comfort of their familiar online relationship, not the strangeness of a phone call on top of all the other weird things going on in her life.

She needed to see Thomas's cheerful *what are you up to tonight?* appear on her computer screen. She wanted to stay up too late chatting with him online about all that had happened to her in the last few days, and ask his opinion about what she should do with all these men who'd come all this way to see her, even though most of them had no clue what romance was beyond buying her more flowers than she'd need in an entire lifetime.

Rufus shot her a quizzical look when she held out her hand as she said goodnight.

"Did you not have a good time?" he asked.

"I had a marvelous time. It's just been a very long day."

It wasn't quite a fib. It had been a very long day, and she was tired. And antsy to get inside and get on her computer.

"Can I see you again?" Rufus asked.

She hadn't quite made up her mind about that. Her libido wanted her to say yes, but the rest of her thought she should give the shy man a chance. He might be dating material as well, and she had asked him to stick around. Not that she'd seen him in the audience tonight (although she hadn't scanned the audience to be sure; she hadn't wanted to turn around in her seat and find all those men staring back at her).

It was one of the things she wanted to talk to Thomas about.

Would she be a terrible person if she asked Rufus to wait around while she went on a date with someone else? He'd been unflappable so far, but every man had his limits.

Besides, no one might be as suitable as Rufus.

"Would it be bad of me to tell you to come by the chapel tomorrow around eleven?" she asked.

"For a date?" he asked.

She considered that. She was expecting a delivery at the store the next morning to replace all the camping supplies she'd sold out of in the last couple of days. Memorial Day weekend was coming up fast, suitors or no suitors. The people who planned to spend the weekend on the lake might not take kindly to having to drive to Hawthorne to get the last-minute things they forgot to pack. She'd need their business again next year, and the key to repeat business was to keep the customers happy.

Still, she'd have to break for lunch sometime. Her first thought had been to talk to Rufus while she restocked shelves, but the whole restocking thing might go quicker if he helped. Besides, she had a wicker basket in stock that had sat on her shelves unsold for far too long.

"How about this," she said. "You help me restock the shelves in the store, then I'll have time to go for a nice picnic lunch down by the lake, just the two of us."

He grinned at her, and the twinkle was back in his eye. "You are a crafty woman, Edwina Morrisey. I happen to like that."

Before she realized what he intended, he bent his head down and kissed her.

Edwina's breath caught in her throat as his lips touched hers. His lips were soft, with a hint of scruff at the edges, and slightly parted. He didn't pressure her, just held his mouth there while he held her hand in his from where she'd tried a goodnight handshake instead of a kiss.

Why again hadn't she wanted a kiss goodnight? This felt marvelous. She'd felt close to him during the movie, sitting in the hollow beneath his arm, but this was a decidedly different kind of closeness.

This was the kind of closeness that could lead directly to nooky, and there were certain parts of her that definitely wanted it and wanted it *right now.*

But she wasn't in college anymore. Love was about more than sex, and romance was about more than giving in to lust at first sight.

Especially on the first date.

With a little sigh, Edwina drew back and opened her eyes. His eyes were still half-closed, and he had the softest expression on his face.

"I happen to like *you,*" he said.

He stepped back and then reached up with one hand to brush Edwina's hair back from her forehead. A happy little shiver ran down her spine.

"Tomorrow at eleven," he said. He brought the hand he was still holding to his lips, kissed her knuckles gently, and then he let go.

Edwina stood on her front porch for a full minute, watching him walk back down her street toward the chapel where he'd left his car. She wondered where he was spending the night. He'd never said. He could have been one of the lucky ones who'd gotten a room at the motel, although he hadn't been one of the first ones to appear at the dry goods store.

Or maybe he'd brought his own camping gear with him. With any luck, maybe he had a sleeping bag built for two.

She blinked, surprised at her train of thought.

"You are in serious trouble here," she muttered to herself. "Lust is not love."

She'd repeated that to herself a dozen times or more by the time she sat down in her favorite chair and turned on her laptop. She really needed a dose of common sense. She needed to talk to Thomas.

Only he wasn't online.

She glanced at the clock at the bottom of the laptop's screen. Only a little after ten. Yes, ten at night was late for some people, but she'd chatted with Thomas until midnight or later more than once. They'd even watched movies together, both renting the same DVD and starting the movie at the same time, then chatting about it just like they would if they were in the same room.

The good feeling Edwina got from kissing Rufus started to fade, replaced by the utter certain dread that Thomas was angry with her and refusing to log in.

Or worse yet, he'd logged in but had made himself invisible to her so she couldn't bother him.

Was their friendship really over?

Edwina sat back in her chair. Thomas had never struck her as the kind of man who'd end a friendship over a simple disagreement. Yes, she'd inadvertently given him the cold shoulder, but it had only been for a couple of days. He wasn't even giving her the chance to apologize.

Well, the heck with that. Edwina wasn't the kind of woman who gave up that easily. She'd made a go of her chapel out here by herself when the prior owner had simply put the place on the market and closed up shop when things got tough. She'd handled two businesses by herself for more than ten years now. She had a decade-long friendship with a man she really cared about, and she wasn't about to let it go like this.

She called up the website for Thomas's chapel and jotted down both the chapel's number and the after-hours number. She didn't really expect to reach him—the chapel closed at eight during the week, and she figured the after-hours number was probably just a message phone—but she could at least leave him a voicemail with her cell phone number. That way, if he didn't call her back, she would have at least made an effort.

She told herself her fingers weren't really trembling when she dialed the after-hours number on her cell phone.

A man's recorded voice came on the line—Thomas, no doubt. He sounded crisp and professional and friendly all at once.

Edwina tried for the same tone of voice for Bluebelles' recorded message. She thought of it as her "social" voice as opposed to her everyday voice.

Her heart sank as she listened to the message. Thomas was out of town for a few days. The chapel would reopen on Saturday for the Memorial Day weekend. He hoped that no one was inconvenienced. If the caller wished to reserve a wedding date, please leave a message and he would return the call.

Edwina didn't want to reserve a wedding date, but she did want to leave a message. She cleared her throat and waited for the beep.

And found she had no idea what to say. She never did like talking to answering machines.

"I hate these machines," she said, then paused as she realized she'd said that part out loud. "Crap."

She'd said that out loud too, and into an answering machine. No taking it back now.

"Sorry, Thomas. This is Edwina." She paused again, then told herself to just get on with it. "And I want to say I'm sorry if I've offended you in any way. My life has gone...well, it's certainly *gone* the last few days. I'm not even sure what day it is anymore."

Lord, she sounded stupid. She forced herself to take a deep breath.

"I haven't been online to chat, and I hope you don't think I did that deliberately because of the way you reacted when I..." Another pause. "I'd like to talk to you about that, actually. It's turned out, well, not exactly the way I'd hoped. Or dreamed. I could really use your advice, and I know you're out of town on vacation. If you have a moment, maybe you could log in so we can chat?"

*I miss you.*

The thought brought unexpected wetness to her eyes. She couldn't say that to a message machine.

"Thank you, Thomas," she said, and pressed the little icon on her cell that would end the call.

It wasn't until after she'd stopped trembling, after she'd wiped her eyes and felt herself settling down, that she realized she'd never left him her cell phone number. That was probably a good thing. She wasn't sure she could face talking to Thomas for real.

Not just yet.

# CHAPTER 17

Sleeping on the cot in the rec center kitchen was better than sleeping in the back seat of his car, but only marginally. Thomas woke to an assortment of aches and pains he didn't normally have when he spent the night in his own bed. The cot certainly wasn't comfortable enough to spend any more time on than necessary, so he set about stretching his legs and arms and attempting to stretch his back so that nothing would cramp up on him when he sat up.

According to his watch, it was eight in the morning by the time he managed to get his stiff muscles to cooperate and let him crawl off the cot.

He blinked at the dial.

He'd slept for nearly twelve hours. He never did that. No wonder he was so stiff! Just went to show how emotionally drained he'd been last night.

Well, enough of that. Last night had been all about feeling sorry for himself. Wallowing in the misery of a man who realized he'd waited too long to tell the love of his life how he felt. Today was about making sure Edwina was happy so that he could go back home and get the chapel ready for the holiday weekend.

Not to mention take a shower. He'd slept in his clothes, and he was sure he smelled a little rank. Did the rec center have shower facilities? If not, maybe he could sponge off in the men's restroom.

Only there was a line of half-dressed elderly suitors at the sinks in the men's restroom. Apparently Thomas wasn't the only one who'd thought of that idea.

Well, he wasn't in a hurry. He could wait.

He wandered back out to the main room of the rec center. The pastor and a young man who looked like he was in his early twenties were setting up folding tables. The man had the fresh-faced, freshly showered look of someone who hadn't spent the night on a cot.

"Could you use some help?" Thomas asked the pastor.

The man smiled at him. "Another pair of hands is always welcome, my son."

Thomas held out his hand and introduced himself. "That way you don't have to call me 'my son.'"

"Father Mills," the pastor said in return. "And I hope you'll excuse my bad habit. I've met so many people in the last few days, I have trouble remembering everyone's name. Coming from a man of the cloth, I think 'my son' is more dignified than 'hey you.'"

Thomas chuckled in spite of himself.

"True. It's just that I think I'm probably older than you are." He shrugged. "Felt odd."

The pastor gazed at him. "Oh, I don't know about that. I've been blessed with a young-looking face and my father's genes when it comes to hair. No one ever took me seriously when I was younger. They still don't."

Something about the way Father Mills was looking at him made Thomas uncomfortable. Maybe his rough night on the cot —or his rough night emotionally—was more evident in his expression than he'd thought.

"Joey," Father Mills said to the man helping him, "why don't you take a look in the restroom and see if any of our guests needs assistance. Or extra toilet paper."

The young man shot the pastor a confused look. He scrubbed at his still-damp hair and a cowlick sprang up in the back, which made him look younger than he probably was.

"Are you sure you don't need my help out here?" the man Father Mills had called Joey asked.

"I have Thomas here to help me." Father Mills glanced at Thomas. "Isn't that right?"

Thomas nodded.

"You're sure?" Joey said again. "I don't think those guys need much help except with that stinky stuff my mom rubs on her shoulders, and I'm not doing that."

"We all have our crosses to bear." Father Mills made a shooing motion. "Consider it a favor."

Joey glanced at Thomas but he left, still looking reluctant.

"See what I mean?" Father Mills said. "No one takes me seriously."

Joey probably knew that Father Mills was just trying to get rid of him. Thomas did, too.

"I didn't see you at the movie last night," Father Mills said once the restroom door closed after Joey. "My choice wasn't to your liking?"

Thomas tried to keep his face impassive. "It was actually one of my favorites. I was just tired." It wasn't quite a lie. He had been tired, but that wasn't why he hadn't ventured beyond the kitchen door.

Father Mills nodded. "I see. I imagine quite a lot of the people here were tired. I would have thought most would have curled up on their cots or gone back to their tents by the lake, but they all stayed. Not that most of them watched the movie."

They'd watched Edwina, the pastor meant.

Thomas hadn't given any thought to how Edwina must have felt sitting in the front row, the center of so much attention. She wasn't comfortable with anyone shining a spotlight on her, much less a room full of virtual strangers.

They'd had long chats about how conducting a wedding wasn't really like being on stage, but rather like being part of the room, a piece of furniture that talked and moved occasionally. Edwina said she liked it that way, which was why the Elvis costume her predecessor had left behind stayed in the closet. Edwina felt, and so did Thomas, that the bride and groom should be the focus of attention, not the person conducting the ceremony.

"She's a good woman," Father Mills said. "I've known her since I was assigned here. You would think that a pastor who marries the faithful before God wouldn't call a woman who performs non-denominational civil ceremonies a friend, but I believe Edwina and I are friends."

Thomas fussed with the last table he'd set up, making sure it was lined up right with the rest of the folding tables, but his attention really wasn't on that task anymore. He was pretty sure Father Mills could tell.

"It's a lonely life out here." Father Mills carried a chair over from the neat rows set up for movie night and set it down next to the table. "Some don't like it, and they move back to the city—Reno or Las Vegas or somewhere else where there are more people than coyotes. Those of us who stay, we're an independent sort, but we look out for each other without being pushy about it." Instead of going to fetch another chair, he put a gentle hand on Thomas's shoulder. "Do you understand what I'm saying?"

Thomas wasn't sure he liked being on the receiving end of this man's sympathy. He definitely wasn't sure he deserved it. Maybe he should have just left the rec center instead of waiting for the lines in the restroom to thin out. There had to be somewhere else he could clean up.

When the pastor didn't remove his hand, Thomas made himself meet Father Mills' patient gaze.

"I'm pretty sure you're telling me that you wouldn't let

Edwina make a mistake," Thomas said. "I'm just not sure why you feel you have to tell me that."

Father Mills smiled, but the smile was tinged more with gentle empathy than good humor. "She's not a woman you just met," he said. "I imagine you came here expecting something quite different than the reality of all this."

There was no point trying to deny it. "How did you know?"

Father Mills gestured at his face. "Older than I look. I've had a lot of experience counseling broken hearts. It's a part of the human experience that never gets any easier to deal with." He sighed. "Or to hide."

So much for putting on an impassive face. "I'm okay," Thomas said. "No need for counseling. As long as she's happy, I'll be fine."

Father Mills nodded. "I imagine you will be. You're still here, after all, and I don't see you as the champion of lost causes."

Lost causes. Edwina's date must have gone well, then. "I thought I'd stay just long enough to see for myself that she's okay."

Father Mills patted his arm, then turned back to the chairs. Thomas took that as a sign the conversation was over.

It wasn't. Not quite.

"She's a strong woman, my friend Edwina," Father Mills said. "I'm sure she'll make the choice that's right for her. I'm sure you will, too."

The restroom door opened and Joey came back out, along with a man who must have been in his early seventies. The elderly man held a cane in one hand and Joey's forearm in the other.

"Which cot is yours?" Joey asked the man rather loudly.

"Eh?" the elderly man said.

"Cot! Which one is yours?" Joey had raised his voice as close to a shout as he could get without actually shouting. "If we're going to find your hearing aid, I need to know where to start looking."

"We should start looking in my cot!" the old man shouted

back.

Father Mills shook his head as he watched the pair. Joey was a big guy who looked like he would be at home playing football, not shepherding an elderly man who was looking for a lost hearing aid.

"I'd better go join the hunt," Father Mills said to Thomas. "Edwina specified teeth. She never said a thing about being able to hear without electronic assistance. I'm beginning to wish she had. Do you mind finishing with the chairs?"

"No problem," Thomas said.

He watched the three of them toddle off toward the cots at the back of the main room. One of Father Mills' other helpers had already folded up all the sheets and blankets. Good luck finding a missing hearing aid back there.

Thomas had just finished setting up all the chairs around the folding tables when the blonde—Nellie—and the very pregnant brunette from the diner came through the main doors of the rec room, their arms laden with platters of pancakes.

"Where do you want the food, Father?" Nellie called out.

"Over by the kitchen," Father Mills said. "Thomas, would you mind giving them a hand?"

Feeling very much like he'd been drafted for an entire war when he'd just volunteered for one small battle, Thomas went over to the brunette and relieved her of her burden. Together, the three of them set up a buffet line on a folding table the priest had set up along the wall outside the kitchen. Nellie made coffee while Thomas and the brunette, whose name was Bessie, found silverware and plates in the kitchen, along with enough napkins to last through the next century. Most of the men who'd spent the night in the rec center were still there, and before long, everyone had settled down to a pancake breakfast complete with syrup and butter and the best coffee Thomas had tasted in a long time.

After the night he'd had, he didn't think he'd have much of an appetite, but he surprised himself by cleaning his plate. After he was done eating, he helped Bessie and Father Mills clean up the dishes and restack them in the cupboards, and then Thomas and Joey folded up the tables and chairs, and put them back in the storage room behind the stage.

When Thomas looked at his watch again, he was surprised to see it was nearly ten o'clock. He still hadn't cleaned himself up, but he felt much better.

Because Father Mills had kept him busy.

Deliberately.

"He's a pretty devious guy, isn't he?" Thomas asked Joey as they walked out of the rec center into the bright mid-morning sunshine. Most of the rest of the men were gone, probably to hang around Edwina's dry goods store or go tell tall tales to each other down by the lake.

"Father Mills? Oh, yeah. Once you're on his radar, he'll work your butt off if you let him. He's got a good heart, though." Joey gave Thomas a thoughtful look. "You ever met him before?"

"No," Thomas said. "Why do you ask?"

"He doesn't usually conscript strangers, is all, especially nobody out of this group. He must like you a lot."

Thomas didn't know about that. The pastor had taken the time to talk to him when he'd still felt emotionally drained, and he appreciated that, but that was all.

"I think he's just a decent guy," Thomas said.

"My mom says we're lucky to have him," Joey said. "He used to pastor this big church over in the Sacramento Valley. I'm not sure why he left, but I'm glad he ended up here."

They walked along in silence for a bit, then Joey asked, "Say, you got a place to clean up?"

Thomas glanced at him. They were close to where Thomas would have to turn to head back to where he'd left his car. "I was going to clean up in the rec center, but the weekend'll be here before I get through that line."

"I hear you there." Joey stopped and pointed in the opposite direction from Edwina's dry goods store. "My mom and I, we have a trailer over this way. It's not much, but the shower works and the water's hot. You don't have a bag with you, so I guess you came out here not planning to stay overnight, unlike some of these guys. They brought those little roller suitcases, like they were expecting to stay in a nice motel. I think the rec center was a shock to their systems."

"Probably why they were in the restroom so long," Thomas said.

Joey laughed. "Most likely. I'm just glad I'm not on bathroom clean up duty."

Thomas had cracked the joke because he wasn't quite sure what to say about Joey's offer. It wasn't every day a stranger offered up his shower. Then again, there had been nothing every day about the last few days.

"So you're serious about letting me take a shower at your place?" Thomas asked. "You sure your mom won't mind? You don't even know me."

Joey shrugged. "You don't know me either, but Father Mills likes you. Besides, my mom always says everybody starts out as strangers until they decide to get to know each other, right?"

Thomas blinked. That was how his friendship with Edwina had started. She'd posted a request for help on a message board for wedding chapel owners, and Thomas had decided to respond.

He hadn't been in town long enough to really get a feel for the place, but Liberty Springs didn't seem to be the kind of small town that made strangers feel unwelcome. Or the kind of small town that seemed to resent the tourist trade even when tourists were the ones who made their businesses successful. If things with Edwina had turned out differently, if Thomas had ended up staying here, he was pretty sure the people in this small town wouldn't make him feel like a perpetual outsider just because he hadn't been born here.

After all, a nearly complete stranger had just offered up his—well, his mom's—shower. So much better than sponging off in a crowded men's bathroom.

"You're absolutely right," Thomas said. "Point the way."

# CHAPTER 18

Nellie brought Edwina breakfast at the dry goods store at seven forty-five.

"This is becoming a habit," Edwina said as she locked the door after Nellie came inside.

Already five men were standing outside the entrance to the dry goods store. Edwina didn't remember seeing any of them the day before.

Good lord, were men still arriving in Liberty Springs hoping for a date? She wasn't that special. Couldn't they see that?

"Here you go," Nellie said, putting a Tupperware container on the counter next to the cash register. "Can't stay long. Father Mills volunteered Gus to cook for all the men who spent the night at the rec center."

Gus? "Are there that many eggs left in town?" Edwina asked. All the man could cook were scrambled eggs and hamburgers, and no one outside of a teenage boy wanted a hamburger for breakfast.

"He's attempting pancakes." Nellie smiled a wicked little smile. "I left him my recipe. I'd stay it was foolproof, but I know better."

Edwina opened the Tupperware container. Inside was a plain waffle with a fried egg nestled in the middle.

"Nothing fancy," Nellie said. "I'm too worn out to think up a daily special. Those boys your ad brought to town, they sure have good appetites. Well, most of them. And most of them are good tippers, too. Bessie sure appreciates that."

Edwina's eyebrows rose. "You have Bessie waiting tables? You want those twins born behind the counter?"

"It was her idea. She thinks she can work those babies into deciding it's time to be born." Nellie leaned a hip on the counter. She was Bessie's birthing coach, which was probably how the whole idea of waiting tables had come up. "Okay, enough with the small talk. Tell me about your date before I have to jet out of here."

Edwina felt her cheeks heating up. "How do you know I had a date?"

Nellie gave her The Look. "It's a small town, Edwina. This is the biggest thing that's happened here since the sailboat races went bust."

Which meant everyone in town knew by now that she'd gone out to the movie with one of the men who'd answered her ad.

"So who was it?" Nellie asked. "The last guy from yesterday, or the one before him?"

The shy man? "Why would you think it would be the shy guy?" Edwina asked.

"Is that what you call him? The Shy Guy?"

Edwina cut into the waffle so she wouldn't have to look at Nellie. "I can't remember his name. I saw so many men yesterday, and most of them were totally forgettable. *Their* names I can remember, but his? Not so much."

Nellie shrugged. "Can't help you there. I didn't save any of the slips of paper from yesterday's group, and I sure didn't keep a sign-up sheet." She poked Edwina in the shoulder with a finger, just hard enough to make a point. "So, you ducked the question. Who did you date?"

Edwina grinned. "Rufus. The last one."

"Oooo." Nellie's eyes lit up. "The young guy. I told you he was pretty. Looks like that movie star, what's his—"

"Yes, he most certainly does."

And he kisses like a superhero, too, Edwina thought, not that she'd tell Nellie that. Some things she wanted to keep to herself, at least until she figured out how she felt about the whole thing.

"So what now?" Nellie asked. "Are you going out with him again?" She nodded toward the front door, where the small group of men were still milling around. "Should I tell these guys they're one day plus about thirty years too late?"

"He's going to help me restock the shelves, then I thought we'd go on a picnic lunch over by the lake."

Nellie grinned. "I'd say that was a date. Good for you."

If Nellie noticed that Edwina didn't answer the rest of the question, she didn't say anything. Which was good since Edwina didn't know what to do about the rest of the men in town or the new ones who were still apparently showing up, ready to give Edwina a look at their teeth, dental work and all.

Nellie straightened up and stepped away from the counter. "I've got to get going. I don't want Gus to burn down the place. Why don't you stop by the diner on the way to the lake, and I'll have a nice lunch for you to take."

Edwina shook her head. "You don't need to do that. I can make my own food." She glanced at the waffle. "Occasionally."

Nellie gave her The Look again.

"You have no idea, do you?" Nellie said. "I've made more money at the diner these last couple of days than I usually make over Memorial Day, Fourth of July, and Labor Day combined. Even giving away pancakes over at the rec center this morning, I'm still coming out way ahead. Ernie at the AM/PM on the highway had to order an extra delivery, he's selling so much gas and snack food and soda. Your manhunt is good for business, girlfriend. I don't mind kicking in a free meal or two to show my gratitude."

Edwina hadn't really thought about it that way. All these extra people in town bought things, which was good for local businesses. Hers, too. She'd sold more tents and sleeping bags and Ben Gay in the last few days than she usually did in an entire year. She was a one-woman economic boom.

How wonderful.

Except... she didn't want to be. She just wanted to be Edwina again, even if she was dateless and alone.

Now where did that bleak thought come from? She did, after all, have a date with Rufus later on today.

She pasted a smile on her face. "Then I'll be happy to take you up on your offer."

Nellie gave her an odd look, then did something she never did —she hugged Edwina. "You hang in there," she said, patting Edwina on the back. "It'll all work out. Things always do." She let Edwina go. "Now come let me out so I can go check on my husband."

After Edwina let Nellie out the door, making sure the lock was firmly engaged, she went back to her breakfast. Not that she was all that hungry, and it wasn't her upcoming lunch—okay, second date—with Rufus that had her stomach tied in knots.

Thomas hadn't called her back.

She knew it was silly to expect him to pick up messages on the chapel answering machine when he was out of town. Everyone deserved a vacation from real life. She couldn't remember the last time Thomas had taken any time off. The man was long overdue. Plus, it was still pretty early in the morning. Wherever he was, he might have slept in.

Her head knew all these things were entirely probable. That didn't make her heart feel any better.

Someone knocked on the glass window next to the front door. Edwina glanced up to see one of the men pointing at his watch and smiling at her. She sighed. Yes, it was eight in the morning, and yes, the dry goods store was supposed to be open.

Edwina put what was left of her breakfast on the shelf beneath the cash register. For the first time since she'd bought the chapel and dry goods store, she didn't want to open up for business, and that just wasn't right. She'd always loved the store. Not as much as performing wedding ceremonies, that was true, but her store was as much her child as the chapel. She loved stocking shelves and tracking down odd items her customers might want. She loved the little electronic gadget that read stock numbers and helped her count her inventory, and she even loved the bookwork and balancing her accounts. But today, all she wanted to do was go home and hide.

Well, nuts to that.

Sigourney Weaver wouldn't let all these men intimidate her.

Edwina carefully printed up a new sign in large, bold letters, and taped it on the window next to the door. She wore her practiced, professional smile as she watched the men read it, give her a disappointed look, and wander away.

She didn't unlock the door until after they'd all left. Then she went back to her now cold waffle in her blessedly suitor-free store and finished it.

When the UPS driver showed up a little before nine, Edwina was busy rearranging the shelves to make room for the extra stock she'd ordered. He gave her sign a quizzical look before he came in with the first load of boxes.

"Come back at three?" he said. "What's that all about? Are you taking the day off?"

"Just half a day," she said.

"Good." He started to unload the boxes along the side wall where he put all the deliveries to Edwina's store. "You look beat, if you don't mind me saying so."

She figured she probably did. "Just so long as you don't say I look old."

"You? Old?" He snorted. "Give me a break. Sigourney Weaver's looking old these days. I just saw her in something—some weird little movie my wife wanted to watch—and she's looking her age."

Edwina blinked. Hadn't she just been thinking about Sigourney Weaver not that long ago?

The UPS driver started back toward the front door. "I got another couple loads for you. Guess you're stocking up for the weekend, right?" Before she could answer, he said, "You, though, you're still a knockout. Anybody says different, they can answer to me."

Then he was out the door and back at his truck, busy stacking the next load of boxes on his cart.

Edwina couldn't believe what she'd just heard. She was still a knockout? She'd never thought she was a knockout to begin with, and certainly not now.

She was just Edwina, a middle-aged woman who was handsome at best with fifty looming in her not-so-distant future. She had laugh lines at the corners of her mouth and the corners of her eyes, and little lines beginning to show on her neck. Yes, she could still fit into her swimsuit, but she couldn't remember the last time she'd worn it. She didn't believe in facials or anti-aging cream, and her idea of a good time was chatting online with her friend Reverend Thomas.

What in the world did all those men out there see in her?

Which was exactly what she asked Rufus when he showed up at eleven for their date.

# CHAPTER 19

When Joey had said his mom's trailer had a shower with plenty of hot water, he hadn't been exaggerating. The water was hotter than Thomas's own shower back home, and he took advantage of it. The hot water helped loosen tight muscles from a long night spent on a cot.

Too bad he had to put the same clothes back on, but like Joey had mentioned, Thomas hadn't exactly come to Liberty Springs prepared to stay overnight. At the most, he'd planned to spend the day getting to know Edwina, with the hope that once they met in person, they'd make plans to get together again. After all, while Lovelock and Liberty Springs weren't exactly next door to each other, the drive wasn't that long that they couldn't get together every week or so.

Or at least that had been the plan he'd had in mind when he'd gotten in his car at the crack of dawn the day before. He had no idea what the plan was now, other than to try to make sure Edwina was happy.

"I've got a couple of days off," Joey said when he showed Thomas to the front door of the trailer. "My mom's out of town, in Reno visiting a couple of her girlfriends. If you end up needing a place to sleep tonight, just knock on my door. I'm just gonna be gaming anyway."

Joey and his mom's trailer was a nice place—a double-wide with more rooms than most apartments Thomas had lived in—and not at all like the dinky thing Thomas had imagined when Joey first mentioned he and his mom lived in a trailer. His mom had inherited the place when Joey's grandfather passed away, and instead of selling it, she'd decided to move to Liberty Springs. She telecommuted for her job, something to do with a tech firm out of California—Joey was a little shy on the details—and Joey drove a big rig between Carson City and Sacramento. He told Thomas that in his down time, he played one of those online multi-player games.

Which was what he'd been doing when Thomas got out of the shower. He'd been sitting hunched over a keyboard, his cowlick now dried into place.

That wasn't all he did in his down time, though. Thomas had passed a small room that held nothing but workout equipment. That explained the football player look.

"If you need it," Joey said, "our couch is probably more comfortable than one of those cots."

Thomas had no doubt that it was. Pretty much anything except the floor or the back seat of his car would be more comfortable than the cot.

Halfway from Joey's trailer to where Thomas had left his car, he remembered the chapel's answering machine. He really should call and check for messages. He hadn't intended to be gone for more than one day. He'd just left a generic message saying that he was out of town until Saturday. If someone wanted to book a wedding for this weekend, he really should touch base so he could set that up. Just because his emotions had been all out of whack (and probably still were, if he was being honest with himself), he shouldn't be ignoring his work.

He called the chapel's number and keyed in the code that gave him access to his messages. There were only two.

The first message was from Judge Julie.

"I didn't see you after court today," she said, "and now I hear, thanks to your very professional message, that you're out of town until Saturday. I'm taking both those things as a good sign. I would take it as the best sign if you called me back to let me know that you haven't ended up as roadkill on a highway somewhere."

Thomas winced. He'd promised to call Julie once he got to Liberty Springs—if he decided to go to Liberty Springs—and let her know what happened with Edwina. He should have done that while he'd been sitting by the lake yesterday, but he'd been too wound up and worried about coming clean to Edwina about who he really was.

He made a mental note to call Julie after he listened to the next message. She'd be on the bench—it was still the middle of a busy workday for Judge Julie—but he could leave a message on her cell phone just to let her know he was alive and was not, in fact, roadkill. Besides, leaving a message might be his best option. Then he wouldn't have to answer any questions about how things were going. He didn't want to tell her that he'd been too late. At least, not yet. He'd have to tell her when he got back to Lovelock, but he hoped by then it wouldn't hurt so much to admit that he'd missed his opportunity.

Thomas pressed a button on his cell for the next message.

"I hate these machines," muttered a woman's voice, followed closely by, "Crap."

Thomas grinned. He hated answering machines too.

Then he stopped dead in his tracks as the message continued.

"Sorry, Thomas. This is Edwina." The message paused, just like his heart. "And I want to say I'm sorry if I've offended you in any way. My life has gone...well, it's certainly *gone* the last few days. I'm not even sure what day it is anymore."

It was Edwina, all right. Now that she'd said more than a few words, he recognized her voice from yesterday. It was just that she'd never called him before, and he hadn't been expecting to hear from her, not this way. Especially not to say she was sorry. What in the world did Edwina have to be sorry for?

"I haven't been online to chat," her recorded voice continued, "and I hope you don't think I did that deliberately because of the way you reacted when I..." Another pause. "I'd like to talk to you about that, actually. It's turned out, well, not exactly the way I'd hoped. Or dreamed. I could really use your advice, and I know you're out of town on vacation. If you have a moment, maybe you could log in so we could chat? Thank you, Thomas."

Her voice had sounded strange on the last couple of words, almost like she couldn't get them out.

She was really upset.

What time had she called? He'd been too startled at the message to listen to the date and time.

He keyed in the command to replay the message and listened to it again. This time he heard the date and time stamp.

She'd called last night at ten thirty-eight.

That was after her date.

What in the world had that man done to her that had her so upset? She'd looked happy when he'd seen her at the rec center. Two and a half hours later, she'd been so upset that she'd called him when she couldn't find him online.

He really should have brought his laptop with him, but he never thought he'd need it. He wasn't one of those people who was attached at the hip to his computer. If it wasn't for his nightly chats with Edwina, he probably wouldn't even turn the thing on every day. Besides, he doubted the rec center had an internet hookup that just anyone could use.

Why didn't he have a smart phone like everyone else? He could have used his phone to check online, then he would have been there for Edwina when she needed him.

And here it was, nearly noon. He'd taken a really long shower, and then spent some time talking with Joey. All the while, Edwina had needed to talk to him, and he hadn't even known it.

Well, just because he hadn't been there last night, didn't mean he couldn't be there for her today. He had a pretty good idea where Edwina would be. He could be here for her in person. He'd have to get over his own nerves about telling her who he really was and his own heartache, but he could still be the friend she needed.

The day was already hot, the smell of sagebrush heavy in the air. A few cars were on the street, but Thomas would never call traffic in Liberty Springs heavy. He walked as fast as he could to his car without running—the last thing he needed was heat stroke—and slid behind a hot-to-the-touch wheel. Thomas drove the few blocks to Edwina's dry goods store far over the posted twenty-five miles per hour speed limit. Luckily for him, no sheriff spotted him.

He got to Edwina's store in time to see a large group of people walking up the steps on the chapel side of the building. The group appeared pretty evenly divided between men and women, the men in wildly printed, baggy shorts and Hawaiian shirts, the women in simple, brightly colored sun dresses and floppy beach hats. Most of them wore flip-flops or sandals, and the women carried large straw tote bags.

There at the front of the group was Edwina. She was busy chatting to one of the couples.

And right beside her was the man Thomas had seen her with at the rec center the night before.

# CHAPTER 20

"What do all those men see in me?" Edwina asked Rufus when he walked through the door of her dry goods store at eleven o'clock on the dot.

"Well, hello to you," he said with a smile. "Have you had a rough morning?"

She hadn't exactly had a rough morning, but by the time Rufus showed up to help her put all the new stock the UPS driver had delivered that morning out on her shelves, she had already pointed out the "Come Back at Three" sign by her front door to enough potential suitors that she was beginning to think she should have put something about good eyesight in her ad along with "must have own teeth."

"I'm serious," she said as she handed Rufus a carton of hearty, single-serving canned soups and stews, big sellers with the sportsmen who camped out by the lake. "Follow me."

She led him to the aisle where the canned goods normally took up shelf space next to flour, sugar, and baking soda. Like most of the shelves in her store, the canned goods had been wiped out.

"Everything in the carton goes here," she said, indicating the middle shelf.

He took out a can of southwestern-style beef vegetable soup and peered at it. "Is this a dry good?" he asked with a grin.

Edwina raised her eyebrows.

"Well, it is a dry goods store," he said, still smiling. "I've never been real sure about what to expect in a dry goods store."

"My mom used to call a place like this the Five and Dime," Edwina said. "I sell a little bit of everything, almost like a grocery store and sporting goods store and a miniature version of Target all rolled into one, but I don't have refrigerated shelves or a dairy case." She tilted her head and looked at him. "This is a very strange conversation."

"Not as strange as you asking what a man would see in you," he responded.

Edwina sighed. "I just don't understand all the attention. I don't even know how all these men found out I was looking for a man. You told me how you did, but the rest of them?" She shook her head. "I never expected all this. I went from having no one pay attention to me to—" She made a frustrated gesture with her hands. "I can't go anywhere without being mobbed. I'm not a movie star. I run a wedding chapel and a glorified corner market, without the fresh milk and vegetables. I live in a town where everyone knows everyone else, and most of us get along. I had to break up a shouting match in the parking lot this morning between two men who could barely hear the insults they were yelling at each other."

Rufus put the carton on the floor and took her chin in one gentle hand. He tilted her head up until she was looking in his eyes, which were still a gorgeous blue. He had a bit of a scruffy beard this morning that Edwina thought gave him a roguishly handsome look.

But he was still so young!

"You are a beautiful, desirable woman," he said. "I know, even with just the little bit of time we've spent together, that you don't believe you deserve half the attention you've gotten. I don't know how they found you. Things have a way of going viral on the internet. Someone must have posted a link to your add on some social network somewhere. That's all it would take. But if it makes you feel this uncomfortable, cancel the whole thing and send them all home. I just have one small favor to ask."

Edwina swallowed. It was easy to think she might really be as beautiful as he said as long as she kept looking in his eyes.

"What's that?" she asked.

He leaned in a little closer. "Don't ask me to leave. Not just yet."

This time when he kissed her, she wasn't taken by surprise. But it was only a brief kiss, one that left her longing for more. From the expression on his face as he drew away, he knew it, too.

"See?" he said. "We're going to have so much fun together, you and I," he said.

Someone cleared their throat loudly.

Edwina turned around to see a man and woman standing at the end of the aisle. She felt a flush heat up her cheeks. They'd clearly seen her with Rufus.

"Can I help you?" she asked.

"The sign on the chapel door said to come to the dry goods store," the man said. "But the sign on this door said to come back at three. Will the chapel be open then?"

"Oh," Edwina said, desperately trying to shift gears and get back in business mode. "No. I mean, the chapel's available for wedding ceremonies pretty much all the time, but the door's only open when a wedding's actually being performed."

"Can we do that now?" the woman asked. "Get married? He popped the question this morning before we left Carson City, and I don't want to wait."

The couple were around Edwina's age, the man a little older, the woman maybe a couple of years younger. They were dressed in what Edwina thought of as beachcomber casual, the man in loose-fitting print shorts and a Hawaiian shirt, the woman in a sundress and sandals.

"Sure," Edwina said, smiling at them. "I'd be happy to help

you out." She introduced herself, explaining that she was the minister for the chapel, but that it was purely non-denominational. "If you'd like to come next door, we can get the paperwork filled out and proceed with the wedding."

"Mind if I tag along?" Rufus asked.

The couple exchanged a look, then smiled a knowing smile at Edwina. "Not at all," the bride-to-be said to Rufus.

Edwina was surprised to see a group of at least thirty people, all dressed in beachcomber casual, some with fake-flower leis, waiting out in the parking lot next to a charter bus.

"We're part of a tour group," the man said. "We're going down to Bishop for a bowling tournament and luau. Elks Club." He was holding the woman's hand. "Jean and I have been dating for six months."

"We've known each other for eight years," the woman—Jean—said. "I met George in a mixed-doubles league, and we went to a lot of the same functions. Tournaments. League dinners." She beamed at her husband-to-be. "I couldn't believe when he asked me to marry him this morning. The bus had just pulled into a pit stop in Carson City when he took my hand and slipped this ring on my finger." She held out her hand for Edwina to see. A modest diamond ring glittered on the ring finger of her left hand. "It's the prettiest thing I've ever seen. Of course I said yes, then I joked that we should get married right away before he changed his mind. One of the other bowlers—"

"It was me, Jean!" called one of the women near the bus.

"Harriett, yes, thank you!" said Jean. "Well, she remembered seeing a billboard for your wedding chapel on last year's trip. Everyone on the bus teased George that he should put his money where his ring was, and next thing you know, here we are."

"So you're sure about this?" Edwina said as she led the group up the stairs to the chapel entrance.

"That we want to get married?" George asked.

"That, and that you want to do this now. Don't you have family you'd like to invite?"

Jean gestured toward the crowd, who had followed them to the chapel. "Our family's right here. Besides," she gave George a hug. "I don't want to wait another minute before I marry this wonderful man. He might change his mind after the tournament."

"She's a little erratic when it comes to bowling," George said, his tone implying that he was spilling a state secret.

"A little?" someone else in the crowd said, which led to some good-hearted laughter.

"Good thing that's not why I'm marrying her," George said.

The couple shared a long look, and Edwina smiled, satisfied. She would have married them anyway—her business was marrying people, after all—but seeing couples like this who were so in love it was obvious to the entire world around them, that was what made Bluebelles Wedding Chapel such a special place.

It didn't take long to fill out the paperwork for the wedding. George and Jean had already picked out their two witnesses. They didn't have wedding rings, only the engagement ring George had given Jean a couple of hours ago.

That was all right. A lot of the couples Edwina married didn't have wedding rings. Nevada had no waiting period where marriage was concerned, and spur-of-the-moment decisions to marry often didn't come with rings involved. George and Jean said they didn't mind, and Edwina had no problem leaving out that part of the ceremony. They said they preferred Edwina to wear her royal blue robe—it was in keeping with the luau theme —and one of the guests provided an iPod with steel drum music to play in the background.

When Edwina and the happy couple stepped back out from her office to the altar at the front of the chapel, George and Jean's friends applauded.

"Not yet," Edwina said, grinning. "We've got a little bit of a ceremony to go through first, then you can applaud to your hearts' content."

"I hope you're keeping this short," a man sitting in the first row said. "Bill's got a schedule to keep."

"The bus driver," Jean said to Edwina. "He's a little anal about his schedule, but he's been a good sport about all this extracurricular stuff this morning."

"He gave us a half hour," George said, "and we're pushing it. Think we can pull this off in the next five minutes?"

"You got it," Edwina said.

She looked out over the audience. She was pretty sure this was the biggest group who'd ever attended a wedding at Bluebelles, but then again, tour buses didn't usually stop for a wedding. All the luau garb made the place look downright festive. It was pretty clear from the sea of happy faces that Jean and George were well liked, and that the wedding had become the high point of the trip.

Edwina was also pretty sure from the rowdy nature of the crowd that the bus had an open bar that served more than plain orange or tomato juice.

Rufus had taken a seat by himself near the back of the chapel. He had a big smile on his face that made his eyes twinkle. She could see that plain as day even from where she stood at the altar with the happy couple.

She couldn't help but smile back, even as it occurred to her that this was the first time she'd performed a wedding ceremony in front of anyone she was even remotely interested in. It gave her a nervous little feeling in the pit of her stomach, like she was back on display again like last night at the rec center when all she'd wanted to do was watch a movie while she got to know Rufus a little better.

She told herself firmly that it didn't matter that Rufus was in the chapel. This was Jean and George's day. She'd have time for Rufus later.

"Okay," she said. "Let's get this show on the road so you can all get back on the bus in time."

She went through an abbreviated version of her standard opening in which she talked about the joy of finding that one other person in the world who was the right person to spend your life with.

"Jean and George found each other," she said, "and I think that's pretty special. They've invited all of you to witness their marriage, and that's pretty special, too. They've told me they don't have vows—precisely—but they do have something they'd like to say to each other in front of all their friends. Jean, would you like to go first?"

Jean turned toward George. Her eyes were shiny bright and her smile was a little on the wobbly side, like a lot of the brides who stood before Edwina, but she held herself together.

"George," she said. "This is the last thing I expected to be doing today, and the one thing I've wanted to do since the day I met you. Even though you beat my high score that day—and no, I've never forgotten that you did that—I have forgiven you for it."

Everyone in the audience laughed, and luckily, so did George. The guy standing next to George who was serving as a witness and the best man clapped George on the shoulder. "Better you than me, buddy," he said.

Jean glared at him, and the man ran a finger over his lips, like he was zipping his mouth shut.

Oh yes, there had definitely been an open bar on the bus.

Jean turned her attention back to George. "Life's too precious to compromise when it comes to who to spend your life with, and too short to wait when you've found that person. I love you, George Hillicot. I want to grow old with you, but I don't want us to ever get old. You know what I mean by that, right?"

George nodded, grinning, and he waggled one eyebrow at her.

Edwina had a good idea what she meant, too, and good for her.

"That's my vow," Jean said.

Edwina cleared her throat before she turned to George. For an off-the-cuff profession of love, Jean had been pretty darn eloquent.

"George?" she asked, giving the groom his cue.

George took a deep breath and let it out slowly. "What she said, except for the high score part."

Everyone laughed again, including Edwina.

These two were going to get along just fine.

"That's it?" Edwina asked.

George gave her sharp nod.

"All right, then," Edwina said once everyone quieted down. "Since we're keeping this short and sweet, let's cut to the chase. Jean, do you take this man to be your lawful wedded husband, for richer or poorer, in sickness and in health, until death do you part?"

"I do." Jean's voice trembled a little, but her wobbly smile had turned radiant.

"George, do you take this woman to be your lawful wedded wife, for richer or poorer, in sickness and in health, until death do you part?"

George hesitated, and Jean lifted one eyebrow. Even Edwina could tell he was teasing. Oh, yes, these two were going to be great together.

"I do," he said.

"Then by the power vested in me by the State of Nevada," Edwina said, "I now pronounce you husband and wife. George, go ahead and give your bride a kiss."

He did, accompanied by an enthusiastic round of applause from their friends, who were all on their feet.

Edwina glanced at the back of the chapel. Rufus was on his feet as well, applauding along with the rest of the audience.

So was the shy man.

Edwina's breath caught in her throat. She hadn't even seen him come in.

She felt a wave of relief. He hadn't left town after all!

But why was he here?

She certainly hoped all the men who'd come to town to date her wouldn't start hanging out in the chapel when she conducted wedding ceremonies. Weddings should be all about the bride and groom. It was bad enough that the flowers all those men had given her were still crowding the aisles. Even Jean and George had commented on the overwhelming number of flower arrangements inside the chapel. At least they hadn't seemed to mind. Edwina had even given one of the smaller bouquets to Jean to hold during the ceremony.

The shy man didn't appear to be intruding on the wedding party, though. He had enough good sense to sit in the back row of the chapel, just like Rufus, only on the opposite side. They looked like bookends—one man a little (okay, more than a little) on the young side but movie-star handsome, and the other a more appropriate age for her, handsome enough to make her heart skip a beat, but in a comfortable, relaxing, we're-going-to-be-best-friends-forever kind of way.

She didn't mind that the shy man had shown up for the wedding ceremony because he obviously knew enough about weddings to be respectful of the happy couple, and Jean had agreed that Rufus could attend (after drawing some fairly obvious conclusions about his relationship—relationship! Did she actually think that word about Rufus?—with her), but Edwina was going to have to do something about the rest of the men in town.

Given the way some of her potential suitors had looked at her the day before when she'd interviewed them, she got the distinct impression they thought she was a prize to be won, not an independent woman who'd be making up her own mind regarding any romantic feelings she might have for them. She didn't want men like that in her chapel when she was performing a wedding. Weddings were about romance and love, not about who won or lost the dating lottery.

The shy man held Edwina's gaze when she looked his way, and he nodded slightly. The expression on his face was odd, a mixture of emotions that she couldn't quite pin down. He didn't look happy, exactly, but he didn't look sad either. Resigned was the word that came to mind, but he also looked like a proud parent whose kid just hit a homerun over the left field fence.

She wished she could remember his name. They'd seemed to connect so well during their brief meeting. What would it be like to spend as much time with him as she'd spent with Rufus? As much as her hormones pushed her toward Rufus, hormones weren't the be all and end all. Hormones eventually took a break. If a relationship was going to last, it had to be based on more than hormonal overload.

There she was, using that word again. Relationship.

Well, wasn't that what she wanted? A relationship?

No. She wanted the kind of love like Jean and George obviously had for each other. She wanted a love that would last.

Like what happened with a lot of the weddings at Bluebelles, these particular newlyweds didn't get a chance to walk down the aisle before their friends crowded around and congratulated them. Rufus joined in the celebration, mingling with the rest of the wedding party to give the happy couple his congratulations.

The shy man stayed in his seat at the back of the chapel. Edwina almost wished he'd come up to join in the congratulations so she'd have a chance to talk to him again.

"So when are you going to marry the minister here?" one of the tipsier men in the audience asked Rufus. His voice was loud enough to carry over the noisy crowd, no doubt on purpose.

The people in the wedding party quieted down and turned to look at Edwina.

She was still standing at the altar, two steps above everyone else. Talk about being put on the spot. She didn't dare look at the shy man at the back of the chapel, not when she felt the worst blush of her life heating up her cheeks.

Rufus grinned at her as she stepped down from the altar. "We haven't gotten that far yet," he said.

"We just started dating," she added, although after she said that, she had a feeling she'd only made matters worse.

Jean turned to Edwina, the happy smile of a newly-minted bride still lighting up her face. "Well, don't let him wait eight years to pop the question. Life's too short. When you've found the right man, I say go for it."

George came up behind his wife and wrapped his arms around her waist. "Go for it? Right here? I'm game, but I thought you'd want to wait for later."

Jean smacked his arm, but she turned her head so that he could lean over her shoulder and kiss her.

Edwina stole a glance at Rufus. He was watching Jean and George with a big smile on his face.

Would things ever be as casually loving between them as they obviously were between Jean and George?

Over Rufus's shoulder, she caught a glimpse of the shy man slipping out the chapel door. She wanted to run after him and ask him to wait, but would that be fair to him? She already had a picnic lunch date with Rufus. Then there were all the other men she'd told to come back at three.

What exactly would she be asking him to wait for?

All of a sudden her life had become far too complicated, and she felt like she had no time to even catch her breath.

She agreed with Jean that life was too short. That's why she'd placed her ad in the first place.

Her gaze kept going back to the empty spot where the shy man had been sitting during the ceremony. She felt like maybe she'd missed out on something special. Rufus was wonderful, but was he the right man for her? Could she actually see herself spending the rest of her life with him?

She wanted to find the right man and start living with him as soon as possible.

But with so many choices and no time to actually spend time with the ones she was interested in, how could she tell when—and *if*—she'd found the right one?

# CHAPTER 21

It had been nearly fifteen years since Thomas had watched anyone else perform a wedding ceremony.

Before he moved to Lovelock, Thomas had worked at a wedding chapel in Reno doing almost everything else except officiating at weddings. While the work was easy, it wasn't as emotionally satisfying as Thomas imagined actually marrying people who loved each other would be. He'd decided to get his own license, but even after he did, the man who owned the chapel only let Thomas perform weddings two days a week. That's when Thomas began looking for a wedding chapel of his own.

The few chapels that went on the market in Reno and Carson City were way out of his price range. He widened his search, and that's when he discovered that the chapel in Lovelock was for sale.

When he went to Lovelock to look at the place for himself and decide if he wanted to relocate, he spent some time watching the husband and wife who owned and operated the place conduct wedding ceremonies.

The chapel in Lovelock certainly wasn't as busy as the chapel he'd worked at in Reno, which Thomas had expected. Otherwise the place wouldn't have had such a bargain-basement price. In the week Thomas spent living out of a hotel room, he'd only seen the couple conduct three weddings.

The ceremonies themselves were all identical. The husband officiated and his wife put some nice touches in the ceremony—including recorded music that Thomas later learned the wife had performed herself—but they made no effort to personalize the ceremonies to the needs of the couple getting married. Neither had the man who owned and operated the chapel Thomas had worked at in Reno.

All of them had made weddings seem utterly routine, utterly boring, and utterly bankrupt emotionally.

As far as Thomas was concerned, if a couple wanted an impersonal ceremony, they could get married before a civil marriage commissioner. Couples came to a wedding chapel for a romantic wedding without all the religious trappings of a church wedding.

When Thomas took over operation of the chapel, he decided he was going to conduct the kind of weddings the bride and groom would remember, and not because the wedding was cheesy or corny, or even a small-town version of what they could get on The Strip in Las Vegas. No Elvis impersonations or fake cowboy, dude ranch ministers would ever conduct a wedding at his chapel. Thomas wanted people to remember their wedding in his tiny chapel in Lovelock because the minister took time to get to know them, to care about them, and to give them the kind of wedding they really wanted.

Which, he supposed, was one of the reasons the Reverend Thomas nickname had stuck. If that was the price he had to pay to give his couples the kind of service that made them truly happy, then so be it. He didn't care. The only thing he'd really cared about back then was making every wedding special, even if he wasn't sure the couples were going to last.

Edwina had just done the same thing for Jean and George.

It was pretty obvious to Thomas that she'd done it on the fly, too. Not everyone could do that, but Edwina clearly cared more about making the bride and groom happy than worrying whether she got the words just right.

And she *had* made this particular couple happy. Thomas could see it on their faces, and what was even better, he could see their happiness reflected in Edwina's expression.

He felt proud just watching her, partly because when she first started talking to him online and asking his opinion about the kind of weddings he performed, he'd told her about how he'd decided to adapt his weddings to what each couple wanted, and how he felt that was more emotionally satisfying to everyone involved. Edwina had obviously listened to him and taken his advice to heart.

But mostly he felt proud of her just because she was so good at what she did. She was a natural because she cared about each and every person who came to her chapel to get married.

They'd talked about that, too. She thought it was silly to get so invested in the happiness of strangers she'd never see again, but she told him she just couldn't help it. That empathy of hers was part of what made Edwina Morrisey such a lovable woman.

He wondered if anyone else who'd come to Liberty Springs in response to her ad understood even just a little bit all the things that made her wonderful. Understood—or cared.

The tall young man with the superhero physique who'd been Edwina's date last night might understand, but Thomas couldn't be sure. Her date had sat in the last row on the opposite side of the chapel from Thomas for the whole ceremony. If he'd been aware that Thomas was here for Edwina, not the happy couple, the man didn't show it. Thomas was certainly aware of him.

Thomas had assumed that Edwina had wanted to talk to her friend, the Reverend Thomas, so badly the night before because something unpleasant had happened on her date with that man. She'd sounded so unsure of herself not to mention fairly upset when she'd left the message last night, yet today she looked just fine. Not to mention that the man she'd been on a date with was here in the chapel, and she didn't seem any too upset about it.

Thomas stayed for the entire wedding ceremony. He laughed when the rest of the audience laughed, and applauded along with everyone else when the groom kissed his new bride. The way she'd performed the ceremony, not to mention the obvious joy and love this older couple had tying the knot, infected him. He hadn't felt this fulfilled by a wedding in a long time, probably about the same time he'd stopped customizing his wedding ceremonies and instead starting going with his tried and true standard versions. Edwina was good for him, no doubt about that.

Except when the wedding was over, a hollow ache settled in his chest again. He certainly wasn't going to come clean to her right now about who he really was. If he did? Talk about your bad timing.

He decided to slip out quietly now that he knew Edwina was okay so that his melancholy mood wouldn't put a damper on the wedding party's happiness, and that's when she looked directly at him.

Their gazes met and held, and Thomas felt the same connection to her that he had the day before.

She must have felt it, too, because she kept looking at him until the friends of the bride and groom rushed the happy couple.

And someone in the wedding party asked the man Edwina had been with the night before when he was going to marry the minister.

An uncomfortable, almost embarrassed expression stole over her face, and her gaze dropped away from his. She stepped down from the altar, and Thomas lost sight of her in the crowd of people at the front of the chapel. But he clearly heard her say that they'd just started dating.

*Just started dating.*

That meant there would be more dates.

It seemed like she'd made up her mind about which one of her suitors she wanted to spend more time with, and it wasn't him.

It really was time to leave.

He slipped out of the chapel while Edwina was still surrounded by the wedding party.

She didn't need him. She might have had a moment of panic last night, but today she looked happy. She'd been in her element at the front of the altar. Her face had the kind of radiance Thomas always imagined it would. She'd told him more than once that when she married people, she always felt honored to be there when they started their lives as husband and wife, that she could feel the love they felt for each other radiate outward to encompass everyone witnessing the wedding.

He didn't need to stay. She'd be fine. He should just go home so he could log on the computer and be there as her friend, the Reverend Thomas, the next time she wanted to chat with him online. She didn't need him intruding on her happiness just to give her some lame excuse about why he hadn't told her who he really was. That wasn't how he wanted her to remember him.

He trudged down the steps of the chapel and without really intending to, headed toward the lake. He'd missed his morning run, and while he wasn't dressed for running, he could take a good long walk around part of the lake.

The sun was definitely hot overhead now, and the bright desert sunlight glinted off the water, making him squint against the glare. Only a slight breeze off the lake made any attempt at all to cool down the day. He walked at a steady pace along the edge of the same road he'd taken the day before, his feet kicking up little dust clouds of dry dirt as he walked.

He should go home. It was the smart, logical thing to do. Getting out of Liberty Springs would be the only way he could start recovering from his self-inflicted broken heart.

So why didn't he just get in his car and drive home instead of lingering in a town that didn't need him?

Because the simple truth was he wasn't ready to say goodbye to his dream, not just yet.

Stubborn, ridiculous man.

In his pocket, his cell phone buzzed.

Thomas pulled his phone out and peered at the name in the little screen.

Judge Julie. Of course. It was her lunch hour by now, and he hadn't called her.

"I'm not roadkill," he said in lieu of hello.

"Then why do you sound like you've been hit by a Mack truck?" she asked.

He sighed. What to tell her?

"It didn't go well, did it?" she said.

He knew it wasn't really a question. Julie knew him too well to need him to respond, but he did anyway. "No. Although I did make a new friend who offered me the use of his couch and his shower."

He could practically see her eyebrows climb her forehead. "Are you experiencing a lifestyle change I should know about?"

"No."

At least not on his part. Thomas couldn't be sure about Joey. He'd never been good about picking up on the subtle signs that signaled when someone was gay. Flamboyantly gay, sure, he could tell that, but Joey didn't seem to have a flamboyant bone in his body. Besides, Thomas would know if a guy was hitting on him, right?

"So tell me," Julie said. "Was she surprised that you traveled all the way from Lovelock to meet her?"

Thomas rubbed the bridge of his nose. "I didn't tell her that part." In fact, Edwina had never asked where he was from. They'd spent too much time discussing love and hope and the possibility of finding the one person in the whole world you were meant to be with. Insignificant stuff like that.

"But you did introduce yourself, didn't you?" Julie asked.

His steady pace had taken him within a block of the lake. A few boats were on the water already, and off in the distance, he could see a skier kicking up wakes behind a speed boat.

A quarter mile away, a few tents housing some of Edwina's suitors still squatted on the beach in spite of the "No Camping" signs posted along the lakeshore. Some of the men had wandered down to the lakeshore, and a couple of them were watching a guy who stood in the lake about ten feet out into the water, casting out his line as little waves lapped at the calves of his waders.

"It's been a little strange here," Thomas said, and before he realized he was going to do it, he told Julie everything. From his arrival in town when he discovered he wasn't the only one who'd responded to Edwina's ad, to his decision to keep his identity to himself when he met her, to witnessing her date last night and his decision today to just go home and never let Edwina know he'd been here.

"My," Julie said when he was done. "What an interesting situation."

To put it mildly.

"And what a complete load of bull," she said.

What?

"What do you mean by that?" he asked

"It's just that I've never known you to give up quite so easily," she said. "Oh, you've managed to talk yourself into the idea that you're leaving because it's the best thing for her, but the real reason you're leaving is because you think it's the best thing for you."

It certainly wasn't the best thing. The best thing would be holding Edwina in his arms and at long last kissing her, and discovering that the kiss he'd been imagining didn't hold a candle to the real thing.

"You're afraid she'll be angry with you, or that she might not return your feelings," Julie said. "That's why you hid your identity from her in the first place."

That wasn't why. "I didn't want to make her think I was trading on our friendship to get a leg up on everyone else," he said, more than just a little annoyed. "I didn't want to—"

"To what? To let her make the decision for herself? To let her have all the information you do so that she can make an informed decision without you making it for her?"

Well, when she put it that way.

"Tell me, Thomas," Julie said. "When a couple comes into your chapel, do you decide what they should or should not say at their wedding? Do you tell them you offer only a short ceremony or a more traditional ceremony? Do you let them decide what room they'd like to get married in, or do you not even offer them a choice at all but pick one for them depending on how you feel at the time?"

She didn't wait for him to respond.

"Of course, you don't," she said.

He didn't have to be hit over the head. He understood the analogy. "I screwed up, didn't I?"

"You screwed up, but you're not alone. In matters of the heart, most of us screw up at one time or another. We all guard our hearts so carefully, it's not surprising that we err on the side we think guarantees we suffer the least amount of pain. It rarely works out that way."

She would know. Thomas specialized in weddings. Julie dealt with people getting divorced.

"Tell me," she said, "would you rather know, one way or the other, or spend your life wondering if you walked away from the chance to be with the one person in the world you were meant to be with?"

Julie was good, and she was right. If he went home now without coming clean to Edwina, he'd always wonder what might have happened if he'd only told her when they first met who he really was.

"I've always hated that movie," he said. He knew Julie would know which one he meant. He'd complained long and loud to her about what a ridiculous plot *You've Got Mail* had for a romantic comedy.

"A Meg Ryan fixation can only take you so far," Julie said.

And now he was living that movie.

What was worse, it was all his own fault.

Well, enough of that. The next time he saw Edwina, he'd tell her who he really was and why he'd come to Liberty Springs. If she never wanted to see or talk to him again, he'd take his broken heart and go home, but at least he would know he'd given himself —and Edwina—an honest chance at being more than online friends.

And who knew, maybe things would turn out all right at the end. He still thought of himself as a romantic at heart, and all romances ended with a happily ever after. After all, if he didn't believe that the kind of love that happened in the movies was inspired by real life, he never would have come to Liberty Springs in the first place.

He just had to give himself—and Edwina—a chance.

$\mathcal{E}$dwina lost sight of Rufus in the rush of getting the marriage certificate signed and in the hands of the bride and groom. Most of the wedding guests had headed back to the tour bus. The driver was no doubt obsessively checking his watch and worrying about his blown schedule. With all the bowling balls that were no doubt crowding the luggage compartment, Edwina doubted he'd be able to pick up much speed on the highway.

"We've got to get going," Jean said, echoing Edwina's thoughts. "You've been a real good sport about the whole speed wedding thing."

Edwina smiled and held out her hand, but Jean surprised her by giving her a hug instead. Then George hugged the both of them, and Edwina had to laugh.

"Okay, off with the two of you," she said. "Be happy together."

"You, too," Jean said, giving Edwina a knowing grin. "I don't know how you snagged him, but for a guy like that, I'd have to think twice about not kicking George here out of bed."

"What?" George blinked at his new bride. He clearly hadn't been following the conversation.

"Don't worry, sweetheart. He'd not on the market anymore."

And with that, Jean hustled her husband down the aisle and out the chapel doors.

The assumptions people made! Edwina had managed to tamp down the embarrassment she'd felt about being asked when she and Rufus were getting married, but still...

Of course, Jean's first sight of Edwina and Rufus had been the two of them kissing. And not just any normal kiss, but a sweet, heartfelt, romantic kiss. A gaze-into-each-other's-eyes-afterwards kiss.

Was it any wonder Jean thought the two of them were an item?

Edwina followed Jean and George out the front of the chapel. She always liked to see the happy couple off when they left Bluebelles. Just because this couple was leaving on a tour bus didn't make any difference.

Except maybe it did.

When Edwina got to the front steps of the chapel, she saw Rufus in the parking lot talking to two women who'd apparently stayed on the bus during the wedding because she didn't remember seeing them inside the chapel.

These two weren't quite as old as the rest of the bowlers she'd seen from the bus tour. They looked like they were in their late teens or early twenties. On them, the sundress and sandals combination looked way more appealing that it had on most of the wedding guests.

Edwina stood on the steps and watched them talking. Rufus had a smile on his face—the same open, friendly smile Edwina had seen often ever since she'd met him—and he was leaning against the bus so casually, it looked like he might have done the same thing every day of his life.

The women (girls, really) were clearly infatuated with him. One was playing with the ends of her long, blonde hair while the other girl was talking to him, her hands gesturing wildly as she told him something that must have been funny. Rufus laughed, and the two girls laughed with him after they exchanged happy glances.

Edwina told herself it didn't mean anything. He was used to being friendly with strangers. He had to do that all the time when he was at work in Las Vegas, and when he was at work, he'd done it wearing much less than the jeans and fairly tight T-shirt he was wearing today.

Why hadn't she noticed before how well that T-shirt fit his body? The girls certainly looked like they'd noticed.

As soon as Jean and George made it back to the bus, a man in an official-looking uniform followed them inside and honked the horn. The girls gave Rufus mock sad-faced looks, and the one who'd been gesturing with her hands touched his arm briefly before they both stepped onto the bus. Rufus gave them a little wave, and then turned back toward the chapel.

When he saw Edwina, his face lit up. "There you are!" he said. He jogged the few yards from where the bus was now pulling out of the parking lot to where Edwina stood. "You were magnificent. Is that how all your weddings go?"

Edwina blinked. He'd gone from flirting with the girls—because yes, it was flirting, at least as far as the girls had been concerned—to being her suitor in the blink of an eye. Which one was the real Rufus? Or were both of them real?

She made herself smile. "I don't normally speed wed anyone," she said. "It's nice to know I can set a land speed record when I need to."

He reached out and took her hand. "So are we done in the store, or do we need to shelve more stock before our picnic lunch?"

Her stomach picked that moment to rumble loudly. Why did her entire body seem to go haywire around him? She was pretty sure her palms were sweating profusely, which was never a good thing on a woman who was holding hands with her date.

"I think that just answered the question," she said, smiling ruefully. "We just need to stop by the diner to pick up the food."

Before she locked up the dry goods store for lunch, Edwina retrieved the picnic basket she'd taken off the shelves that morning and stashed behind the checkout counter. It was one of her favorite items in the store, a sturdy wicker basket with a red-and-white checked lining, and just big enough to hold lunch for two.

She'd never had a reason to use it before today, and now that she did, she felt a little sad about it. It was silly really, but the longer that picnic basket remained on the shelves unsold, it had come to represent her fantasies about how her life with the perfect man would be, full of peaceful noontime picnics beside the lake talking about everything and nothing in particular.

None of her fantasies had included her perfect man flirting with women who were less than half her age.

Rufus carried the basket in one hand on the short walk to the Lickety-Split and held Edwina's hand with the other. His hand still felt warm and strong in hers, but it didn't feel quite as right as it had the night before when they walked to the rec center for the movie.

She wished she could quit thinking about him with the two girls by the bus. Edwina had never considered herself the jealous sort. As far as she was concerned, jealousy was nothing but overblown mistrust.

She didn't know Rufus well enough yet to know whether he was trustworthy, which was part of the problem. He certainly treated her well, and he had flat out told her he was tired of dating women who were only attracted to him for his looks.

Only...

She'd been attracted to him at first because of his looks, too. Yes, she'd told herself they had a deeper connection, but whenever they were together, it was her hormones that were doing the talking, not her heart and certainly not her head. One of the reasons she'd decided to spend more time with him was her hope that the more she got to know him and the more he got to know her, they'd discover more things they liked about each other, and then they both could figure out if they were truly right for each other, age difference or not.

But what if that wasn't going to happen? She was getting to know Rufus just like she wanted to, but her heart still wasn't convinced he was the right man for her. If he was, shouldn't she know it by now? Besides, if she really cared about Rufus all that much, she wouldn't still be so intrigued by the shy man who'd been to the wedding but who'd disappeared before anyone else left.

She shouldn't be giving the shy man another thought, but she'd felt her heart skip a beat (in a good way) when she'd seen him so unexpectedly in her chapel. And then when their gazes locked...

It wasn't anything like lust or love at first sight. It was something deeper. Even though she'd only felt it for a second (and hadn't admitted it to herself at the time), she felt like she *knew* him and he knew her—the real her—and definitely not in a creepy, stalker kind of way.

But he'd left before she could even talk to him.

And she was on a second date with Rufus. What was wrong with this picture?

What was wrong with her?

Rufus was clearly everyone's idea of a dream date, and here she was, obsessing over a guy she'd only talked to once. Rufus might not be perfect, but if she waited for the perfect man to come along, she might as well resign herself to growing old alone.

The Lickety-Split was busier than usual, considering Nellie's usual noontime crowd consisted of maybe a couple of customers who took up one of the tables. Today it was standing room only inside the diner. All the customers were men—older men. Her suitors, in other words.

Lovely. She hadn't thought of that when she'd suggested getting a picnic lunch. In fact, she'd suggested that specifically so that she and Rufus could have some alone time without being the center of attention.

Gus was out waiting tables. Edwina could just see the top of Nellie's blonde head in the kitchen.

"What's she doing back there?" Edwina asked Gus.

"Putting the finishing touches on your lunch." Gus grinned at Rufus. "So is this the lucky guy?"

Rufus held out his hand and introduced himself. "I think I'm still on probation," he said.

"Call backs," Edwina said, sticking to her audition analogy.

"But it's looking good, right?" Rufus said to her.

Edwina lifted an eyebrow, trying for a teasing look. "I still have to meet with the money men," she said. "You know how these decisions go."

From the way Rufus's expression dimmed, she could tell she hadn't been entirely successful with her attempt at humor. Not only that, she had inadvertently attracted the attention of every single man in the diner.

"Hear that fellas?" shouted someone from the end of the counter. "We still got a shot!"

Now that was met with hearty laughter all around.

Once again, she felt like crawling into a hole and disappearing until everything went back to normal.

"Hey!" shouted Nellie from the kitchen. "Settle down out there, or no desert for you."

Nellie's deserts were almost as famous as her waffles. Apparently everyone in the diner had figured that out, because the noise level dropped back down to nearly nothing.

"That's better," Nellie said. She came out from the kitchen carrying two Tupperware containers. She must have a nearly endless supply. "Here," she said to Edwina. "A new daily special, just for you. No peeking until you get where you're going."

Rufus smiled at Nellie as she put the containers in the basket. Gus added a bottle of wine and two plastic cups.

"Wine?" Edwina asked. "That wasn't part—"

"Oh, hush." Nellie gave Edwina a hug. "You need to live a little," she whispered in Edwina's ear. "If it takes a bottle of wine to get you to realize that, well…I have no problem helping things along.”

Heat started building up in Edwina's cheeks again. Why in the world had she ever told Nellie about wanting some nooky before she died?

“Conspiring against me?” Rufus asked when Nellie let go of Edwina. “I have fairly good hearing, you know.”

Nellie swatted him on the arm. “Trust me, if you heard what I told her, you'd be blushing, too.”

Which Rufus promptly did.

On him, it looked adorable.

Gus cleared his throat. Edwina looked around the diner and realized they were still the center of attention.

This was getting ridiculous.

“Three o'clock,” she said to the men in the diner. “Auditions resume at three. Until then, I'd like a little privacy. Is that too much to ask?”

The men all promptly turned back to their meals.

“She's tough,” Rufus said to Gus, like they'd been best buds for years.

Maybe that was just Rufus's superpower—the ability to achieve instant friendship with anyone—and that's all it had been with the girls next to the bus.

Except the girls hadn't been flirting with a new friend.

Edwina told the annoying voice of doubt inside her head to shut up and let her live a little. Like Nellie said.

“She's good,” Gus said, giving Edwina a wink.

Nellie rolled her eyes. “You both have it wrong.” She smiled at Edwina. “She's the best.”

“Oh, brother,” Edwina muttered, then she turned her attention to Rufus. “Are you hungry, because I'm starving.”

Rufus shut the lid on picnic basket and grinned at her. “Lead the way.”

BACK IN THE days when Liberty Springs still had a lot in the way spare funds in its budget to spruce up the town, thanks to the first year of the sailboat races, the same city council who'd come up with that idea had realized that in order to keep attracting tourists, the town had to turn itself into more than a simple blip in the great Nevada desert.

The council had decided to use some of the revenue from that first race to build not only the lakeside walking trail, but install what passed as a lakeside park, only with desert landscaping. The town had installed benches complete with shade covers and low-maintenance bushes that blended in with the rather sparse vegetation that surrounded the lake. Here and there wrought-iron tables and benches covered by corrugated metal umbrellas dotted the walking trail, and a small cluster of the tables and umbrellas huddled near the lake about a quarter mile from the entrance— the city's idea of a park.

All the wrought iron had been painted white to reflect the heat of the summer sun, and the umbrellas were big enough to keep anyone sitting on the benches from getting a serious sunburn. The park had no grass—the desert would have killed it anyway—and thankfully none of the odd decorations that dotted the landscape around Hawthorne thanks to the weapons storage facility out in the desert near the town. Edwina had always thought decorating the landscape with old bomb casings was kind of creepy.

She had a favorite table close to the water, and that's where she took Rufus for their picnic. She liked to sit at that particular table and read, or just generally watch the wildlife that populated the lake. In addition to the gulls that seemed to flock near the campgrounds, the lake had a large population of snowy white pelicans.

Why in the world these particular pelicans had decided to make a desert lake their home was beyond her. Maybe they were as tired of life on the coast as she had been of city life. Whatever the reason, the large white birds were some of the silliest things she'd ever seen. They were clumsy and graceless on shore, but oddly elegant when they flew low over the water on the hunt for their next meal. She loved to watch them skim the surface of the lake, taking advantage of wind currents to glide seemingly unfettered by gravity. Neat trick. Sometimes she wished she could shed gravity and fly over the lake just for the sheer fun of it.

Over the years, she'd come to see herself as something like the pelicans—clumsy and awkward in situations she wasn't suited to, but graceful and competent when she was in her element, standing at the front of her chapel, marrying two people who were in love.

All these men coming to town just for her had put Edwina in a situation she wasn't suited for, and she'd handled the whole thing horribly.

The first time she'd felt at all like herself since all her suitors had shown up in town was when she'd lost her patience at the diner. Until then, she'd been as clumsy as a pelican on dry land, bumbling around trying to please everyone but herself.

The men made her feel so uncomfortable. She hated being the center of attention. She felt like she couldn't go anywhere without their eyes on her. Just walking to the lake with Rufus, they'd run across more of her suitors hanging out in groups of two or three on benches near the lake, and they'd all stopped whatever they were doing to stare at her as she walked with Rufus to the park.

Rufus hadn't seemed to mind, but she knew herself well enough to realize she was just about at the end of her rope. The idea of conducting more interviews this afternoon made her want to crawl into a hole. She couldn't face more elderly men whose smiles looked like corpses with their lips drawn back and away from their teeth. They were sweet—most of them, anyway—and while she didn't want to disappoint them, she couldn't keep doing what she'd been doing, not if she wanted to maintain her own sanity.

"You look like you're a million miles away," Rufus said, interrupting her thoughts.

She realized with a start that she hadn't even been paying attention to him, and apparently not for quite some time. He'd spread the little red-and-white checkered cloth that came with the picnic basket across the wrought-iron table and put Nellie's two Tupperware containers on top of the cloth. He'd been in the process of opening the bottle of wine, but he'd stopped before he actually got the cork out of the bottle.

No, she wasn't a million miles away. She'd been right there, right where she belonged, rediscovering herself.

Finally.

She gave him a long look. Yes, he was definitely the most gorgeous and attentive man she'd ever known, and he'd been so nice to her, but she hadn't really been herself with him. She'd been so blown over simply with the fact that he was paying attention to *her*, out of all the women in the world he could have spent time with, that she hadn't realized she'd been trying to mold herself into the type of woman she thought he might like.

She'd even spent more time on her hair and makeup getting ready for their date last night than she'd ever done in her life!

Did she want to spend the rest of her life doing that? Trying to be someone she wasn't?

No, she didn't.

When she really thought about it, she realized that deep down she must have known all along that Rufus just wasn't the man she was looking for.

She put a hand on his wrist to keep him from uncorking the wine.

"We need to talk," she said.

# CHAPTER 23

Telling himself—even telling Julie—that he would come clean to Edwina the next time he saw her was one thing. Thomas was discovering that finding Edwina in order to have that conversation was turning out to be another whole thing entirely, even in a town as small as Liberty Springs.

First he went to her dry goods store, but the door was locked and there was a *Be Back Later* sign in the window. The sign was one of those old-fashioned things with a clock-face and movable hands for the minute and hour. The hands had been arranged to point at three o'clock, which was the same time as the hand-printed sign Edwina had put in the window telling her potential suitors to come back at three.

Four other men had apparently decided to stake out the dry goods store. All of them stood next to the locked door, glaring at Thomas. He didn't bother to glare back. He already knew that Edwina had made her choice, and it wasn't him—or any of them, either.

He went from the store to the chapel, thinking that she might have retreated to her office after the wedding, but the chapel doors were locked as well and the parking lot was empty. Thomas couldn't tell if anyone was inside.

Where else would she go? The wedding had ended about twelve-thirty—Thomas knew that because that was when Julie had called—which meant that Edwina hadn't had lunch yet. Thomas walked over to the diner to see if she was there. Not that he'd interrupt her lunch. That would be rude.

The diner wasn't nearly as crowded as it had been the night before. The very pregnant brunette was nowhere to be seen. Instead, a paunchy middle-aged man with a once-white apron tied around his middle was busy serving food. The pretty young blonde, Nellie, was in the kitchen cooking. Apparently she had a much larger repertoire, if the food Thomas saw on nearby plates was any indication.

"Just take a seat anywhere you can find one," the man with the apron said. "I'll be with you in a minute."

Thomas didn't really want anything to eat—his stomach was too nervous for that—but he was thirsty. The free breakfast at the rec center had been a while ago. He could at least have a cup of coffee.

He sat down on an empty stool at the far end of the counter. He hadn't planned on staying, especially since Edwina was nowhere to be seen in the diner, but he'd run out of places to check. He had no clue where she lived, and he wasn't about to go door to door looking for her. That might sound romantic in the movies, but one thing he'd learned living in rural Nevada was that people you'd never think would own a gun might have a few tucked away for emergencies. It was better not to show up unannounced at a stranger's front door. So far all the residents of Liberty Springs he'd met had been exceptionally nice. That didn't mean everyone in Liberty Springs would be exceptionally nice to a stranger—especially one whose clothes weren't the freshest anymore.

At least he knew Edwina would be back at the dry goods store at three. He'd hoped to catch her before then, but if he couldn't, he'd take what he could get.

"Hey," called the blonde from the kitchen. "I remember you."

Thomas looked up to see Nellie craning her neck so she could look at him through the pass-through window where three steaming bowls of soup sat waiting for the guy in the white apron to pick up.

"What's your name?" she asked. "You never said when you came in last night."

"Thomas," he said, before he remembered that he'd given his name as Tom when he'd gone to see Edwina the day before.

Had it really just been the day before? So much had happened, it seemed like he'd been in Liberty Springs for a week at least.

Nellie grinned. "Hang on just a minute," she said, and her head disappeared from the window.

She came out from behind a swinging door that reminded Thomas of the kitchen door at the rec center. The diner looked like it had been constructed about the same time as the rec center. Whoever had built these things seemed to have a fascination with swinging doors.

"What can I get you?" she asked him.

Thomas slid the coffee cup and saucer at his place setting in front of himself and turned the cup right side up. "Just a cup of coffee," he said.

Nellie took a pot of coffee off the warmer and filled his cup with practiced ease. "We have pretty good pie today," she said. "Made it myself. Peach or Dutch apple. I can heat you up a slice and top it off with vanilla ice cream."

That sounded marvelous. Thomas would have taken her up on it any day but today. "No, thanks," he said. "Just the coffee will be fine."

Nellie peered at him. Her gaze was so direct it made Thomas uncomfortable, so he concentrated on blowing on his coffee to cool it enough to drink without burning his mouth.

"I see why Edwina calls you the shy guy," Nellie said. "Though I don't think you're really all that shy. Except maybe around her."

Thomas had the cup halfway to his mouth when she said that. He was glad he hadn't actually been taking a drink, or he might have spluttered coffee out all over himself and the counter.

Edwina talked about him? She remembered him enough to talk about him?

"Uhm..." Thomas had no clue what to say. Maybe he should have ordered the pie. That way, if he'd had his mouth full, he would have had an excuse not to talk.

The guy with the white apron passed by Nellie on his way to pick up the three bowls of soup from the pass through. "Are you trying to give our customer here—"

"Thomas," Nellie said.

"—Thomas—a heart attack?"

Nellie gestured with her head toward the man. "My husband, Gus. Gus? Meet Edwina's shy guy, Thomas."

Gus's eyebrows climbed his forehead. "That's the guy? Didn't we see him in here last night?"

"But I didn't realize who he was last night."

"Honey, we were so busy last night, the president could have stopped by and you wouldn't have realized who he was."

Thomas put the coffee cup down. Did the whole town know that he was Edwina's "shy guy?" Had Father Mills known that this morning when he'd had such a compassionate conversation with him?

Thomas was tempted to jump in his car and leave town right then, but he'd promised himself—and more importantly, he'd promised Julie—that he wouldn't leave without coming clean to Edwina.

He needed to say something. Both Nellie and Gus were looking at him like they expected him to jump into the conversation, but he couldn't think of anything to say.

Good lord, maybe he *was* shy. Funny, but he'd never thought of himself that way. All those years conducting wedding ceremonies. Shy people didn't choose professions like that, did they?

Well, not unless they adopted a public persona. A persona like Reverend Thomas.

So what would Reverend Thomas say?

"Uhm..." Thomas started again.

Oh, this was ridiculous.

Nellie patted him on the arm. "It's okay. I shouldn't have startled you like that. If it helps, Edwina was pretty impressed with you."

"She was?" Not enough to go out with him, a petty part of him wanted to say. Then again, that wasn't really fair. Thomas couldn't compete with someone like the man he'd seen her with the night before and again today at the chapel.

"Well, she didn't come right out and say it," Nellie said, "but I've known Edwina for a long time, and the only time I've seen her with such a dreamy expression on her face is when she talks about some of the couples she marries."

Dreamy expression? When she talked about him?

That couldn't be right.

Maybe these two were just teasing him. He didn't know them well enough to tell.

"I've been..." He cleared his throat. "I've actually been trying to find her. I'd like to say goodbye before I leave. You don't happen to know where she is?"

Nellie frowned at him. "You're leaving? Why?"

He shrugged, then made a vague gesture at the diner, still mostly filled with Edwina's various suitors. "I didn't quite expect this when I came here." Which was true. "I didn't expect any of this."

Like dealing with the knowledge that Edwina had chosen someone else. Which was also true.

"Ah."

Nellie shared a look with Gus. Without a word, he went to deliver the bowls of soup while she poured a cup of coffee for herself and leaned on the counter in front of him.

"You have to understand something about Edwina," she said,

looking down at her coffee cup instead of at him. "She's a smart woman, but sometimes she can do the dumbest things. See, she cares more about making other people happy than making herself happy. That's why she's a wedding chapel minister, you know? She'd rather live out in the middle of nowhere, even if it means she'll never meet anyone she might like to spend her life with, so long as she can run that chapel the way she wants, and she can make people happy by doing the kind of ceremonies they want. You understand?"

"I watched her marry a couple today," Thomas said. "The ones who came in the tour bus. They wanted a quick wedding, and that's what she gave them. But she still made it special."

"Exactly." Nellie added a good-sized dollop of cream to her coffee and stirred it in. "See, she cares so much about making other people happy, I'm sure that's why she hasn't told half these guys to hit the road. They're totally unsuitable for her, which they'd realize if they only took half a minute to figure it out. But they're all acting like Edwina's the prize in some wedding lottery they want to win, so they just can't admit to themselves they're out of the running."

Out of the running, like Thomas was.

"That's why I'm leaving," he said. "I figured it out."

Nellie shook her head. "You're about as clueless as she is, I swear." She put her spoon down on the saucer. "She talked about you. You made an impression. Sure, I know she's been going out with that other guy, the one who looks like he stepped out of a superhero movie, but I think she's just flattered at the attention he's giving her. I know Edwina, and let me tell you, that kind of thing is going to wear real thin real fast. She hasn't talked about anyone else, just you. She won't even discuss Mr. Young and Handsome with me. I think she's actually kind of embarrassed by the whole thing."

Thomas thought about that. Was it just a matter of being flattered by the attention? He didn't think so, but then again, how would he have reacted if a beautiful woman a decade or so younger than he was paid the same kind of attention to him that this other guy was paying to Edwina? Thomas knew he'd be just as flattered. Everyone—even supposedly shy wedding chapel reverends—liked being liked by someone they thought was out of their league.

"Wear thin real fast, huh?" Thomas said. "Does this mean you think I should stay?"

"This means I think you should give her a chance to catch a clue, which, if I know Edwina, could be happening any minute. Now, if you'll excuse me, I'd better make book on all this extra business before Edwina gives all these guys the boot." She gave Thomas an appraising look, then bent over as close as she could get to his ear. "They went on a picnic lunch down by the lake. Edwina likes to spend time at the little park the city built over there. Benches, picnic tables, a nice walking trail. She likes the lake."

Thomas blinked at her. "You're ratting her out?"

Nellie grinned. "Nope. Not me. I'm not telling you what to do with that information." She paused for a moment, then added in an even softer whisper, "Don't you mention what I said to any of these guys, or she'll never have a moment's peace."

"Aren't you worried about me?"

"You? I figure you're an honorable guy, or you would have just bugged out without saying goodbye."

She stood up and clapped him on the shoulder like they were good buddies. Her eyes were twinkling with good humor.

"Thank you," Thomas said, standing up himself. He wasn't quite sure he wanted to go interrupt Edwina's picnic date, but at least now he knew the general direction of where she'd be.

He dug in his wallet and came up with a five dollar bill, which he put on the counter next to his coffee cup.

Nellie's eyebrows rose, and she grinned at him. "For that," she said, "you could have had pie ala mode." Her grin got bigger. "*Reverend* Thomas."

Thomas felt the blood drain from his face. "You know?" he managed to choke out.

"Guessed," she said. "But it wasn't difficult. You care way too much about her for someone who just met her yesterday, and the 'Thomas' thing gave it away. You really need a better secret identity."

He swallowed hard. "Does she know?"

Nellie chuckled. "I doubt it. Oh, she probably would have figured it out by now if she hadn't been so distracted by Mr. Young and Handsome and been under siege from all these geezers."

"Hey!" said an old man sitting at a table near the counter. "I heard that!"

Nellie shrugged. "There goes that tip."

"Think she'll be mad when she finds out?" Thomas asked.

She shrugged again, this time with her eyebrows. "Depends on what mood she's in when you tell her."

No kidding.

The only thing Thomas knew for sure was that he couldn't put it off any longer.

Coffee—and advice—downed and paid for, Thomas left the Lickety-Split and went in search of the one woman he was pretty sure he'd be in love with for the rest of his life.

Even if she kicked him out on his ear and told him, in no uncertain terms, she never wanted to see him again.

# CHAPTER 24

The picnic basket, complete with uneaten meals and unopened bottle of wine, looked pathetic sitting on the desk in Edwina's office. Especially when it occurred to her that just the afternoon before—right around this time, in fact—the man she'd been on that picnic lunch with had walked through the connecting door into this very office, and she'd thought he was the handsomest man she had ever met.

Of course, she'd also thought he was too good to be true. As it turned out, he was, but not because of anything he'd done. Not really.

No, he was too good to be true because she just couldn't see a happily ever after for the two of them no matter how hard she tried.

Telling Rufus that he wasn't the right man had been one of the hardest things Edwina had ever done in her life. She was sure of her decision—well, mostly anyway—but she had hated seeing the hurt-puppy expression in his gorgeous blue eyes and the way his muscular shoulders had slumped in defeat.

To give him credit, he hadn't tried to talk her out of her decision.

In fact, he honestly hadn't looked all that surprised, which made Edwina think he'd figured out before she did that she was going to call things off. He'd put the unopened bottle of wine back in the basket along with the two plastic cups and asked her if she wanted him to walk with her to wherever she wanted to go. When she told him no, she'd be fine, he'd got up from the picnic table, kissed her hand, and told her she was a fine woman.

He also told her that he'd be going back to his job in Las Vegas, and if she ever changed her mind, to let him know.

She was pretty sure they both knew she wouldn't.

He'd stuffed his hands in the pockets of his jeans and walked away from Edwina's favorite picnic table at Sutter Lake with his held his head high.

She'd had a tight little feeling in her chest watching him leave, but it wasn't enough to make her want to call him back even though he'd been her best shot for truly memorable nooky.

She hated hurting anyone's feelings. She wanted people to be happy. That's why she'd wanted to work in the marriage license bureau in Reno all those years ago instead of working in the clerk's office. She'd seen plenty of people come to the courthouse to get divorced. They always looked so unhappy. Even when she overheard them talk about what a great thing it was to finally be rid of that bastard of a husband or that bitch of a wife, they'd never seemed really happy. Not like the couples who came in to get their wedding licenses, many of whom were surrounded by family and friends while they stood in line waiting their turn. Some of the brides even wore their wedding gowns to the clerk's office, and their husbands-to-be wore tuxes.

That was also why when she'd had a chance to buy Bluebelles Wedding Chapel, she hadn't taken her usual amount of time to mull over the decision. She'd seen two paths in life spread out before her clear as day: one was a lifetime spent making other people happy, or the other was a lifetime spent filing papers for people who were suing each other. The decision of which path to take had been a no-brainer.

She'd learned an important lesson in the last day or two,

though, with all the men in town, and especially with what had happened with Rufus.

She had to stop focusing all her attention on making other people happy. She deserved to be happy, too, especially in the romance department. While she hadn't been miserable with Rufus, she hadn't been all that happy with him either.

She'd taken her time walking back to her store, lugging her full picnic basket, complete with the red-and-white checkered tablecloth that she'd folded up and placed on top of the food. While she walked, she mulled over her current situation.

The plain truth of the matter was she really wasn't happy with all these men hanging around town vying for the right to date her. This wasn't at all what she'd wanted, or what she'd hoped for when she put her little ad up on the chapel's website. Not that she'd given it much thought beforehand, but still...

She wasn't a prize in a lottery. She just wanted to meet some-one, not a whole slew of someones all at once. How could a person be happy with all this fuss going on? She was beginning to think that if she wanted to meet a man, one of the online dating services might actually be her best bet. One date at a time, not these cattle-call mass auditions. That was the way to go.

She really wished she could talk to Thomas about all this, but he hadn't called her back. She'd checked her cell phone on the way back to the chapel just in case, but she hadn't missed any calls. There had been no messages on the chapel's answering machine either.

She wasn't ready to kiss her friendship with Thomas goodbye, not without giving it her all.

She booted up the computer on her desk, the one she used strictly for chapel and dry goods store business. She never chatted from this computer, but it was nearly three o'clock in the after-noon. She had no doubt that another group of men were congre-gating around the front of her store, just waiting for her to unlock the door, and she didn't want to go out there. Not just yet.

After the computer finished its warm-up routine, she logged onto the chat site hoping that she'd catch Thomas online.

The tight feeling in her chest got a little tighter when the chat window on her computer screen displayed a sleepy-faced icon next to Thomas's ghosted-out screen name.

She'd missed him again, if he'd even been on.

She tried to tell herself that he was just out of town and hadn't checked his messages yet. She had no idea whether he was the kind of person who'd take a computer with him on vacation. For all she knew, a vacation for Thomas meant getting away from everything, computer and phone and especially an annoying online friend who wouldn't recognize good advice if it bit her in the behind.

She sighed. She'd have to handle this on her own, and the first thing she had to do was reclaim her own life. Hiding out in her office because she didn't want to face the men at the front door was not how Edwina Morrisey wanted to live her life. This all started because she'd posted that silly ad to the chapel's website. She didn't need Thomas to tell her she needed to take that ad down.

It took her all of five minutes to put the chapel's website back the way it had been—almost. After debating with herself—and looking at previews of the site with and without her picture—she decided to leave her picture there.

Thomas was right. She should have always had her picture on the site. It really should be a picture of her standing on the chapel's front steps. She'd have to see if Nellie or Gus would play photographer without trying to make her laugh. That competent, friendly, professional smile she had in the picture she'd taken with her laptop's camera would be hard enough to duplicate without the person behind the camera cracking jokes.

That done, Edwina glanced at the clock in the lower right-hand corner of the screen. Now it was ten after three. If she didn't go do something soon, the guys waiting in front of the dry goods store would probably break down the door.

She was tempted to post another sign calling the whole thing off and run back to her office so she could hide until everyone left town, but that would be the cowardly away out. She'd summoned up the courage to break up with Rufus in person. Whether she liked them or not, those men had driven all the way out to Liberty Springs just to meet her. Some of them were sleeping in tents or sleeping bags that they'd bought at her store. Others had spent the night on uncomfortable cots at the rec center. If she was going to call this whole thing off—which she realized was actually what she'd decided to do—they deserved hearing about her decision from her in person.

The crowd in front of the dry goods store wasn't as big as she'd feared it might be. Still, a good twenty or so men, all well past retirement age, stood on the front porch and in the parking lot waiting for her. Most of them—except the ones leaning on canes—stood up a little straighter when they caught sight of Edwina through the plate glass windows of the store.

She expected a rush when she unlocked the door, but the men surprised her by moving out of the way when she stepped out onto the front porch.

"First of all," she said, "I want to thank you all for coming."

"Eh? What did she say?"

The question came from the back of the group. Edwina couldn't tell who asked—the crowd was too big to let her see everyone—but the voice sounded wheezy and more than a little grumpy.

"I said, I want to thank you all for coming," she said, louder this time. "Can you hear me okay now?"

A round of affirmative murmurs came back at her, but the tone was subdued, like they all knew what was coming. Maybe they did.

"Good," she said. "You've all made me feel wonderful with the attention you've given me, and for those of you who've sent me flowers or candy, I want to let you know I really appreciate that. But I think it's made me realize that all this is a little too much for a woman my age who's spent a lot of years alone."

"Does this mean you're breaking up with us?" asked another man at the back.

"I'm pretty sure she is," said another man. "I seem to remember a conversation or two in my lifetime along these lines."

"What do you mean, only two?" said the guy next to him, and pretty much everyone in the group chuckled.

When they quieted down, Edwina said, "You're a great group of guys—all of you are, even the ones who aren't here."

"They're down by the lake fishing," one of them said. "They got a pool going on who catches the biggest trout."

Of course, they did. Edwina sighed, but it was a happier sigh this time. They'd all be fine. She was no longer the prize; now it was a fish. Somehow, that was fitting.

"I'm calling an end to the auditions," she said. "I took the ad down. I'll talk to Nellie over at the diner. As a way of thanking you all, if you'd like one last meal before you head out of town, your meal's on me."

They applauded.

Edwina felt herself blush. She didn't deserve their applause. A happy life? Her own life back? She deserved that, but she didn't deserve applause for disrupting their lives like this.

The men started to shuffle off the porch, and as they went, Edwina noticed that none of them walked away alone. They grouped together, sometimes just a couple of guys chatting with each other, sometimes in a small cluster.

Go figure. They'd made friends with each other.

When she thought about it, it made sense. They'd spent a lot of time in a town that didn't have a lot in the way of entertainment, so they'd done what men usually did—found someone to buddy up with. Maybe their trips to Liberty Springs hadn't been such a waste of time after all.

The last man to leave the porch was a spry-looking white haired man who walked with a cane. She was about to offer to help him down the couple of steps to the parking lot when he held up a liver-spotted hand to stop her.

"I'm fine, dear," he said. "Been getting around on my own for seventy-one years now, don't see a need to change. I would like it if you told me one thing, though."

Edwina smiled at him. Her smile felt lighter than it had in days. "What's that?"

He frowned a little. "Who won? You never did say."

She knew he meant who had she chosen. She was actually a little surprised that he was the only one who'd asked.

But instead of responding the way he no doubt expected, she took his question literally.

Who won?

"Me," she said, her smile a little wider.

She went back inside the dry goods store, and this time it felt good not to have to lock the door behind herself.

# CHAPTER 25

Thomas made it halfway to the lake when he saw the man Edwina had been with at the rec center walking back toward town.

Alone.

Edwina was nowhere in sight.

The sight made Thomas stop in his tracks. It was pretty clear from the droop in the man's shoulders and the resigned look in his face what had happened.

Edwina had told him no and sent him on his way.

But why? They'd looked so happy together last night. They'd even looked happy this morning at the chapel, and clearly the people in the wedding party had considered them a couple. That meant they must have done something to make everyone assume they were together.

So what had happened?

Had Edwina "come to her senses," as Nellie'd put it?

Thomas glanced toward the lake. Nellie had told him where to find Edwina, and he'd been headed down that way, but now he thought better about it.

If Edwina had just told someone goodbye, she probably wouldn't be in any mood to hear Thomas come clean about who he really was. Just because she'd talked to her friends about him—calling him the shy guy, like she couldn't remember his name—didn't mean she'd want to see him right after she broke up with a man who was twice as handsome and half as old as he was.

No, right now he needed to give her some space.

She'd be back at her dry goods store at three. He'd left his car in the parking lot. He could wait for her in his car, and after she got back at three, wait his turn along with the rest of the men who'd been congregating around.

Yes, that's what he'd do. He'd give her some space and some time to herself. He doubted she'd had any time to herself the last few days. He'd keep his promise to Julie, and keep his promise to himself, but it didn't need to be that minute.

He hadn't taken his morning run, what with helping Father Mills set up for the pancake breakfast at the rec center, then with the tear down. He hadn't even thought about going for a run before he took Joey up on the offer of a shower. While he didn't want to run now—not a good idea to work up that kind of sweat before he went to talk to Edwina—a good walk around part of the lake would stretch out his legs and give him something active to do before he went to talk to her.

He'd just make sure he walked in the opposite direction from the little park so he wouldn't risk running into her before he was ready.

~

THERE WAS A PRETTY healthy crowd around hanging around the front of the dry goods store by the time Thomas got back. He unlocked his car and almost immediately regretted his decision on where to wait.

The inside of his car was like an oven.

He'd been so distracted he'd forgotten what Nevada heat and sun did to the inside of locked cars. He rolled all the windows down and left the driver's side door open. There was a little breeze coming off the lake, but it wasn't nearly enough to cool off the inside of his car. Rather than start the car to turn the air conditioning on, he decided to stand outside until three, and then take a seat behind the wheel so Edwina wouldn't be able to see him when she unlocked the door.

Three o'clock came and went. His car cooled off enough for him to sit inside, but the door to the dry goods store stayed closed.

Had she come back from the lake?

From where he sat, he couldn't see the front of the wedding chapel. She could have gone in through the chapel side of the building. In fact, she probably had just to avoid the crowd by the dry goods store's front door. But if she was inside, why wasn't she opening the door?

The men started grumbling among themselves, but it was a good-natured grumble. The conversations that weren't about the way women never could get anywhere on time were centered more on fishing and baseball and the number of good-looking women in bikinis on water skis and jet skis out on the lake now that the recreational area had opened and Memorial Day weekend was getting in full swing, and whether any of those bikini-clad women would be interested in a date.

Given the average age of the men pondering that question, Thomas was pretty sure the answer would be no.

Shortly after three-fifteen, Edwina unlocked the front door to the dry goods store.

With the window down in the car, he heard her thank the men for coming. He couldn't see her well from where he was sitting—too many men were in the way—but she sounded happy. Happier, in fact, than she'd seemed since the first time he'd met her in person. Relieved, almost, which seemed odd. She'd looked so happy at the rec center the night before. Had she only been pretending to be happy?

Then she shocked him—along with a good portion of the men waiting for her—when she called an end to the auditions and told the men to go home—after a meal at the Lickety-Split, if they wanted one, and she'd pick up the tab.

But...she hadn't chosen the guy she'd been with last night. Thomas knew that for a fact. If she had, she wouldn't have sent that guy packing, and it was pretty obvious she'd done exactly that.

So what did it mean that she was sending everyone away?

Was she calling the whole thing off?

Thomas stayed in his car after Edwina went inside her store and the men started to leave. A few of them exchanged phone numbers, and others made plans to meet back here next year to go fishing at the lake and see whether Edwina had changed her mind. Some headed down to the tents by the lake, others toward the rec center. A few, like Thomas, had left their cars in the store's parking lot. Those men unlocked their cars, opened the doors to let the heat escape, and then got in and drove away. Only a couple of the men looked like they were heading back to the diner.

So what should he do now?

She'd just told everyone to beat it. In a very nice way, of course, because she was Edwina, and his friend Edwina Morrisey didn't have a cruel bone in her body. But it was clear she wanted everyone to go away and leave her alone. She might not welcome an intrusion from him because as far as she knew, he was just the shy guy. Just another one of her suitors, not her friend Reverend Thomas.

If he disappeared now, he'd always be the shy guy as far as she was concerned. He could go back home, and they'd go back to being online buddies who chatted and never met.

And they'd never be able to meet anytime in the future, either. Because when they did, she'd realize immediately how he'd deceived her.

If he drove away now, this was it. He'd never be able to see her again.

And he'd made himself a promise. He'd made Julie a promise.

Then there was the fact that Nellie knew who he really was.

Would she tell Edwina? They were good friends. If Julie was in Nellie's position, Thomas knew Julie wouldn't keep information like that to herself.

One way or the other, he had to come clean to Edwina. He didn't want her to think that he didn't have the guts to face her in person. If she got angry with him, it was his own fault. He should have learned his lesson from *You've Got Mail*. Never deceive the person you love.

Thomas got out of his car. He didn't bother rolling up the windows. He was pretty sure he'd be driving away soon anyway, and he'd rather not create another oven inside his car.

He'd talk to Edwina and make his confession, but first he wanted to see her chapel again. She'd been so at home there. Even with all the unexpected flowers all over the place, the chapel was where Edwina's heart really lived.

If he was truly saying goodbye to Liberty Springs, Thomas wanted to see the place one last time before he left.

# CHAPTER 26

 *E*dwina felt remarkably good having her dry goods store all to herself. No men leering at her through the windows, no old geezers trying to show her their teeth. The only customers she'd get now would be the campers and fishermen in town for Memorial Day weekend. After the last few days, a normal holiday weekend crowd would be a relief.

Chalk this one up to experience and move on.

At least no one seemed to be mad at her. True, she hadn't forced any of those men to drive all the way out to Liberty Springs, but she still felt like the worst kind of con artist. She'd had the best sales month ever at her dry goods store, and all the men had gotten out of the deal was sunburn, aching backs, and a return trip to wherever they called home.

Of course, they had made new friends. Men always did seem to make friends with other men no matter where they went.

She wouldn't have minded being friends with some of them. The shy guy, for example. They'd seemed to hit it off pretty well in the few minutes they'd talked to each other. If only she knew who he was and how to get in touch with him. She might be tempted to call him or chat with him online, like she did with Reverend Thomas.

Who still hadn't called her back.

Edwina sighed. She hoped she hadn't wrecked their friendship. She hoped he was just off on vacation somewhere, enjoying whatever he was doing, and he'd be back soon and things would go back to normal there, too. She hadn't realized how important he was in her life until he suddenly wasn't there anymore.

Her stomach took that moment to rumble loudly. She hadn't eaten her picnic lunch with Rufus, and she hadn't even thought about food when she got back from the lake. Now that she'd taken care of the men waiting out front, she realized she was actually hungry.

She went back to the little office that connected the dry goods store with the chapel. The picnic basket still looked forlorn sitting on the top of her desk. She hadn't found her Mr. Right, someone to share lunches with down by the lake, but maybe it just wasn't meant to be. Would it really be such a bad thing if she lived the rest of her life alone in this little town as long as she could keep making other couples happy by performing the type of wedding ceremonies they really wanted?

No, she decided. It would be a pretty good life. She had her friends, she had her store, and most of all, she had her chapel.

Which was currently stuffed to the gills with rapidly wilting flowers from her would-be suitors.

She'd noticed during the rush wedding for the couple from the tour bus that morning—had it really been just that morning? She'd been so busy (and so preoccupied) that it seemed almost like a lifetime ago—that almost all of the flower arrangements had started to look a little stale, but she hadn't had time to do anything about it. Jean and George hadn't seemed to notice, and neither had the wedding party. After the wedding, no one had stuck around long enough to pay attention to the flowers.

Well, unless the Memorial Day crowd at the lake included a couple who just couldn't wait to tie the knot, she doubted she'd be officiating at another wedding before the flowers totally wilted. Better to get rid of them now.

She opened one of the Tupperware containers in the basket. Nellie's famous BLT, complete with extra bacon, just the way Edwina liked it. If she sat down at her desk and attacked the sandwich, she might not have the ambition—or the heart—to do anything about the flowers later.

That didn't mean she couldn't have a few bites now to appease her growling stomach.

A few bites turned into half the sandwich (Nellie's sandwiches were to die for, but with how swamped the diner had been the last few days, where in the world had she gotten all the bacon?), but Edwina made herself stop before she ate the rest. Instead, she put the Tupperware containers in the cold case in her store where she kept a small selection of sodas and a larger supply of bottled water for the campers. Thanks to Nellie, she wouldn't have to make herself dinner tonight or lunch tomorrow.

On her way back to the chapel she grabbed a couple of large trash bags from the closet where the Elvis costume hung. Then she thought about the sheer volume of flowers in the chapel, and grabbed two more bags just to be on the safe side and the plastic watering can she'd used to water the flowers.

She started with the arrangements surrounding the altar. The red roses were definitely drooping their heavy heads, and the frilly edges of the pink carnations were turning brown. Flowers never did seem to last long in the desert.

Just like the majority of the men who'd answered her ad. She knew most of them wouldn't have stuck around Liberty Springs, not for her. The brief auditions she'd conducted had convinced her of that. Rufus had said he would—well, he'd hinted at it, although he hadn't come right out and told her he'd stay in Liberty Springs with her—but the rest of them?

Most of the men she'd met with had talked about the lives they had back wherever they called home. Bowling leagues and poker nights with the boys for those young enough to still partake in those things. The older gentlemen, the ones who soaked their teeth in a dish at night, they talked about their buddies down at the Lodge or the neighbors they saw on their daily walks around the neighborhood where they'd lived for thirty years. One man had even waxed nearly poetic about how, armed with only an electric leaf blower, he did battle every morning with the leaves that had blown in his yard overnight.

The shy man had been different. She'd asked him a serious question—why so many men had driven all the way out to Liberty Springs just for a chance to date her—and he'd given her a serious, heartfelt answer. He'd talked about the possibility of finding that one true love that would make the rest of life worthwhile.

She'd been so enchanted with him that they'd never even gotten around to discussing where he came from or what his life was like back wherever he called home. She didn't even know if he'd ever been married.

She picked up the last bunch of red roses and held them for a moment before placing them in the trash bag. She'd been looking for the one true love of her life. Not necessarily to make the rest of her life worthwhile or even complete, but because she firmly believed that everyone deserved to find the love of their life.

Had she been aiming too high? By holding out for her one true love, had she overlooked someone who could be Mr. Right if she'd only given him half a chance?

Well, it was too late to find out now. She'd sent them all away. No doubt the shy man was on his way back to wherever he'd come from as well. He hadn't been in the crowd outside the door to her store, but he'd probably heard by now that she'd called the whole thing off. Gossip had a way of spreading in a small town faster than wildfire, which was too bad, because she wouldn't mind asking him that question and hearing his honest answer.

And she was pretty sure he would give her an honest answer.

"Quit being silly," she muttered to herself. "You've got a good life here, don't you forget that."

But where had the good feeling gone, the one she'd had after she'd made her decision to call this whole thing off? The one that had let her tell the old geezer that she was the one who'd won her contest?

Maybe she should have eaten all of her lunch before attacking all these wilted flowers after all. Indulging in a little self care might bring that good feeling back. If that meant eating all of her lunch, she should do that. She could also turn on some music that she enjoyed, and then tonight she could draw herself a nice hot bubble bath, light some candles, and pour herself a tall glass of iced tea before she let the water go to work on the sore muscles she'd have after dealing with all these wilted flowers.

She had just tied off the first very full trash bag when she heard the door to the chapel open behind her.

Of course.

One of the couples who'd come to the lake for Memorial Day must have decided to kick off the weekend by getting married. And right after she'd thrown out all the flowers on the altar, too. She just hoped the bride and groom-to-be wouldn't mind a naked altar, so to speak. At least she hadn't tossed the rest of the flowers.

She turned toward the door, a warm smile on her face, ready to meet the latest happy couple who wanted to exchange their vows at the Bluebelles Wedding Chapel.

Except the man standing inside the chapel wasn't a groom-to-be.

Standing there like a deer caught in the headlights was the last man Edwina expected to see again and the one man she'd been sorry she wouldn't get another chance to talk to.

The shy guy.

He'd come back.

And she couldn't believe how happy she was that he had.

# CHAPTER 27

Thomas hadn't expected to find Edwina in the chapel.

Yes, he wanted to talk to her. He *needed* to talk to her, to tell her who he really was, but first he just wanted to sit in her chapel and experience the place one last time before she told him to get out of her life forever.

He was pretty sure that would be the outcome of their talk. He'd deceived her, after all. Deliberately. He hadn't put "Thomas" on that first slip of paper, just "Tom T." Oh sure, he'd had his reasons at the time, but looking back now, he realized his friend Julie was right. They'd been bullshit reasons, and he deserved whatever he got. Because what friend did that to another friend, much less to a woman he was sure was the love of his life?

He hadn't given one thought to the possibility that he might find her in the chapel. Of course, the dry goods store opened into Edwina's office, which opened into the chapel. A smart man should have counted on the possibility, but he wouldn't be in this predicament if he was as smart as he thought he was.

He swallowed hard. He really should just get this over with and take whatever lumps came his way.

But then she smiled at him. *Really* smiled at him, like he was the one thing she'd been waiting for in the whole wide world, and all his resolve melted into a puddle of happy goo.

Thomas felt a silly grin stealing across his own face.

"You're still here," she said.

He swallowed again and hoped that his voice would work.

"Couldn't leave without seeing your chapel one last time." Amazingly enough, he managed to get the words out without a single squeak. "Although I think I'm interrupting your work."

She glanced at the big black garbage bag next at her feet. The very full big black garbage bag.

"It's a shame," she said, "but flowers just don't last long in this heat."

He had artificial arrangements in his own chapel to save the expense of replacing real flowers every couple of days. If a bride and groom wanted real flowers for their ceremony, Thomas called the local florist and had them deliver an arrangement.

Extra trash bags lay next to the full one. A lot of half-wilted flowers still lined the outer walls of the chapel and the entrance.

"How about if I give you hand?" he asked.

If he kept himself busy, it might be easier to tell her what he needed to tell her. Especially if he didn't have to look at her while he came clean, didn't have to see that wonderful smile leave her face.

"I can't ask you to do that." Her smile turned a little on the bashful side. "Especially not after I just called this whole silly thing off."

Silly thing? Is that what she thought? She'd seemed so adamant about placing her ad the last time they'd chatted online. Of course, that had been days ago and before a ridiculous number of suitors had answered her ad. They hadn't really had a chance to talk much since then, just that one brief meeting (audition) in her office.

*You have an opportunity now,* he could practically hear Julia say.

Okay, fine.

"You didn't ask," he said. "I offered."

"Then I accept."

She handed him one of the empty garbage bags and nodded toward the flower arrangements lined up against one wall of the chapel. "Let's start with this side."

Thomas held one of the bags while Edwina dismantled the colorful arrangements that were definitely showing their age. She carted along a plastic watering can for any leftover water.

"For the plants outside," she said. "No water gets wasted in the desert."

He understood that well enough. Keeping growing things alive in the desert was no small feat. The plants on the sides of the chapel's front doors looked well cared for, just like the rest of Bluebelles.

She put all the glass vases carefully in one bag and tossed everything else into the garbage bag he held.

"You're not keeping anything as a memento?" he asked.

His mother used to keep a single flower from every arrangement his father had given her. She'd pressed them in what she called the world's largest dictionary, a huge book that had to weigh at least five pounds. Then again, his mother had never been inundated with this many flowers at once.

"Good lord, no. I only keep mementos when I know there's genuine emotion behind the gift," she said. "These were just to make a favorable impression."

"Oh, good," he said. "Now I don't feel so bad about not giving you anything."

He'd thought briefly about buying something for her when he'd driven down to Hawthorne the day before while he'd been killing time waiting for his audition—had that only been yesterday morning? It seemed like a lifetime ago—but when he'd stopped by the only florist shop he'd found, a little place connected to a nursery that seemed to carry more yard decorations than plants, he'd seen a group of elderly men already in line waiting to buy flowers. He'd decided against flowers, and he'd never been a big fan of candy himself, so he never even thought about buying her a box of chocolates. As his audition time had grown closer and he'd been standing in her store waiting his turn with men older than he was who had flowers or boxes of candy in their arms, he'd felt like he was blowing first-date etiquette.

"You gave me something better," she said as she separated another flower arrangement from its glass vase.

He blinked at her. "I did?"

"Honesty," she said, looking at him full in the face. "I asked you a serious question, and you didn't give me a glib, pat answer. After the day I'd had, I couldn't have asked for a better gift."

He couldn't hold her gaze.

Right. He'd given her honesty by giving her question the gravitas it deserved, but he'd lied to her about the most important thing of all.

He needed to come clean, but he couldn't think of a good way to do it. Why was this so hard?

Because he was going to break her heart, and that was the last thing he wanted.

She clearly had feelings for her "shy guy," or she wouldn't have been so happy to see him walk through her door. She wouldn't have accepted his invitation to help her with the flowers. She wouldn't be casually touching him now as they shuffled their garbage bags down the outside aisle of the chapel, disposing of the flowers and saving the water and the vases for recycling. Little touches on his arm to move him along. She might not even realize she was doing it, but to him, each touch felt like a caress and left little tingles behind once her fingers were gone.

So how was he going to spoil all of this by telling her who he was?

As it turned out, she gave him the perfect opportunity.

They'd reached the end of the aisle. They'd been talking about things in general—how the weather was really starting to heat up, her love of all things bacon (something he already knew about her since they'd talked about that online), and the silly pelicans who'd decided to make the lake their home. She had the last flower arrangement, the one closest to the chapel's front door, in her hands, when she glanced at him rather shyly.

"I hate to admit this," she said, "but I can't remember your name. Isn't that terrible of me?"

No, he didn't think that was terrible at all.

"I met so many people yesterday, and I didn't want to keep a list of names—I wanted to see if I remembered the person, not the name, and I didn't want to jot down notes during my meetings because that would just be too much like a job interview, which sounds lame now but made perfect sense to me yesterday."

A few things made a lot more sense to him, now, too. Including that new nickname.

"That's why you call me the 'shy guy,'" he said.

"What?" Color infused her cheeks, which only made him love her more. "How..."

"Nellie told me," he said, and then he took a deep breath. It was now or never. "After she guessed who I am."

A frown built between her brows as she looked at him. "So," she said, drawing the word out. "Who are you?"

He took another deep breath, then he put down his garbage bag and held out his hand.

"Thomas," he said. "Reverend Thomas Trask, and I can't tell you how happy I am to finally, officially, meet you in person."

The color fled from her face and the vase she was holding slipped from her fingers. If the floor of the chapel hadn't been carpeted, the glass would have shattered into a million pieces. As it was, the vase rolled to the nearest pew, spilling water along the way.

"Thomas," she breathed, stepping away from him. "Why didn't you... Good lord, I *called* you, and you were right..." She took another step back. "I thought I'd—"

The door of the chapel slammed open, interrupting her.

Nellie burst in through the open doors. "Don't you ever answer your phone?" she demanded, glaring at Edwina.

Edwina gave him a last unbelieving look then turned toward Nellie. "I guess I left it in the office."

"Great timing," Nellie said, which Thomas thought was the ultimate in irony, especially since it had to be obvious to Nellie that he and Edwina had been in the middle of something serious.

"What's wrong?" Edwina asked, because it was also fairly obvious by Nellie's disheveled appearance that something had gone seriously haywire. Thomas had seen Nellie handle standing room only crowds at the diner without breaking a sweat.

He let his outstretched hand drop. Whatever was going on, it was pretty clear his conversation with Edwina was over.

Nellie shoved her blonde hair away from her face. "Bessie's gone into labor," she said. "Gus is out on the lake, and we can't wait for an ambulance." She finally spared a look at Thomas, then turned her attention back to Edwina. "Girlfriend, I'm sorry, but I need your help."

# CHAPTER 28

At first Edwina thought Nellie needed help running the diner while she drove Bessie to the hospital in Hawthorne.

She'd given Thomas—*Thomas!* Her friend, Reverend Thomas, was the shy guy, and he'd never even given her a single *hint!*—one last, reproachful look, then she'd raced out of the chapel after Nellie, expecting to run back to the diner and handle what was left of the crowd until Gus got back from the lake.

Not that she had one idea of how to cook the things on the diner's menu. She did just fine cooking for herself, but cooking for Nellie's customers? She might burn down the place if she tried making anything on the flat top.

Instead Nellie headed toward the old Plymouth Gus had given her to celebrate their tenth anniversary. Nellie had fallen in love with old cars during a trip to Reno one summer for the city's classic car show-and-shine festival, and Gus had spent nearly as much time scouring online classic car websites as he did tying flies until he found the perfect—and affordable, he kept stressing—car for Nellie.

The Plymouth was parked in the lot outside the dry goods store, the motor running, with Bessie in the back seat.

"I can't drive," Nellie said. "I thought I could, but…"

She ran a hand through her messy hair, and for the first time, Edwina noticed that Nellie's hands were shaking.

Nellie never got flustered. Ever.

Except, apparently, when she was hit in the face with the reality of helping a friend deliver not one baby, but two.

"I'm a wreck," Nellie said. "I'd be a hazard on the road, so I really hope you can drive us to the hospital."

In Hawthorne.

Edwina had never driven Nellie's car before, but a car was a car, right? She got behind the wheel while Nellie got in the back seat next to Bessie.

"Sorry about this," Bessie said. "We tried calling for the ambulance, but they're stuck out at a wreck on 359."

She grimaced as another contraction must have hit her.

Hawthorne only had one ambulance. Highway 359 ran south of Hawthorne, which was in the opposite direction from Liberty Springs. From the look of Bessie's strained and sweaty face, she didn't have an hour or more to wait for the ambulance.

Thank goodness Nellie's car was an automatic. Edwina snapped on her seatbelt and pulled out of the chapel's parking lot onto the main road. She'd driven past the tent city her suitors had put up—at least half the tents were dismantled now—when she remembered that she hadn't grabbed her cell phone or her purse or her keys, much less her wallet with her driver's license.

"I don't have my license," she said. "I need to go back—"

Bessie chose that moment to let out a loud groan.

Nellie gave Edwina a stricken look. "These babies are coming fast," Nellie said. "I'm really not ready for them to come into the world in the back seat of my car."

Okay, then. No wallet. No driver's license.

No speeding.

Edwina pasted a determined smile on her face. "I'll get you there," she said. "Don't you worry."

She spent the entire twenty-five mile drive—twenty-two to get from Liberty Springs to Hawthorne and three to get to the hospital once she hit town—concentrating on nothing but driving according to every law on the books. Luckily they didn't pass a single highway patrol car on the way.

By the time they reached the hospital, Bessie was telling Nellie that she felt an overwhelming need to push.

Edwina put the car in park by the emergency entrance and ran into the hospital. She corralled the first orderly she saw, and they both raced back to the car, the orderly pushing a wheelchair like he was headed for the finish line in the Olympics. The orderly took one look at Bessie, hustled her into the chair, and wheeled her into the hospital nearly as fast as he'd run out to the car, Nellie hurrying after them.

After they were gone, the steam seemed to run out of Edwina all at once. She leaned against the car, her knees threatening to collapse. The car's motor was still running, and she really needed to go find a parking place, then find the nearest restroom to wash the sweat off her face, but all she could think about was Thomas.

She'd managed *not* to think about him on the drive to Hawthorne, but now that the immediate emergency was over, her mind wouldn't let her think about anything else.

He'd deceived her, pure and simple.

And more than that, he'd deceived her *deliberately.*

He hadn't told her who he was when he walked through her office door for his audition. She remembered now—he'd called himself "Tom," not "Thomas"—and even though they'd talked for the entire ten minutes (no uncomfortable silences, unlike some of the men who'd come to see her and simply sat there staring at her, like they were sizing her up for something she probably didn't want to think about), he hadn't said a thing about himself that would have given her *one single clue* that he was her online friend, Reverend Thomas.

She'd been shocked when he told her who he was, but now that the shock had worn off, she was just plain angry.

How could he?

He'd treated her exactly like Tom Hanks' character had treated poor Meg Ryan's character in a movie *Reverend* Thomas professed to hate—*You've Got Mail.*

He'd manipulated her. He'd lied to her. The only thing he hadn't done was put her out of business.

Unless he'd come to Liberty Springs expecting her to pack up shop and move with him to Lovelock, and that would have effectively been the same thing.

Well, forget that, mister.

She wasn't about to fall into his arms with a simple "I knew it was you all along," or some such nonsense.

No matter how much she'd felt herself falling for the "shy guy" more and more while they worked together in her chapel, cleaning up all those flowers.

She took a deep breath. Her knees felt strong enough now to hold her up without leaning on the car to keep herself upright. She could probably navigate Nellie's boat of a car into an open parking space without doing the car—or anything else—any harm. Provided the empty space didn't have a car or pickup truck on either side.

She'd worked up a sweat standing out in the hot afternoon sun while she had her own little freak out, and she had to push hair away from her face as she got behind the wheel. Now that she had a chance to look around instead of zoning in only on the emergency entrance, she realized the hospital must be having a slow day. The few "Physician Only" parking spaces were full, but the rest of the lot had more empty spaces than cars or trucks.

She pulled the car into a spot that was partially in the shade of the hospital building. She didn't know how long she'd be here. Car services and taxis were as rare out here in the desert as cowboys without pickup trucks, and who knew how long Nellie would need to be here helping Bessie deliver her babies. For now, at least, the driver's side of the car was in shade.

Edwina sat behind the wheel for a few minutes after she turned the motor off. She needed time to finish pulling herself together before she went back inside the hospital to begin the wait for Bessie's babies.

She wasn't a woman scorned, but she was a woman deceived. Friends didn't do that to friends.

Especially not a friend who knew all her insecurities. All of her thoughts and hopes about love and life and finding that one special person to spend the rest of your life with. About the joy she felt when she wed two people who stood in front of *their* friends and professed their love for each other, just like Jean and George had done that morning.

How could Thomas have done such a thing?

How could he have come to her chapel, of all places—the one place in the world where she felt the most at home—to tell her how he'd fooled her into thinking he was someone else?

Would she ever be able to stand at the altar in her chapel, stand before two people who loved each other and had chosen Bluebelles as the perfect place for their wedding, and *not* remember what Thomas had done to her?

Only if she finished this business with him.

She hated the term "closure," but that's what she needed. She hadn't had the opportunity to respond to him in any meaningful fashion. The few words she'd managed to blurt out before Nellie arrived didn't count. She wouldn't be able to get this out of her head—get him out of her head *and* her chapel—until she could give him a piece of her mind.

Which she planned to do as soon as she could get back to Liberty Springs. It's what Sigourney Weaver would do.

"You better watch out, Reverend Thomas," she muttered to herself as she crossed the parking lot toward the hospital to begin her baby watch vigil. "You think you know me because we've been 'friends' for so long, but you ain't seen nothing yet."

It never occurred to her that when she got back to Liberty Springs, he might not be there.

## CHAPTER 29

 ell, that had gone over like a lead balloon, as his mother used to say.

Thomas stood inside Edwina's chapel, garbage bag at his feet, not sure what to do.

She was gone.

Things between them had felt so good, so *right*, as they'd worked together to clean up the inside of the chapel. They'd chatted while they worked like the old friends they really were, but they were clearly more than old friends. The longer they worked together, the surer he was that he'd fallen deeply in love with her. And what's more—that she was falling in love with him.

Her face had a certain kind of softness, an inner glow that he'd seen on the faces of the brides who'd stood at his altar who were truly in love with their husbands-to-be. The utter happiness he'd seen in the expressions of wives who'd come to Lovelock to renew vows with their husbands of twenty or thirty or even forty years. She'd started touching him as they moved around the chapel, and her touches on his arm had been magic. He'd had to restrain himself from simply taking her in his arms and kissing her like he'd wanted to ever since he'd realized he had feelings far deeper than friendship for her.

But he couldn't kiss her, couldn't hold her, without telling her who he really was. That would have been unfair to her, and he'd already been more than unfair to her.

He'd known from the start who she was. He hadn't given her the same courtesy.

He bent over to pick up the glass vase she'd dropped when he'd introduced himself using his real name. The water that had spilled out of it on the carpet would dry just fine, thanks to the desert heat, but he didn't want to leave a mess for her to clean up when she got back.

Which might not be for some time.

He hadn't run after her, not exactly. But he had gone down the front steps of the chapel, intending to... what, offer his help? He wasn't quite sure, but he had seen Edwina get behind the wheel of an old Plymouth, the kind of car that was twice the size of Thomas's own fuel efficient model, and take off toward the highway. He hadn't gotten a clear look at the car, but he was pretty sure Bessie, the pregnant waitress, was in the back seat.

Liberty Springs didn't have a hospital of its own as far as he knew from his drive around town the day before. Hawthorne might have a hospital. That town was much bigger, at least compared to Liberty Springs, and just because he hadn't seen a hospital didn't mean there wasn't one.

If she was going to Hawthorne with a woman in labor in the back seat, and if she stayed until the pregnant waitress—Bessie— gave birth, she might be in Hawthorne for hours.

Would she be glad to see him when she got back?

No, she wouldn't.

She most definitely wouldn't.

He'd expected her shock. He'd even expected anger. What he hadn't expected was the way she'd backed away from him.

That simple move spoke volumes. Far more than the words she couldn't quite manage to get out.

She'd *backed away from him.* Twice. Like she couldn't stand being next to him, when only a few moments earlier she'd been touching him, brief little caresses that left him longing for more.

Thomas picked up the next vase full of half-wilted flowers. He dumped the water in the plastic watering can, dropped the flowers in the garbage bag, and carefully placed the vase—ceramic this time—into the recycle bag.

He didn't know what to do with himself. Should he stay here and keep working? Should he simply leave? Only no one was in the store and no one was in the chapel, and Edwina hadn't locked up. He didn't even know if she had her keys. Did she carry her keys with her all the time, or did she leave them in her desk in the office? He didn't want to go look. After what he'd already done to her, he didn't want to go poking through her things. That would have felt far too intrusive.

He could call her and ask her what she wanted him to do. He did have her number on his phone, in the voicemail she'd left last night.

Last night seemed like a lifetime ago.

Last night at least they'd still been friends. Now he wasn't sure if they could ever be friends again.

"You're being foolish," he could almost hear his good friend Julie say. "You gave the woman a shock. Give her a little time to get over it."

Time. He was more than willing to give Edwina that. He'd give her as much time as she needed.

Right now he had to give her at least a half hour for the drive to the hospital in Hawthorne, if that's where they were going. He didn't want to call her while she was still on the road.

In the meantime, he kept working on the flowers inside the chapel. He filled up the garbage and recycle bags and found more on the altar at the front of the chapel. When the plastic watering can got full, he took it out front and watered the plants near the chapel entrance, then went back inside to keep working. He glanced at his watch every few minutes, both willing the time to go by faster and dreading the call he would have to make to ask Edwina what she'd like him to do.

Most of all, he missed her company. Time had seemed to fly by as they worked together on the flowers, but now? The seconds were crawling by, and it seemed like he hadn't made a dent in the flowers lining the aisle on the other side of the chapel.

But he couldn't get out of his mind the way she'd looked at him when he'd told her his name, her face a mask of shock and betrayal.

And most of all, how she'd backed away from him.

Finally, when enough time had passed for him to make the call, he took his phone out and listened to her voicemail again, just to make sure he had her number right. He took a deep breath and swiped at the sweat on his forehead. The chapel was cool enough —Edwina kept her chapel air conditioned and the temperature pleasant for a nervous bride and groom—but the air conditioning wasn't enough to calm his nerves.

Would she even take his call?

Only one way to find out.

He punched in her number, listening to the ring.

A corresponding ring sounded from somewhere behind the altar.

Thomas hung up. The ringing stopped.

He called her again. The ringing, a pleasant tone that he didn't recognize, started up again.

She didn't have her phone with her.

Of course not. Unlike the younger women who came to his chapel to get married, Edwina wasn't attached at the hip to her phone. She didn't carry it everywhere, especially not when she was working in her chapel. She'd run out in such a rush with Nellie that she didn't think to grab her phone before she left.

Now he had no way to reach her.

Which, when he thought about it, seemed like the perfect metaphor for his whole trip to Liberty Springs.

He'd come here to meet Edwina, to connect with her in real

life, to tell her how he felt about her and hope that she felt enough affection (if not outright love) for him that she'd realize how perfect they were for each other. Instead he hadn't been able to talk to her because of the rush of men who'd come to town in response to her ad, and then when he finally did have the chance to talk to her, he'd been foolish enough that he hadn't introduced himself as who he really was. Yes, he'd done that for what he'd thought was a good reason, but had it really been all that good? Not in hindsight, but hindsight always had better vision than the present.

Now, even after all the other men were gone, he still couldn't seem to connect with her. He'd managed to properly introduce himself—finally—which had gone terribly, but he still couldn't simply sit down and attempt to explain himself.

He'd come to Liberty Springs with such hope in his heart, but the universe apparently had other plans.

Maybe he should take the clue-by-four (another one of his mother's sayings) the universe was trying to hit him with and just go home.

But he couldn't leave without locking up the place after himself. From what he'd seen, Edwina kept the chapel doors open while she was in the chapel or the store, but he was the only one here now and he didn't want to leave the place unattended.

As it turned out, the universe—this time in the form of Gus —solved the problem for him. Less than five minutes after his attempt to call Edwina, the chapel doors opened and Joey came in.

"Oh, hey," Joey said, clearly surprised to see Thomas. "Gus sent me over to lock up. He didn't think anyone would be here."

He held up a keyring with two keys on it.

"Gus and Nellie have spares in case of an emergency," Joey said to Thomas's unasked question. "He knew I was home, and he's stuck at the diner now. In his fishing gear. He finally got a few hours out on the lake now that all the old guys are going home, and..."

He trailed off, apparently realizing that Thomas was one of the "old guys" who should have been on his way out of town.

"And the imminent arrival of twins certainly constitutes an emergency," Thomas said, deciding to skirt the issue of why he hadn't left town yet with the rest of the old geezers.

Joey's face lit up. "Bessie's going to be so glad once they're finally here," he said. "She's had kind of a rough patch, being alone with babies on the way. I offered to help out when I'm in town, but she's real independent. My mom says that'll change once she brings those babies home. I can't wait to see 'em."

That wasn't something Thomas expected to hear a man Joey's age say, especially about a woman he wasn't involved with.

Or was he?

Or maybe she was a woman he hoped to be involved with someday.

Thomas silently wished him well.

Especially since he wouldn't be around to see how it all turned out.

# CHAPTER 30

Edwina unlocked the door and flipped on the "Open" sign for her dry goods store an hour earlier than normal on Memorial Day only to find Nellie standing on the front porch with a Tupperware container in her hands.

"What are you doing here?" Edwina asked as she held the door open for her friend.

"You know I detest sunrises, don't you?" Nellie said as she came inside.

Edwina took the Tupperware from her friend's hands. "If you detest sunrises, why do you own a restaurant that serves breakfast?"

"Because I own a restaurant next to a lake, and the damn fishermen think they need to be out on the water at the crack of dawn." She stifled a yawn. "Jacob and Jess kept me up until two last night."

Jacob and Jessica, two of the cutest little babies in the world. Aunt Nellie, as Bessie had started calling her, had volunteered to help Bessie out on her first night home from the hospital with her babies. Bessie had surprised everyone—Nellie included—by accepting the offer.

Edwina knew better than to offer her help. She'd been an only child, and she'd never even babysat when she'd been a kid. She had no idea how to care for babies, and she was a little too old to learn now. That didn't keep her from admitting the babies were cute, if a bit on the loud and fussy side.

"So what brings you to my door bearing gifts?" Edwina asked.

Instead of answering right away, Nellie went through the door at the back of the store that led into the office connecting Edwina's two businesses. A moment later she hauled out the metal folding chair from the office.

The same chair all of Edwina's suitors had sat in for their interview.

The same chair Thomas (the traitor) had sat in when he'd met with her.

Edwina clamped down on that train of thought. The day had dawned bright and beautiful, the sun casting a golden glow over the desert. Liberty Springs was full of sportsmen (and women) out for a long weekend on the lake. Her store was sure to be busy, and she might even have a wedding or two to perform, although Sundays during the Memorial Day three-day weekend holiday were traditionally the busiest day for her chapel. She wasn't about to ruin this glorious Monday morning by thinking about Thomas and how she hadn't been able to give him a piece of her mind because when she'd finally driven Nellie home from Hawthorne after Bessie had delivered her babies, the chapel had been locked up tight and Thomas was gone.

Nellie dragged the chair over to the end of the checkout counter and sat down with a sigh.

"Have I told you before how glad I am that Gus never wanted kids?" she asked. "I mean, I have nothing against kids in general—and Bessie's in particular—but at this moment in time, I'm really thankful I never had any of my own."

Edwina never had any thoughts about children one way or the other. Life just hadn't worked out that way for her.

Like it hadn't worked out for her to find the love of her life.

Although Thomas had come close. She'd definitely felt herself falling for the "shy guy" the way she'd always imagined finding her true love would feel like.

Right up until she found out what a louse he was under that fake "shy guy" persona.

Nellie closed her eyes, and for a moment Edwina thought her friend was going to fall asleep right there in that uncomfortable chair, until she cracked one eye open and asked, "So, you hear from Thomas yet?"

The question didn't exactly surprise Edwina. Nellie probably would have asked sooner if she hadn't been so busy with Bessie's twins.

"No," Edwina said, and the unexpected pang that came along with the answer did surprise her. Wasn't she still mad at him? Why in the world would she be upset that he hadn't called?

"You call him?" Nellie asked.

"No," Edwina admitted.

She wasn't about to take the first step. If he wanted to talk to her, he knew where she was. He could call her. She wasn't going to make it easy for him by calling him first. She'd already called him first—just a few days ago, in fact, when she'd really needed his advice, and she thought she'd blown their friendship.

She hadn't even visited the "Join Your Hands Together" forum or logged in to the chat program. She'd been too tired ever since the tense drive to Hawthorne with Bessie trying not to give birth to the twins in the back seat of Nellie's classic car. And she'd been too busy since then with the influx of the regular Memorial Day crowd.

Or at least that's what she'd told herself.

"You do realize, don't you," Nellie said, "that the two of you are acting like butt-hurt teenage girls."

Edwina felt her back stiffen. She was *not* a butt-hurt teenage girl. She was a woman who'd been deliberately—

"He lied to me," she said. "He didn't tell me who—"

"What was he supposed to do?" Nellie asked, opening both eyes. "Come in here that first day, introduce himself, and drop to one knee while he declared his love for you? Would you have taken him seriously?"

"Well, I—"

"Don't kid yourself, girlfriend," Nellie said. "You would have thought he was making fun of you. Didn't you tell me he thought your ad was a bad idea?"

Edwina didn't need to answer. She'd shared that little bit of information with Nellie even before the whole influx of wannabe suitors had arrived.

Nellie rubbed at her face with one hand. "Yes, he was an idiot for not telling you who he was sooner." She yawned so deeply that Edwina couldn't help yawning in return. "But as I recall," Nellie went on, "you were fairly busy with the Hemsworth lookalike at the time."

Edwina felt heat rise in her cheeks as she realized she hadn't thought about Rufus once in the last few days. She hoped he got home to Vegas all right.

"Look," Nellie said. "I'm tired and I'm cranky, and mostly what I'm tired of and cranky about at this moment is watching my best friend blow a shot at love and happiness. Yes, the whole situation the last few days—the last week—has been far from ideal. But who gets 'ideal' in life, anyway? You get what you get, and if you're truly lucky, you don't have to settle for making the best of a bad situation." She yawned again. "Right now your ego's the only thing standing in the way of something that's pretty damn close to ideal."

Ideal?

"He left me," Edwina said, surprised—and a little dismayed—to hear the tremble in her voice. "He didn't stay so we could work this out. He just left."

"So?" Nellie said. "You do know where he lives, or at least where he works. You want happiness?" She leaned forward in the chair, elbows on her knees. "Sometimes you have to work for it." She punctuated that with a groan as she got to her feet. "And with that, I need to get back to work."

Edwina got her second surprise of the morning when Nellie hugged her.

"You want that man," Nellie said. "I know you do, so go get him. I have a feeling about him, that he's one of the good guys. He just did a stupid thing." She shrugged. "What do you want, perfect? He's a guy. Guys do stupid things."

Did she want that man? She hadn't been able to stop thinking about him, no matter how hard she tried.

"I can't close up the store now," she said. "It's the start of the busy season."

"Gus'll get Joey to run the store," Nellie said. "Joey's just sitting on his butt playing video games for the next week or so while his truck's in the shop. Gus told me."

"Joey can't perform weddings," Edwina said.

"So if any people show up wanting to get married, Joey can call Father Mills to come over."

Could she really take time off? She hadn't taken time away from the chapel or the store in years, not more than a day or two to go to Reno, and then only during the off season.

"No matter how it turns out," Nellie said, "if you don't go now, you'll regret it. And trust me, Bessie has enough regrets for all of us, and she's only half your age."

Bessie had apparently told Nellie things during labor that she hadn't told anyone else in town. What, exactly, Edwina didn't know. All Nellie would say was that Bessie'd had a hard life before she'd moved to Liberty Springs last year. That had been right before she'd found out she was pregnant. Boy, the town gossips had had a field day with that—new young woman in town pregnant and the baby's (er, *babies'*) father nowhere in sight—but Edwina had always thought that was Bessie's business. Everyone had a past.

Could Edwina really leave the store—and her chapel—and go to Lovelock just to see Thomas? After what he'd done to her? That's not how *You've Got Mail* ended, but that movie had a stupid ending anyway. Sigourney Weaver wouldn't have just fallen into Tom Hanks' arms like that.

Then again, Sigourney Weaver wouldn't let anything stand in the way of getting something she really wanted.

And what Edwina wanted, no matter how it turned out, was to see Thomas again. Because Nellie was right. Edwina would always have regrets about Thomas if she didn't get to see him one last time.

Nellie patted Edwina on the back and then pulled away just far enough to look Edwina in the eye.

"So?" Nellie asked.

This time Edwina was the one who drew in a deep breath and let it out with a sigh. It didn't do much to settle her nerves, but this time they were nerves caused by anticipation.

She wouldn't leave the store today, not on the actual Memorial Day holiday. But later this week? After the folks who only had the long weekend off went home? After her restock order came in and she put all the goods out on her shelves? Yes, she could take a day off then for a quick trip to Lovelock and back.

Edwina gave her best friend a rueful smile. "Looks like I'm going to see Thomas one last time after all," she said.

# CHAPTER 31

Thomas put on his best professional smile for the couple standing at his altar.

They'd chosen the western-themed room for their wedding. The bride wore designer jeans, brand new from the crisp look of dark blue denim and the way the fabric hugged all her curves, a red-and-white checked shirt, and a huge silver belt buckle on a wide leather belt around her narrow waist. The groom, a good twenty years older than his bride, also wore dark blue jeans (although his jeans had a well-worn look), a blue-and-black plaid flannel shirt (open at the neck), and huge silver belt buckle on a narrow belt circling a not-so-narrow waist. The bride held a bouquet of white daisies, and the groom wore a white cowboy hat that looked like a custom job. All their friends in the audience were dressed in Hollywood's version of western-style clothes as well.

The matron of honor wore a bright yellow dress with a huge, floofy skirt that looked like it would be right at home in a square dance contest. The best man's snakeskin cowboy boots looked fresh out of the box.

This couple clearly had money. Their driver's licenses had southern California addresses, they'd arrived at the chapel in a newish black Porsche, and the engagement ring on her finger sported an impressively large diamond. Thomas had no idea why they'd chosen his chapel for their wedding, much less why they'd expected their friends and family to drive all the way to Lovelock for the ceremony. He knew for a fact that at least one of the wedding chapels in Reno had a western-themed room, and the room was probably in better shape than his.

Ever since he'd arrived home from his trip to Liberty Springs, his chapel had looked especially shoddy.

Of course, compared to Edwina's chapel, any other chapel would look shoddy.

He tried not to think about Edwina as he went through the ceremony. He'd already spent too much time thinking about a friendship that was clearly over. When he'd finally gotten up the nerve to log back into chat program on the "Join Your Hands Together" forum, LibertyBelle had been offline. As far as he could tell, she hadn't logged back in at all ever since she'd placed her online ad for a suitor.

That didn't stop him from looking for any missed calls or voicemails from her whenever he glanced at his phone.

Which was far too often.

But then again, whenever he'd thought about calling her instead, he always found something that needed doing around the chapel and his gift store. She clearly didn't want to talk to him, and he wasn't about to bother her by calling her.

So he'd washed all the seats—rough-hewn pews and wrought iron chairs alike—in both his chapel rooms.

Then he'd rearranged all the stock in his gift shop, and washed and polished all the shelves before he put the stock back in place.

He'd even ordered new wallpaper and silk flowers for the meadow-themed room.

Talk about avoidance behavior.

Judge Julie, who'd left town to travel to the next courthouse on her circuit, had read him the riot act on the phone the night before.

"You are a grown man, right?" she'd said.

The question seemed rhetorical, so he hadn't answered.

"Why are you acting like a spoiled child?" she said.

That question wasn't rhetorical.

"I haven't—" he began, but she cut him off.

"Do you know the number one reason people get divorced?" she said. "Failure to communicate. They stop talking to each other, and when people stop talking to each other, they stop understanding how the other person feels. And when they stop understanding each other, the relationship is doomed."

He refrained from pointing out that he and Edwina weren't married and therefore couldn't get divorced.

"Pick up the damn phone," Julie'd said. "Communicate before it's too late. You're not getting any younger. You did a stupid thing, but you had the best of intentions. In my courtroom we call that mitigating circumstances."

"So I should call her," he'd said. "Whether she's made it clear she never wants to see me again or not. I should call."

"Don't be an ass," she'd said and hung up the phone.

Someone in the chapel cleared their throat rather theatrically, and Thomas realized he'd paused in the middle of his standard wedding ceremony while he relived his conversation with Julie. The bride was looking at him with something like impatience in her expression, even though her eyes were still shiny with unshed tears, which made Thomas wonder how many acting classes she'd had in her life, and exactly how rich the groom really was.

Cynical. When had he gotten so cynical?

And why, exactly, was he still in this business if that's how he really felt? From what he knew of her, not to mention what he'd seen when he'd watched Edwina handle an off-the-cuff ceremony, she didn't have a cynical bone in her body.

Of course not, he almost heard Julie say. She makes every ceremony about the couple standing in front of her. She doesn't stick to a script.

Was that the secret? Thomas hadn't done that in years, but there was no time like the present.

"Communication," he said, deciding to ad lib just a little. "I was just thinking about how important communication is to a successful relationship."

He glanced from the bride to the groom, who was gazing at his bride with unabashed love clearly etched in every fiber of his being. Thomas sincerely hoped, for this man's sake, that the bride was only impatient with Thomas because his mind had clearly wandered from what was the most important day of her life.

"The two of you are here today because you love each other and want to spend the rest of your lives together," he said. "You've communicated your feelings to each other, shared those feelings with your friends who are here to celebrate this special day with you. You might have told your family how deeply you love each other, told distant friends and relations, might even have told the hotel staff or the waitress who served you breakfast this morning. You shared your joy. Shared the fact that you're in love and you're making a commitment that your love for each other will last." He grinned a little. "You even shared your love of Western clothes."

That got a chuckle from a few members of the audience and a sheepish look from the groom.

Thomas's grin faded just a little as he realized he'd blown his own opportunity to share his joy with the most important person in his life. Whether or not he'd hoped his feelings for Edwina would be returned, he should have given her the opportunity.

"That's what this town's name invokes," he said. "Sharing love with a community that understands your feelings. But I guess you know that since you traveled all the way here to tie the knot. So what do you say, shall we make this official?"

Thomas had meant the question to be rhetorical, a transition between his unexpected—but heartfelt—off-the-cuff commentary back into the meat of the ceremony, but the groom answered anyway.

"Sounds good to me," the groom said, which garnered him a

brilliant smile from the bride—a smile that reached her eyes and appeared (to Thomas anyway) completely genuine. The groom's remark generated a few more chuckles from the audience.

Thomas finished the ceremony by sticking to his tried and true script. After the couple exchanged simple vows and impressive-looking rings, Thomas pronounced them husband and wife, and the groom proceeded to kiss the stuffing out of his very willing bride.

Maybe he'd been wrong about them. He hoped so. He hoped he'd been wrong about a lot of the couples he'd married.

The couple had brought along their own wedding photographer. As the wedding party posed for pictures near the altar, Thomas quietly took a side aisle out of the chapel. The bride and groom had rented the room for an additional half hour for photographs, and he wanted to leave them to their own post-wedding photo shoot.

He kept his head down, his mind a million miles away (or a couple hundred, at any rate) as he mulled over his multiple failures to communicate with Edwina even though he'd had more than enough opportunities to do so. But he could fix that, or at least he hoped he could, but he couldn't wait any longer. Julie was right. He needed to call her, and the sooner the better.

Which was why he never saw the subject of his thoughts standing just outside the door to the western-themed chapel until he ran smack dab into her.

# CHAPTER 32

*E*dwina had never considered just how solid a man Thomas really was until he barreled into her and nearly knocked her over.

She couldn't help the little "oof!" that escaped her lips as she backpedaled, wind-milling one arm as she fought to maintain her balance.

That would teach her to eavesdrop on a wedding ceremony. At least when Thomas had watched her perform a ceremony at Bluebelles, he'd had the good sense to actually come inside the chapel and sit down like a normal person, not lurk near the doorway like some little kid trying to get a peek at the tree in the middle of the night on Christmas Eve to see if Santa had shown up yet.

"Edwina!" Thomas said, shock turning his thoughtful expression comical.

She giggled. She couldn't help it.

"I didn't see you there." He held out a hand to steady her, which she took gratefully.

"I've been accused of many things," she said, "but never of being invisible."

His hand felt good holding hers, so when he kept holding on, she was happy to let him.

"I... uh..." He looked down at their hands, clearly at a loss for words. "What... I didn't..." He cleared his throat. "What are you doing here?"

He was adorable when he was flustered, and for the first time since he'd revealed who he was, she saw him as just a person—and a damn good-looking one—and not her friend who'd deceived her.

She smiled at him. "We have a conversation to finish, I believe. I didn't want to do that over the phone. And I wanted to see you in action," she added, gesturing with a little nod of her head toward the altar. "You looked good up there, but I have to ask— do you always lecture your couples on the value of keeping the lines of communication open?"

A flush rose in his cheeks—also adorable—making him look like a kid who'd just been caught taking an extra cookie from the cookie jar.

She gave herself a mental shake. She never thought about kids this much. Must be the influence of Bessie's twins.

"I decided to take a page out of your book," he said. "You looked really good up there at your altar when you made the cere-mony special for that couple." He glanced over his shoulder at the wedding party still taking pictures at the altar. "How about we leave them to their wedding shoot?" He tugged on her hand. "I have some things I'd like to say to you too, and I'd rather not do it here."

Her heart started thudding heavily in her chest as she let him lead her to a little office tucked in behind the checkout counter in the gift shop portion of his chapel. At least he hadn't said "we need to have a little talk," which according to the movies always spelled the kiss of death for any relationship.

Not that they'd had a chance to *have* a relationship.

Yet.

Which was exactly what she wanted to do. Have a relationship with him.

She didn't intend to let him off the hook all the way about keeping her in the dark about who he was. But she'd come to the realization during the long drive to Lovelock that Nellie was right. True love wasn't perfect. Neither were people. Sure, Thomas had done something stupid, but he hadn't done it maliciously. They'd been friends for years, and her friend Thomas didn't have a malicious bone in his body. No matter how—or when—he'd introduced himself when he got to Liberty Springs, she probably would have been upset. Especially after he'd told her what a bad idea her ad had been.

And he'd been right about that too.

Sort of.

She never would have met Rufus except for the ad, and having a movie star lookalike pay that kind of attention to her had certainly made her feel special—at least for a little while. She'd never regret that.

Thomas though…

She had a feeling he could make her feel special for the rest of her life.

The office he led her to reminded her a little of her own, only it didn't have any windows, and the only thing decorating the walls was a framed certificate authorizing him to officiate at weddings. The certificate had yellowed around the edges and had a slight stain on one side. The desk was functional gray steel, as was the room's one filing cabinet. No framed photos decorated the top of the desk. No little knickknacks adorned the top of the filing cabinet, only two wire baskets. One in-box and one out-box, no doubt. No free-standing closet, and most definitely no Elvis costume.

Altogether, it was the saddest, most utilitarian office Edwina had ever seen in her life.

"I should have brought you a plant," she said.

One of his eyebrows arched toward his hairline. "What?"

"Or flowers. Although I might not ever want to look at another bouquet again."

At his continued look of confusion, she gestured with her free hand toward his walls.

"Thomas, this office has all the charm of a prison cell," she said.

He shoved his hands in the back pockets of his black denim jeans. "I don't spend a lot of time in here," he said. "Mostly I'm out in the gift shop unless I'm performing a ceremony. And I don't do a lot of those during the off season."

"Off season?"

The winter was the off season for Bluebelles. Memorial Day to Labor Day was the busiest time of the year for her, but come to think of it, Lovelock probably wasn't a tourist town. Not that she'd ever done any research into what the town was like.

"Any time of the year that isn't Valentine's Day," he said, shrugging one shoulder.

"Ah," she said. "I don't get a lot of business on Valentine's Day."

He'd told her about the Lovers Lock Plaza celebration during one of their online chats.

And just like that, it struck her that they were back to chatting like the old friends they were. Except instead of chatting online, here they were doing it in person.

No awkwardness. No recriminations or stuttering apologies or indignant outrage.

But no nooky either.

Don't beat around the bush, right?

That had been one of her father's sayings, and it sure seemed to apply here. If she wanted nooky, she'd have to make the first move from friendship to something deeper. Her "shy guy" clearly wasn't about to do it. He was too busy talking about Valentine's Day in Lovelock, falling back to the tried-and-true comfort of their previous relationship before he no doubt thought he'd spoiled everything.

Well, forget that. Sigourney Weaver wouldn't hesitate to show a man what she really wanted.

Neither would Edwina.

Taking a deep breath to steady her nerves, she closed the distance between them, put her hands on his shoulders, and proceeded to kiss the stuffing out of a very shocked Reverend Thomas.

# CHAPTER 33

Of all the things Thomas expected Edwina to do—read him the riot act, tell him she never wanted to see him again, or maybe even slap his face in the best outraged movie actress style—kissing him in his office was the very last thing on his list.

Not only kissing him, but *kissing* him. Thoroughly. Wonderfully. Every good –ly word he could think of, which wasn't a lot because his brain was currently focused on the woman in his arms.

Thomas didn't think he'd ever been kissed like that. Not even when he'd finally gotten around to kissing the first girl he'd ever had a crush on back in high school. Back when kissing was the most amazing thing in the world and he never wanted it to end.

Edwina felt so good. He had his hands in her hair, and she'd wrapped her arms around his waist, and the kiss was so much better than anything he'd daydreamed about while he'd been trying to figure out how to properly introduce himself when he'd been in Liberty Springs.

But why wasn't she mad at him?

Which was the first thing he asked her when the kiss finally ended.

"Oh, I was," she said. "It's not nice to fool a lady like that."

"I know," he said, "and I'm so sorry I—"

She stopped him with another kiss, this was far sweeter and far, far shorter.

"Enough," she said. "We've wasted enough time on silliness like that, don't you think?"

He definitely did think. "So what now?"

She still had her arms around him, and he had one hand cupped on the side of her face. Part of him wondered if this wasn't a particularly vivid daydream, and he'd wake up any minute to find himself alone and still trying to figure out whether to call her.

"Now," she said, stepping back just a bit but taking his hand, like she was trying to reassure herself neither of them were going anywhere, "how about you show me around your chapel, and then, if you're willing, we can go get something to eat? I'm starving!"

She explained that she'd been too nervous to eat anything before she left Liberty Springs that morning. So after he gave her a (brief) tour of the chapel, and after the wedding party left—after spending an inordinate amount in his gift shop—Thomas put the *Be Back at 1:00* sign on the gift shop door and locked the place up.

Then he took her to The Player's Club for lunch.

Stan Otto's eyebrows might have disappeared into his non-existent hairline when he caught sight of the two of them holding hands in line, but he had the good graces not to say anything about the fact that Thomas appeared to have a date.

"The usual, Reverend?" Stan asked.

The corner of Edwina's mouth twitched in a grin at the title, and Thomas felt his cheeks heat up a bit, but all he said was, "Sounds good."

"Anything for the lady?" Stan asked.

Edwina peered at the menu on the wall behind Stan. "I think I'll have the Go Fish," she said. That was tuna salad on a whole wheat roll. "Is the tuna good today?" she asked, and she gave Stan a smile that was brighter than the desert sun outside.

"The tuna's good every day," Stan said. "It's my wife's recipe."

Edwina chuckled. "Good to know."

After they got their drinks from the self-serve soda machine—iced tea for the both of them, Thomas noticed—they sat down at a little two-person table off to the side.

"A little bigger than the Lickety-Split," he said.

"Everyplace is bigger than the Lickety-Split."

He leaned toward her and lowered his voice. "Don't tell Stan, but Nellie's a much better cook. Stan's only good with sandwiches."

She put her hand on the table, and he took it in his. It felt so natural, sitting here, holding hands with her. He'd never felt so right before in his life, like there was nothing else he should be doing except spending time with her.

He was head over heels, all right.

"Nellie's the reason I'm here," she said, staring at their joined hands. "She read me the riot act."

He winced. "Sounds like my friend, Julie."

"You told someone about me?" Edwina asked.

"Of course. You're the best thing that's ever..." He stopped to clear his throat. He hadn't meant to say that out loud. "Besides, she kind of guessed how I felt about you. She's a judge, and trust me, she knows how to get the truth out of people."

Thankfully, Edwina didn't ask him what truth. She probably already knew, just like he already knew how she felt about him. They'd get around to saying it to each other, he was sure of that now. Just not today. Today everything felt fresh and new. Even though they'd been friends forever, this was all different and special and entirely wonderful.

Edwina did ask him about his friend, the judge, so while they waited for their sandwiches, Thomas told her all about the Honorable Julie Wilkins, district judge, and taker of absolutely no shit from anyone. While they ate, she told him about her friendship with Nellie, which was a little different since he'd already met Nellie and her husband, Gus. She told him about Bessie's twins, and about how Joey had stepped up to the plate and offered to help Bessie out when she needed it.

"I think he's sweet on her," she said, "although he won't admit it."

"I know he's sweet on her," Thomas said, and explained how Joey had talked about the babies before they even arrived.

As they talked, it occurred to him that it already seemed like he'd known the people he'd met in Liberty Springs his whole life, even though he'd only been there a very short time, and most of that time he'd been focused on Edwina. He felt comfortable in Liberty Springs in a way that he hadn't felt comfortable in his own life in Lovelock in quite some time.

Maybe that's why he hadn't personalized his office. Deep down, he must have always felt like he was just passing through. He spent more time on the internet chatting with other wedding chapel owners across the country than he did talking with people who lived in town. He'd always thought he was a loner. Or what had Edwina called him? Her "shy guy"? Maybe he just hadn't found the right people—the right place—or the right person to connect with.

Well, he had now. They had a lot to talk about, a lot to figure out, but he knew they'd get there. He was a believer in true love, and a big believer that when two people found true love with each other, things worked out.

Edwina was his one true love, and it sure seemed like he might be hers. And if that was the case, he had a feeling Liberty Springs would be playing a big part in his future.

# CHAPTER 34

Edwina opened the doors of her chapel to let in a little early morning sunlight and fresh air. She wouldn't keep the doors open long. July 4th promised to be sunny and hot. Already she could hear the faint burr of a motorboat engine out on Sutter Lake.

She might actually have a wedding or two in the chapel today. The campground was stuffed to the gills, even though this year July 4th fell on a Wednesday. There'd be (carefully controlled) fireworks out over the lake tonight, and the high school band from Hawthorne would be performing patriotic songs on the lakeshore near the campgrounds. Nellie and Gus had prepared a slew of picnic food they'd be selling from a tent, and Father Mills had organized the church's women's league (all ten members) into an apple-pie-baking machine, so there'd be plenty of good old-fashioned 4th of July desserts to go around.

This day seemed especially bright and wonderful, but then again, every day since Edwina had traveled to Lovelock had been bright and wonderful. Nellie had only teased her once about her "glow" and managed not to say "I told you so" at all.

"I'm just so happy for you," was all Nellie'd said.

She'd been Edwina's matron of honor, and Joey (Joey!) had

been Thomas's best man. Judge Julie, who turned out to be a hoot in real life, had traveled to Liberty Springs to officiate at their wedding, which had been held right in Bluebelles.

It seemed like half the town had shown up for the ceremony. Bessie had even brought her twins, Jacob and Jessica, who'd been perfect little babies right up until the time Judge Julie asked if anyone knew of any reason why Edwina and Thomas shouldn't be married. One of them had squalled, then the other one took up the cry, much to Bessie's embarrassment.

"They're just telling us to get on with it," Joey said, which made everyone—including Edwina and Thomas—laugh, and Judge Julie did, in fact, get on with it.

Thomas was spending this July 4th morning straightening up the dry goods store. He'd decided to take a break from "Reverend Thomas" for a while.

"I might even start calling myself Tom," he'd told her when they discussed his move to Liberty Springs.

"Don't you dare," she said. "It's Thomas or nothing."

After all, Thomas was who she'd fallen in love with after being friends for ages.

"Thomas it is, then," he'd said.

She'd been worried at the beginning that giving up performing ceremonies might be too much after giving up his life in Lovelock for her. Didn't he still believe in true love?

"I do," he'd said then just like he'd said at the altar. "I found it with you."

He said he was happy working in the dry goods store, and she believed him. With his help, she'd expanded her stock and even put in a self-serve soda machine and a freezer stocked with ice cream bars, popsicles, and frozen candy bars. Not exactly dry goods, but then again her store had never been a typical small town dry goods place. And they certainly sold a lot of ice cream.

Edwina turned to look at the altar. The chapel had always been her special place, but now it had even more meaning for her. Her best memories came from here. Standing at the altar with her own Mr. Right at her side, saying "I do" and meaning it with every beat of her heart. Her friends had cheered when Thomas kissed her and she kissed him back.

She'd never been happier in her life, and she was still that happy every morning when she woke up with Thomas by her side.

She wanted to give that same feeling to the couples who came to Bluebelles to get married. She wanted to give them nothing but happy memories, whether they arrived in fishing gear and waders, Hawaiian shirts and bowling attire, or a traditional wedding dress, tux, and tails. Heck, she decided she'd even wear that Elvis costume she kept in the closet in her office if someone wanted her to badly enough.

True love was worth it.

True love was worth everything.

True love was what Bluebelles Wedding Chapel was all about, and she'd finally found hers.

And wonder of wonders, he still had all his own teeth.

# ABOUT THE AUTHOR

Liz McKnight is the pen name for award-winning writer Annie Reed. While Annie writes a wide variety of fiction, primarily mysteries, fantasy, and science fiction as well as romance and the occasional non-fiction, Liz writes the sweet romance *Liberty Springs* novels. *Wedding Belle Blues* is the first novel in this series.

You can find Liz on the web at lizmcnight.wordpress.com. Annie can be found at anniereed.wordpress.com.